Had she a blade on her, she'd certainly have run him through.

Unarmed, Cassie settled for jabbing a stiffened finger in the middle of his chest. "Stop mincing words and say what you mean, you blackguard, else I'll cut out your heart and make you eat it. Don't think I don't dare. You're beginning to make me very angry."

Robert caught her hand and restrained it, infuriating Cassie even more. Her already flushed face hovered just under his in a delicious temper. The urge to pull her into his arms and kiss her quivering lips was almost more than he could bear. He hesitated to be that imprudent.

"Let go of me!" Cassie tugged to get her hand free. He didn't let go.

"Och! You're a proud Highland maiden, full of temper and spirit and as hotheaded as your own fearless father!" Robert laughed

D1049372

Dear Reader,

If you've never read a Harlequin Historical, you're in for a treat. We offer compelling, richly developed stories that let you escape to the past—by some of the best writers in the field!

Author Elizabeth Mayne is notorious for her alpha heroes, and has won the hearts of many readers with previous books such as *Heart of the Hawk* and *All That Matters*. Her latest, *The Highlander's Maiden,* is a tension-filled Medieval tale about a handsome Scottish mapmaker who, by king's decree, must join forces with a fearless female mountain guide from an enemy clan. He vows to make this the partnership of a lifetime!

Be sure to look for *Hawken's Wife* by talented Rae Muir. In this continuation of THE WEDDING TRAIL series, a beautiful tomboy falls for an amnesiac mountain man. *A Rose at Midnight* by Jacqueline Navin is a dark and passionate Regency tale about a powerful earl who thinks he's dying and must find a wife to have his child. He never intended to find love....

Rounding out the month is *For Love of Anna* by multipublished author Sharon Harlow. In this sweet, heartwarming Western, a young widow with children finds her happily-ever-after in the arms of a cowboy who is running from his past. Don't miss it!

Whatever your tastes in reading, you'll be sure to find a romantic journey back to the past between the covers of a Harlequin Historical® novel.

Sincerely,
Tracy Farrell, Senior Editor

Please address questions and book requests to:
Harlequin Reader Service
U.S.: 3010 Walden Ave., P.O. Box 1325, Buffalo, NY 14269
Canadian: P.O. Box 609, Fort Erie, Ont. L2A 5X3

The Highlander's Maiden

Elizabeth Mayne

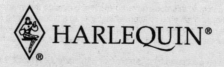

HARLEQUIN®

TORONTO • NEW YORK • LONDON
AMSTERDAM • PARIS • SYDNEY • HAMBURG
STOCKHOLM • ATHENS • TOKYO • MILAN • MADRID
PRAGUE • WARSAW • BUDAPEST • AUCKLAND

ISBN 0-373-29049-7

THE HIGHLANDER'S MAIDEN

Copyright © 1999 by M. Kaye Garcia

This edition published by arrangement with Harlequin Books S.A.

® and TM are trademarks of the publisher. Trademarks indicated with ® are registered in the United States Patent and Trademark Office, the Canadian Trade Marks Office and in other countries.

Printed in U.S.A.

ELIZABETH MAYNE

is a native San Antonian, who knew by age eleven how to spin a good yarn, according to every teacher she ever faced. She's spent the last twenty years making up for all her transgressions on the opposite side of the teacher's desk, and the last five working exclusively with troubled children. She particularly loves an ethnic hero and married one of her own eighteen years ago. But it wasn't until their youngest, a daughter, was two years old that life calmed down enough for this writer to fulfill the dream she'd always had of becoming a novelist.

For Gabriel

You promised all,
and wouldn't settle for anything less.
My hero.

Chapter One

Glencoe, Scotland
February 20, 1598

"Aunt Cassie." Five-year-old Millicent Mac-Gregor caught a handful of Cassandra MacArthur's snood and yanked on it urgently. "Did Lady Quick-foot sink to the bottom of wee Black Douglas's bog?"

"Millie!" Cassie exclaimed as her eyes were blinded by the sudden drop of her cloak's deep hood over her face. Thick wool muffled the rest of her words. "I'm trying to tie this skate on your brother's foot. You'll hear the rest of the Lady Quickfoot story tonight."

"But now is a verra good time to tell it." Millie smiled winsomely.

"Annie Cass, lookie! Soldiers!" Ian swung his hand over Cassie's head to point behind her.

"One thing at a time!" Cassie pleaded. She pushed

the cloth behind her head, and gave more effort into fastening a wooden skate to a child's wiggling brogue. "Sit still, Ian!"

"Tickles!" Ian chortled, squirming restlessly as Cassie's fingers tied the laces firmly around his ankle.

"Lord, for another pair of hands," Cassie proclaimed, pulling a knot secure.

"I dinna think I can wait till bedtime to find out if Black Douglas saves the last jewel of the Highlands." Millie danced about, looking for the soldiers Ian had spotted.

"We've come here for a skating lesson." Cassie firmly redirected the girl. "You'll hear what happened to Lady Quickfoot, Black Douglas and the bard of Achanshiel at bedtime, not a moment sooner, lassie." She sat back on her skates, muttering, "How does your mother keep clothes on your back, wiggle worm?"

"Whisht, Aunt Cassie," Millie scolded. "Those men will think y'er daft. Y'er always talkin' to yerself."

"And what makes you think I care who hears my private conversations, eh?" Cassie winked at her dark-haired niece before she glanced over her shoulder. "Maybe I'm talking to my angel."

"'Twouldn't be an angel," Millie proclaimed. "'Twould be a fairy."

"No difference there." Cassie shrugged "I hear fairies were angels in the beginning of time, till God sent them to stay in the Highlands because their queen was so vain."

"Go on." Millie shook her head. "What they need

a queen for if they had God to look upon all the time?''

Cassie tweaked one of the girl's braids. ''Now that is a very good question, lassie. I don't pretend to know the answer...save that fairies were the most beautiful angels God ever made...and I think it must have something to do with vanity. So God had no choice but to banish them from everyone's sight. Vanity is an excessively awful sin to this very day, is it not?''

''Aye,'' the child agreed solemnly.

They were high up in the north meadow, a wee stretch of the legs from Euan MacGregor's farmstead. Within hailing distance, Euan claimed—if one had lungs as capacious as a blacksmith's bellows—as Euan did. Cassie had heard him yell his clan's battle cry once. He'd scared the daylights out of her.

This was a time of peace, a lull between the clan wars. Still, it paid to be alert at all times. Cassie continued to look for men in sight of the frozen pond. Here the air was frosty enough to keep ice solid until April. Lower on the mountain, everything melted in today's mild sun.

Cassie spied the men on the mountain. Two scruffy travelers hiking through the mud-bound mire of Mac-Donald's cow pasture. They led two packhorses weighted down with a great number of rucksacks, poles and bags. Cassie's eyes narrowed in suspicion. Tinkers, maybe.

A small alarm ran deep in her chest. *They weren't the Watch or king's soldiers if their dun-colored plaids meant anything. No, they couldn't be from the king, not coming from the south.* No one knew Cassandra was at Glencoen Farm save her parents. Cassie shielded her eyes to lessen the glare of the wintry sun, studying the men more intently.

"Da says it's fey to talk to yerself. You do it 'cause y'er redheaded. Tha's why he married Mama instead of ye," Millie continued, proud of her scolding. So big she sounded and all of five. Cassie looked back at her niece and laughed over what she'd said.

"Och, and marrying yer mam wouldn't have anything to do with the fact that yer da wanted a woman to wed when he sweet-talked my poor sister Maggie into taking on this farm of his, eh? And me naught but a flat-bosomed lassie like you at the time." Cassie tapped her niece's nosy nose. "Fey, am I?"

She turned her chin in the direction of the two strangers, saying casually to the children, "Do you know them, then?"

Ian's baby blue eyes rounded as he shook his head.

"They're no' MacGregors!" Millie's identical eyes fixed upon the newcomers with calculating interest. She had the soul of a gossip and knew all her kinsmen and everyone who lived within thirty miles of Glencoe. "Could be MacDonalds. Da says they're thick as flies 'round shite hereabouts."

"Millie! Mind your tongue!"

"Weel, Da says it."

"And ladies don't!" Cassie scolded.

"How come Da can say things that *leddies* shouldn't?"

"Och, that's because men say wicked things to keep all the wickedness inside them from festering like a rotten egg put on the boil. It can't do anything but explode and ruin everything around it for a little while. Men can't hold their passions quiet like we ladies do.''

"So we're gooder?" Millie asked.

"Aye, we are *better*." Cassie stressed the correction on the assumption that Millie's grammar would improve with exposure to proper speech. "It's nice to be a lady and refined like your dear Grandmother MacArthur. We must strive to be more like her every day. Besides, my child, men like doing hard and dirty work. Why, even the best of them can't keep clean from the time they crawl out of the cradle until they fall into the grave.''

"Tha's verra true." Millie cast a wise look at Ian.

Not many strangers wandered into Glencoe in the wintertime. The pass to the north was beautiful but stark. You had to know what you were about to travel it in the winter. Neither of Maggie's children had any innate fear of Highlanders walking the land their father worked. Soldiers, Englishmen or reivers were another matter. Cassie decided to wait and see.

"No' stalkers neither." Ian mimicked his sister's acumen for quick judgment. "No bows or spears."

"You're right there, my lad," Cassie murmured, though she saw the butt of a musket poking from between the saddlebags, and both men wore claymores and dirks, slung from broad leather belts fitted around their hips. That told her they were prepared for trouble if they came upon it.

"Can I run and ask who they are?" Millie said eagerly.

"I think we'll wait and see if they have any business with us, first," Cassie decided. "Speaking of which, we did come here to skate, did we not? Up you go, Wee Ian."

She set the little one on his feet and guided him to the icy pond. His legs wobbled unsteadily on the rough skates, but he was game to give it a try.

Cassie kept a cautious eye on the strangers as they came up the steep incline from MacDonald's meadow. They weren't showing the slightest interest in the activities of the children or the cattle in the high field. Not reivers, then. But who were they? A sinking feeling in the pit of her stomach told her they were the king's surveyors, damn their eyes. What luck! That didn't mean they knew who she was.

They seemed absorbed in the tall one's pacing. The other stood back and counted his companion's steps, letting out a cord, the end of which the other carried.

At the stony rise where MacGregor's high field jutted up and away from MacDonald's grazing pasture, they stopped and talked heatedly. The drum of their conversation carried on the north wind. At the peak of the hill, the lean one made a great commotion of pointing east, north, south and west, all of his motions becoming a sort of comic dance.

They were lost, then, Cassie concluded. Some mapmakers these two were, if they were Messrs. Hamilton and Gordon of the king's surveyors' ilk. She wondered which one was the Gordon, and how it could be that they'd traveled through Glen Orchy and were still alive. She wouldn't waste a king's penny betting on their odds of survival if they ventured into Lochaber without protection. Say, the certain protection of Cassandra's Lady Quickfoot reputation. Then she smiled, because she would see to it that they never found the elusive Lady Quickfoot, the best guide in the Highlands.

The tall one put down his cord and stacked a few nearby rocks on the cord to hold it in place. Then he walked back down to the horses and took a brown folio from the packs. He settled the folio in his arms, using his back as a shield against the sharp wind. He shuffled parchment after parchment to the top, pulled a stub of a pencil out of his sporran, moistened the point with his tongue and began to scribble, it seemed to Cassie's curious eyes.

The stout one took this pause to help himself to a healthy swig of the liquid his pocket flask contained. He offered a drink to his companion. That man shook the offer aside—too busy with his scribbling to break from it. When he finished and began putting the folio away, the stout one took hold of the string lying on the snow-dappled ground and began winding. It was a very, very long string with many knots in it and made a large and oddly bumped ball.

"How curious," Cassie observed aloud.

"Faster!" Ian called her attention back to him.

Cassie caught the loose ends of her wind-ruffled hair together and tucked them back inside the hood of her cloak. She needn't advertise her marital status to outright strangers. "Shall we teach this little ram how to really skate, Millie? Take his other hand."

"I kin do it," Ian yelled boldly, legs splitting and wobbling underneath him.

"No, Ian, you have to learn how first." Millie sounded very much like her mother, Maggie.

A week of skating lessons on the pond behind the farmhouse had turned Millie into a very confident skater. She was bright and quick and it only took someone with a little time on their hands and energy to keep up with the girl to teach her anything. Unmarried aunts like Cassie suited that task perfectly. Sadly, the unusual winter warm spell had turned that convenient pond too slushy for Ian's lessons.

Taking firm hold of opposite hands, Cassie and Millie wheeled the little one around the sheltered mountain pool. Euan had brought the sheep up to this field himself this morning and tested the ice's thickness and strength before telling his children at dinner that they could continue skating lessons this afternoon.

Ian laughed and laughed, delighted by the wind that was so cold it stung his cheeks bright red and took his breath away in big puffs of frosty air.

"I do it m'self!" Ian grew impatient with their steadying hands.

Millie's small face formed the perfect picture of long-suffering sisterhood. She sighed before letting go of her little brother's hand. Cassie also thought it time to let him try skating on his own. When he fell on his bottom a couple of times, he'd accept their help more readily.

"You're on your own, little man." Cassie saw him turn around and head into the soft snowdrift on the north bank of the pond. Here, the ice was thickest. She had no fear that it would shatter under his little weight, no matter how hard he fell. If she remembered it right, this pool was deep and treacherous in other seasons because of its wicked currents.

He inched away, his little body struggling to keep his balance. His arms flopped in great awkward circles. His knees and ankles wobbled. His bottom went up and down and back and forth. Somehow—through all the gyrations, one little wooden skate inched forward after the other.

"Slide yer feet!" Millie shouted, skating in front of Ian on gleaming skates her father had made her last evening at his forge. Her old wooden skates now graced Ian's nimble toes. She stopped and dropped to her knees, holding out her arms for the little boy to come to her. "Oh, Auntie Cassie, you should see Ian's face, he's trying so very hard! Why, it's all screwed up like the last apple in the stillroom and red as the devil's toes!"

"Is not!" Ian grunted and threw himself at his sister's arms. He crowed in triumph, "I did it!"

"So you did, wee Ian-Dhu." Cassie came to a graceful stop beside them, put her knee to the ice and hugged Ian affectionately. She was so pleased with his efforts she even rumpled his dark curls till he laughed with glee.

"Mumph," grunted a male voice nearby, making that throaty sound every Highland woman recognized as a preamble to actual speech.

Expecting to find Old Angus scowling at her for spoiling the boy, Cassie looked up to find both travelers standing at the edge of the pond, grinning like a pair of loons.

"Pardon me, goodwife..." the taller one began. The second man cleared his throat as if he was correcting his companion without words.

"Och, Auntie Cassie's not a goodwife," Millie declared impulsively. "If y'er looking for a goodwife, you'll be wanting to see my mother. She's at the dairy, churning butter."

"'Tis my auntie Cassie," Ian chimed in possessively, patting Cassie's wind-stung face. "'Tisn't married."

"Whisht, children," Cassie said repressively as she came gracefully to her feet. "May I help you, gentlemen?"

"We hope you can." The taller one spoke for both of them. "My friend and I were given directions to Glencoen Farm, though by our measurement, we seem to be north of it. We have a packet for Euan MacGregor who lives there, and a letter of introduction from his kinsman, Laird Malcolm MacGregor of Balquhidder. Do you know the precise location of that farm?"

The children giggled, but Cassie managed to shush another outburst with a stern glance. She wasn't as good at that as her sister. Maggie could get these two imps to shush by just quirking one dark eyebrow. But then they probably couldn't tell when Cassie's pale eyebrows twitched or moved. Nobody could.

"Actually, sir, you're standing on part of it as we speak. This is the north meadow of Glencoen Farm. You missed the turn coming through MacDonald's cattle field."

Cassie pointed to a narrow path beyond the snow-dappled rocks and foraging sheep. "You'll find the right track there at the twisted pines and the sheep-fold. The snow is melting, so be careful where you walk. Some of it is quite muddy. You can't miss Glencoen Farm. It's the only two-storied house in twenty miles. Just keep moving downhill." She added a smile and a few extra words. "South by the south-west."

Her addendum brought a sudden smile onto her questioner's face. He thanked her and wished them a good day, then raised his hand to his brow in a polite salute on parting.

That gesture drew Cassie's attention to a pair of very wonderful blue eyes and his hands. He wore mittens just like she and the children did. Simple finger-less tubes of knitted wool stitched at the great knuckles. His fingers were so dirty and chapped raw from winter's cold that she could hardly tell where dark wool left off and skin began. That wasn't unusual for any man trekking the hills in winter, but it certainly didn't go with his gentle-seeming eyes.

Those eyes tilted deeply at the outer corners. While his skin was stung from exposure, the sparkle in those blue eyes and the length of his eyelashes betrayed his age. He was somewhere close to her own. She was days away from twenty. Those eyes declared he wasn't older than twenty-five, if that.

As they strode away, her own eyes narrowed in revision of her earlier impressions. The two men were very nearly the same weight. The one she had thought stout was only larger boned and wore heavier clothing under his winding plaid. The other, the one she'd spoken to wore only a leather jerkin and woolen sark beneath his plaid. His slender frame was practically bare in comparison. Warm enough garments for most Highlanders. The leather surrounding his chest was as close as one could come to being waterproof—definitely a boon in Glen Orchy and Lochaber.

She noted another detail. His kilt was separate from his plaid and stitched. Precise knife pleats encircled his hips and fell in a neat swirl 'round his knees. His plaid swung over his shoulder and was firmly clipped beneath a hunting brooch. Both ends were secured under his belt, keeping the cloth close across his chest and loose on his back. She recognized that habit, knowing intuitively that there walked a ready man whose garments wouldn't betray him if he had to draw dirk or sword suddenly to be ready for battle. A murdering Gordon to be sure.

Other than both being garbed in serviceable Wallace hunting plaid, she could not tell from where they came or to which clan they gave allegiance, though she'd have had to be blind not to pay notice to his straight back and proud bearing—another giveaway of his clan affiliation. He moved with the proud strut of an invincible warrior, which the bloody Gordons were, curse their souls!

She could be wrong. The more slender man could simply be a soldier or officer in King James the Sixth's garrison. God forbid he was a Gordon or Douglas scout, reconnoitering for rebels hidden in the pass. This was MacDonald territory and a Campbellton shire. Rebel earls and their war parties weren't welcome here.

Both men hitched their plaids close over their backs as the brunt of the strong wind caught them and their overloaded pack animals descending the mountain.

Cassie saw that they had slogged through deep mud, probably in crossing the mire of MacDonald's cow field. The hems of their muddy plaids slapped against the backs of their legs.

"You didn't find out who they are!" Millie fussed when they went 'round the bend and out of sight.

"Why should I want to know that?" Cassie responded, turning her attention back to Ian as he fell soundly on his bottom. Cassie winced at his impact, knowing that the fall had hurt. His bare shanks were exposed to the ice. He was so surprised he didn't know whether to howl or pound his fists. Cassie waited to see what he would do.

"They could be im-por-tant!" Millie insisted as she pulled hard on Ian's arm. "Whisht, Ian, get up. Let's try again."

Ian rose so unsteadily he clutched Millie's waist, then leaned too far into her. His sturdy little body overbalanced Millie as well. Down they both went as quick as a blink, a small mass of tangled legs and banging skates.

"Ian, leggo! Y'er choking me!"

"Am not," Ian insisted, mad now. He did a split getting up, both of his hands pushing heavily into Millie's tummy. Cassie came to their rescue.

"Shall we skate together for a little while?" she suggested, righting the little one, firmly steadying his balance. Without argument, Ian gave her his hand. Millie dutifully took the other and they circled the pond without further mishap, restoring Ian's confidence.

"The dark one had a signet ring, so he must be somebody im-por-tant!" Undeterred, Millie returned to her prior topic. She was like a dog that had dragged off a bone, determined to savor it down to the very marrow.

"One was dark?" Cassie repeated, adding under her breath, "Who could notice for the mud?"

"Och, y'er doin' it again! Saying things ye don't want me to hear but ye say them anyway. Mama says it's because y'er always doing yer thinking out loud."

"Your parents make a habit of discussing me in front of wee bairns, do they?" Cassie asked, teasing Millie naturally, the same way her older brother and sisters had teased her at Millie's age. "Your da calls me fey and my own sister accuses me of being so witless I say every thought out loud like a five-year-old."

Not one to be distracted, Millie continued. "'Twas a gold ring on his little finger with a blue jewel in it. I saw it plain as day, winking at me from the edge of his ragged mitten."

"Well, there. If your father gives them leave to have supper at his table, you'll have time to knit the poor dark man a new pair of mittens," Cassie said. "I didn't see any ring, myself."

"Tha's 'cause ye weren' lookin'! You only looked at his face."

Cassie shook her head, baffled by the girl's powers of observation. The man had very nice blue eyes and came with an endorsement from Euan's father. That was better than a king's seal of approval in this part of the Highlands. Even so, if he was who she thought he was, he was a dead man. Like the rest of her Mac-Arthur and Campbell kinsmen, Cassie had been brought up believing the only good Gordon was a dead Gordon.

Cassie loosened her hair from her hood. It spilled down the back of her cloak to be played with by the wind and tangled and blown about her face. The sun picked up its fiery colors and turned it into burnished gold. That was the only time she liked it, when she was in the sun.

One of these days she hoped to get the privilege of putting her red hair up in neat coils like her mother and all of her sisters. Until the day she was actually married, to put her hair up was the next worst thing to a sin. She had heard her brother James say that in England unmarried girls past a certain age were allowed that wonderful privilege…if they attended Queen Elizabeth at court. The day that happened in Scotland, Cassie would turn cartwheels up and down the nave of St. Giles Cathedral.

In her mind, she should have been granted that privilege when she and Alastair Campbell became engaged. But her mother had said no, and insisted the answer was still no, even when they'd buried what was left of poor Alastair in their chapel cemetery alongside his parents' infants that hadn't lived through childhood. Cassie still felt as if her heart had gone into the cold earth with him. It had been over a year since Alastair's death. In that time a peace treaty had been signed and no further battles had disrupted the return to normal life.

In just a few days Cassandra MacArthur would be twenty. How could she hold up her head at the spring fetes if she was still wearing her hair down at twenty? Cassie sighed and gave up brooding over the impossible.

Ian was content to hold Millie's hands and let her pull him along. So Cassie skated away, concentrating on making her figures with her blades in the pristine ice. Eights were easy, requiring little more than the careful management of her skirts. The circle within a circle was harder.

The children's voices filled the high meadow with laughter, making Cassie realize she was happy at Glencoen Farm, happier than she was anywhere else in Scotland.

"Auntie Cassie," Ian called to her. "I'm hungry."

She'd come prepared for his inevitable hunger and produced two apples from her pocket. Millie left him standing on his skates and came to her, grabbing both apples greedily.

"Sit you down then." Cassie instructed the girl firmly. "We don't need to tax either of your skills with eating and skating, too."

"I'd best take off Ian's skates. Mama will want us home well before dark," Millie added wisely.

Night came on quickly and early during winter. The sun was already sinking to the west. Millie skated as fast as she could back to Ian while biting into one of the apples. Then a devil got inside her and she circled the boy, holding his apple just out of his reach.

"Give it to me!" Ian demanded.

"Come and get it yerself," Millie taunted. She skated far ahead of him, close to the rockbound edge where granite stones were frosted with a coat of dripping ice. She executed a sharp, quick stop on her iron skates. "Come get it, piglet!"

"Gimme!" Ian yelled.

Crack! went the ice at Millie's feet. The sun caught the jagged line as it ripped across the length of the frozen pool.

"Millie, don't move!" Cassie yelled, horrified as that jagged line zigzagged under Ian's feet.

"Gimme it!" Ian screamed again, his hunger turned to temper.

Millie froze, clenching both apples, and looked to Cassie, who sped Millie's way as fast as she could.

"Children—" Cassie's heart thudded in her chest, but she kept her voice as calm as she could make it "—don't move, please. I'm coming to you."

"I want mine no-ow!" Ian stomped his foot.

The crack underneath him shattered like glass and roared with the voice of a cupboard full of pots and pans toppling onto a flagstone floor.

"Millie!" Cassie screamed a command. "Throw yourself on the rocks!"

"Owwww—iieee!" Ian screamed as he went down into the icy pool.

Millie scrambled onto the icy rocks, terrified by the sight of the ice closing over Ian's head. "What do I do? Ian!"

"I'll get Ian! Get help! Get your skates off and run, Millie. Run!" Cassie raced to the fracture.

The little girl moved quicker than Cassie could speak, catching hold of the buckles over her boots as an entire sheet of ice tilted crazily under Cassie, sending her skidding downward into a shockingly cold ice bath.

"Get your father!" Cassie screamed one last instruction before she, too, plunged under the ice.

Cassie's arms and legs thrashed against the cloud of ice shards that accompanied her descent, in a failed effort to swim. Her cloak and heavy wool skirts rose as she sank. Then they tangled around her arms until she touched the rocky bottom. There the cold water was crystal clear save for a cloud of dark mud stirred up by Ian's violent thrashing. Cassie bent her knees and pushed against the bottom to propel herself more quickly to Ian.

The little boy was trapped under a huge slab of unbroken ice. Even with the momentum of a firm thrust of her legs, getting to Ian quickly seemed to take Cassie an eternity in her heavy clothes. She grabbed the boy and pulled him to her, swiveling, looking for the hole in the ice, out of breath and as desperate for wind in her lungs as he was.

Ian's fingers clawed at her, tearing at her billowing hair. His shoes, skates and knees pounded her as if he were trying to walk to the surface on a ladder made of her very body.

Their heads broke the sparkling surface at the same time and the cold air on their water-chilled skin was a second shock as they each gasped for wind. "Whisht, shh, shh, now, laddie," Cassie gasped, lifting him above the water's surface so he could breathe deeply. "I've got you, sweetheart, be calm. It's only water."

He coughed out mouthfuls of water, choked and gasped and sputtered like a floundering fish. While he got his wind back, Cassie looked for Millie and carefully gauged her own precarious position. Millie was nowhere to be seen, but the ice under the rocks where she'd been standing was intact. Her gleaming skates and the two apples lay negligently cast aside on the rocks. That gave Cassie a moment's deep relief. One child was safe.

Ian, still thrashing, became heavier by the moment. Now how was she to get herself and Ian out of the mess they were in?

Cassie had nothing to grab hold of near her. As Ian came to his senses, he took a breath and coughed more normally. His little arms and legs clamped onto her body, limiting her own movements severely.

The coldness of the water had ceased being important. In fact, it almost felt warm compared to the air above the water. "Ian, let go of my arms. I've got to swim to get us out of here, sweetling."

His jacketed arms clutched her so tightly, he strangled her. He was crying, too, a frightened little boy, and no wonder that—trapped under the ice as he had been. Cassie hugged him a moment longer as tightly as he hugged her, using her strong legs to keep their heads afloat. Her skirts and cloak tangled in her legs. Their weight, along with her boots and skates, made every circling motion an effort.

Mentally, she prayed, *Millie, Millie, sweetheart, run as fast as you can!*

The silence of the mountain pool paid a credit to its isolation. If she and Ian were to be rescued, she had best see to getting them out of the water herself.

Chapter Two

Glencoen Farm was clearly in the travelers' sight when the little girl from the skating pond came screaming and tumbling down the track, out of breath and too terrified to speak clearly.

She got out the words ''ice broke'' ''Auntie'' and ''Ian'' before she took off running for the farmstead, howling like a banshee again.

''What the devil?'' Alexander Hamilton sputtered, confused by the child's terror and slurred Gaelic words.

Robert Gordon understood the child's terror-driven message. Dropping the measuring cord in his hands, he turned and bolted back the way they'd come, running for dear life to the top of the first hill and up the twisting path to the high meadow. Pines hid the pool from sight, but he ran onward at full speed, dread building with each pounding step across the stony ground for what his eyes would find when the pond came into view.

It was worse than he'd had scant heartbeats to envision. The mountain pool had no skaters on its glistening, windswept surface. The southern corner of it thrashed with a froth of broken, disturbing shards of ice and the fractured glare of lights reflecting from it.

Broken ice, treacherous footing and no purchase anywhere, Robert stopped at the edge of the rocky pool, mentally assessing what he saw. A solid sheet of ice extended forward from his boots thirty feet. From there to the southmost bank, it had become a mire of sharp, fragmented shards. The young woman and the boy struggled to stay afloat at the edge of the solid sheet. Their heads bobbed up and down in his sight, competing with chunks of ice for space on the surface of the pond.

Robert shed his weapons, belt, sporran and plaid. In two quick jerks he removed his boots, flung off his cap, then his jerkin, and went out on the still firm ice. He felt the shock of the terrible cold underfoot.

He sighted the girl as she vainly struggled to put the little boy onto the slippery ice ahead of her. It broke, and he went under again only to be grabbed by her, and caught by her, forced forward and onto the ice again. Their dark wools performed that slow, exhausted dance over and over again as he watched, gaining only inches and losing vast ground as more and more ice shattered underneath them.

Likewise, Robert's progress toward them felt like a snail's dance. His heart dropped when her last effort put the boy on a floating island of ice, but caused her to sink in utter exhaustion as the island tilted and wedged under the remaining sheet of solid ice on which Robert made such laggard progress.

The child began to scream pitifully at having lost sight of his aunt. Robert picked his next steps carefully, eyeing hairline stress marks in the fractured sheet as he lay down on his stomach and inched onto the ice floe. He caught the boy by his sodden clothes and firmly tugged him off the icy island.

He turned the startled child in the direction of the shore, telling him calmly, "Stop yer bawling. I'll fetch yer aunt. Go this way to the shore. Go!"

Ian found new hope. The other stranger was stretched out on the ice near Ian, holding open arms that promised safety and warmth only a few feet away. Beyond him, Ian's father rode into sight with all his men from the farm, laying a whip on the horses hitched to his hay wagon. "Da!"

Robert took one look back, making certain Alex was close enough to reach the small boy to get him if the ice should break again. Satisfied, Robert shed his kilt and slid feetfirst into the ice bath. He sank to the bottom, his eyes open, actively searching for the girl among the water weeds and shards of ice that followed his quick descent.

The cold stopped his heart and his breath instantly. He found her on the bottom, struggling to remove her weighty woolen cloak from her neck. Pale white fingers clawed at her throat, unable to manage the simple work of unfastening a corded frog and eyelet. The most beautiful cloud of red curls billowed around her like an angel's halo, sparkling with silvery bubbles of trapped air.

The maiden's blue eyes were stricken wide with terror. She startled as he made eellike progress to her.

He caught her under her arms, pulled her to his chest and kicked his legs hard, trying to lift them both to the surface. She didn't budge. She was caught on something.

He couldn't hold his breath any longer. He let go of her and raced to the surface, broke it and took huge gasps of air, filling his lungs to capacity. Alex was there at the edge of the ice, concern written all over his long face.

"What's wrong, Robbie?"

"She's trapped. Give me your dirk."

He pressed the blade into Robert's palm instantly.

Robert plunged downward, swimming back to the bottom, feeling the length of her legs for her feet. He found the trapped foot and the skate wedged into the rocks, and, pushing the billowing wools aside, slit the laces of her boot clean to the top and hauled her foot free of the shoe.

Her arms floated out at her sides as he again gripped her chest, drawing her close, then he kicked for all he was worth and rose to the surface. Their heads broke water. Robert gasped for air as she fell limp against him. Fluids ran from her nose and mouth. Her lungs rattled in a faint reflex as Robert tightened his arm around her chest, expelling fluids.

There was no fight left in her. None. Her arms were limp and legs wooden as Robert gripped her chest securely and cut the heavy cloak loose before it sank them both. He let the cloth drop, then tossed the knife back to Alex and conserved his strength to keep them next to the firm edge of ice.

Alex had his own finely woven tartan stretched out

like a rope for Robert to grasp. The men from the farm had planks laid out across the unstable ice and rope to finish the rescue.

Sweet Jesus save us, Robert prayed fervently as he moved the woman enough to tie the rope around her chest. If she was breathing at all, it was as shallow as a sleeping baby.

Robert knew why, too. The icy cold did that, robbed the body of all its strength and numbed the brain worse than 100-proof whiskey. His own deft fingers slowed down to abominable dexterity.

"Here, now!" he commanded. "Wake up, lass! We'll have you out of here in a trice." He grasped her chin, lifting her face, and marveled over her sweet, freckled beauty. Her cheek fell against his shoulder and water lapped at her jawline. They had to get out of the icy water soon. Alex hauled on the rope with all his might but it wasn't enough to pull her out of the water—not in her sodden woolens. It was taking too long!

Some other sense told Robert to lend her what he could of his own supply of warmed breath. Her slackened mouth offered no resistance as he covered her full, colorless lips and filled her flooded lungs with his own warmed breath.

That action roused her more than his underwater rescue. Her eyelids fluttered open, her gaze fixed on his eyes and remained there. Again, Robert laid his mouth upon hers and breathed for her. That awoke her from her numbed lethargy, bringing forth a cough and a veritable flood of water bubbling up from her chest.

"Good, good!" Robert let her head rest on his shoulder. He stroked her cheek and throat encouragingly, treading water between breaths.

When the bubbling cough stopped he gripped her chin fast and breathed again into her mouth, giving her the only warmth he could under such intolerable conditions. The same gurgling expulsion of the pond's water from her chest followed.

Alex held his place, flattened out on the planks of wood stretching across the ice. "Robert, they've got the ropes secure, man. Can you hold on? Is the woman tied?"

"Aye!" Robert released her chin and let her head fall to his shoulder as he adjusted his own hold on the rope and the familiar plaid of his companion. "Tell them to pull us out, now. Quicklike. You know how much I hate cold baths."

"Aye," Alex muttered to himself, backing off the ice on hands and knees, knowing that when the horse pulled, all hell was likely to break loose on this ice.

He was right, too, to anticipate that the whole pond would shatter at the intrusion of the horse-powered rescue. Euan MacGregor cracked his whip. His lead horse lurched, then pulled, pushing the remaining sheet of ice backward up the bank till it wedged on rock and the weighty human burden at the end of the secure rope came free of the water and slid across the ice, cracking what was left all the way to the shore.

Horror etched Euan MacGregor's broad face as he knelt over his young sister-in-law, untying the tightened bad knots under her limp arm.

"Get my children away from here," he said over his shoulder to his men. "Cassie's dead."

"Nay, she isn't." Robert let go of the heavy blanket someone had thrown around him and reached for the woman one more time. "She's just frozen, the poor brave thing."

He gathered Cassie into his arms once more, opened her slackened mouth and kissed her with life and breath once more. Her fingers fluttered over her sodden dress, then her arm lifted to reach up and touch his face softly before weakly pushing him away so that she could cough and breathe on her own again.

Without the slightest compunction, Robert turned her over and helped her to expel more water onto his lap. His efforts were rewarded by her first sputtering intake of breath. Granted it was no more than a short, choking breath that was followed quickly by another deep and raucous cough. The involuntary motion was started anew and continued, one labored breath after another.

"She'll be all right," Robert said confidently. His large hands rubbed between her cold shoulders blades to warm and soothe her. Her eyelids fluttered and her cheeks began to pinken, losing the bluish color of drowning.

Euan MacGregor laid another blanket on her. That helped greatly, but Robert knew getting her out of the wind and the elements would help best.

Euan sat back on his heels, realizing that a miracle had taken place before his eyes this day. He kissed Cassie gratefully on her cheek, thanking her for his son's life, then gathered her and the layer of horse blankets into his huge arms and lifted her out of the lap of her savior.

"Bring the wet traveler along and his friend," he briskly told his men as he moved his sister-in-law to the bed of the wagon. "He's earned a place at my board whenever he wants for a hot meal."

Chapter Three

Robert Gordon and Alex Hamilton jumped off the hay cart when it came abreast of the two packhorses tethered to the trees right where Alex had tied them. Cassandra MacArthur, as he now knew the young woman's name to be, was conscious and on the road to recovery from her icy submersion.

It was the tidbit of bona fide information regarding her name, conceded by her solemn brother-in-law, that made Robert smile wryly as he watched the hay cart roll away.

Euan MacGregor paused only long enough to repeat his heartfelt extension of hospitality. Wrapped in rough wool, Robert thanked him for his kind offer and promised he and his companion, Alex, would be down directly. By the same token, Robert refused to be treated as some vaulted, kingly guest—accepting honors that he didn't deserve and that these austere Highlanders would resent giving, heroic deeds or no. He'd only done what any thinking man should.

On the other hand, Robert would be grateful for a

warm meal at this day's end, provided he owed MacGregor no more than he was willing to give.

Taken back, Euan paused a moment longer, eyeing both strangers intently, understanding exactly where they stood. He was like that, too, a renegade of sorts from the eternal bonds of the Highlands' all-pervasive feudal system of loyalties. Euan also preferred to stand on his own two feet, his word of honor his sole moral code after the word of God Almighty.

"Then ye are welcome to sit amongst the free men at my table if ye pitch the hay that was dumped from this cart into the pigs' byre where it was intended. Do ye finish the task before sundown, the barn is free for yer beds this night. A fairer offer I couldn't make any strangers this time of the year."

"That will be sufficient to our needs, and I thank you again, sir." Robert nodded his acceptance.

As the farmer's cart rolled noisily off, Alexander Hamilton moved to their saddlebags and Robert huddled under the weight of the dry woolen blanket draped over his shoulders. Alex tucked up Robert's weapons and handed his shivering friend a dry sark and kilt and dug in a pack of rolled garments for dry stockings.

In this part of Scotland, Alexander Hamilton was a man of few words. A Lowlander by name and association, he was better known in England as the wandering grandson of the wealthy and powerful Earl of Arundel, where he could lay honest claim to lands and estates of his own in Sussex. His heart, though, seemed permanently bonded to Scotland.

When Robert finally began stripping off his wet

sark, Alex spoke for the first time since they'd been left alone by their packhorses. "I wouldn't have objected to being transported inside yonder warm house and treated like a hero for a month or so."

"Would you now?" In spite of his blue-tinged, goosebump-pebbled skin, Robert managed to hike a dark brow over that absurd statement. "And how long do ye think ye would last with the women of the house flutterin' and cooin' all 'round ye, before that loquacious tongue of yours proved ye a Sassenach, a bloody Englishman, by birth and mother's tongue, eh?"

"Ah, well, a week, no more, if my luck holds." Alex grinned, speaking the queen's English. His born-and-raised-in-Sussex accent rang in his voice as clear as a bell. He had his English mother to thank for that. His Scottish father blessed him with other virtues: his easy smile, his height and his untainted Hamilton lineage.

"Humph!" Robert grunted. He dropped the blanket and stood stark naked in the icy air, rubbing himself down briskly with the rough wool before grabbing the dry sark Alex offered him and pulling that over his head and shoulders.

"You realize of course that we've found our elusive Lady Quickfoot?" Robert inquired mildly. He made fast work of pulling on socks and boots, bending to fasten the buckles.

Alex cast him a dazzling grin and ducked his head twice before looking around to make certain there was no one about to hear him speak out loud. "And here I was believing the lady a figment of fertile imagi-

nation. What a piece of luck that was. That wouldn't
happen again in a lifetime, eh, Robbie?''

Alex used the familiar nickname he'd known Robert Gordon by since childhood, before they had attended university. The moniker was used sparingly
nowadays and in these hills. Only when they each
knew they were safe and unattended, did either of
them use their Christian names.

''My thoughts exactly,'' Robert added crisply.

Alex's words reminded Robert that the king's letter
to Lady Quickfoot, Cassandra MacArthur, had gone
unanswered since November. Robert knew better than
to consider finding Cassandra MacArthur lucky. The
renowned Lady Quickfoot preferred not to be found,
or so he and the king had assumed since early in
December.

Personally, Robert thought finding her in this particular circumstance and saving her life the way he
had just done a piece of bad luck that boded little
good for his mission in the Highlands. Now he knew
for certain that Cassandra MacArthur was still a
maiden. A minor detail of the sort King James rarely
attended, but very problematic to the two surveyors
who supposedly were in need of her guidance through
the politically dangerous, Campbell-controlled shire
of Lochaber.

Robert fitted his plaid across his shoulders last. His
blood already ran warm again, for he was weather-
hardened to the bone like every Highlander worthy of
his salt. He shrugged his shoulders after he'd fitted
his weapons back about his hips. ''No matter, my
friend. We'll persevere. Gordons always do.''

* * *

By the time Cassie rose from the tub, her recovery, as far as she was concerned, was complete.

"I should think you'd be terrified." Maggie insisted, handing her younger sister a mug of hot mulled wine.

"Och, I was when I saw Ian trapped under the ice," Cassie admitted as she wrapped her cool fingers around the napkin-covered cup. "But as to the rest of it, I can't really say that I remember very much."

The whole terrible accident had assumed an unreal, dreamlike quality in Cassie's mind. Only two things were really clear: Ian's desperate struggle under the ice and the sight of the stranger swimming like a fish to her from deep in the pond's icy depths.

She had a very vague image of the stranger kissing her, but surely that wasn't real. It couldn't be, because the image that came right after that one was disgustingly flavored with the fear that she might have vomited in his lap. That particularly revolting thought went against every ladylike behavior she had acquired from her beautiful mother, Lady Claire, wife of John James Thomas MacArthur.

So Cassie put that thought aside and refused to dwell upon it just as resolutely as she refused her sister's urgings to sleep.

Maggie didn't allow a pair of idle hands any more than their mother, Lady MacArthur, did. For that matter, when she stayed at Glencoen, Cassie rarely saw her abigail, Dorcas, or her gillie, Old Angus, during the day long enough to say hello. There was too much work to be done, work that everyone pitched in to help finish. The farm's three most frequent visitors loved every minute of the bustle, work and commotion.

Old Angus couldn't be found indoors unless someone opened a cask of whiskey and wanted his fiddle-playing after sunset. Dorcas couldn't stay out of Glencoen's kitchen. She reveled in being allowed to bake all her favorite dishes from Maggie's overflowing larder. At Castle MacArthur, Cassie's parents' home, Cook wouldn't allow anyone from upstairs in his kitchens unless to pick up a tray or give instructions.

Cassie dressed quickly and went to the kitchen. There, Ian sat, devouring a bowl of brose and a biscuit. Millie had just finished her lessons at the table. Maggie handed wee Willie to Millie and told her to take the sleeping baby up to the nursery. Ian dogged his sister's steps out of the kitchen as Millie complained that she had enough to do with numbers and entertaining the baby without Ian coming along, too. Life was going on as usual without a single look back.

Cassie took that as her own cue for the balance of the day.

With a flash of her petticoats rustling about her quick feet, Maggie went out the door with Cassie following her. They were much alike, both sisters, but their faces and hair were very different. Maggie's lampblack curls were as dark as their mother's had once been. Cassie's hair was the cursed color of her father's, and she wished it weren't.

Just as she had her father's red hair, she had his blasted freckles. No man she had ever met took seriously a woman with pale lashes, colorless eyebrows, flaming hair and a face full of freckles.

Maggie, with her fine dark brows and flawless clear skin, was taken seriously by all men. None had dared to call Maggie by some silly childhood nickname the way Cassie had been called Lady Quickfoot since she'd won a boys' footrace in the Highland Games at the age of nine. On top of that, Cassie's slender body might be similar in shape and size to her mother's, but her face was the mirror image of her father's. She had his long straight nose with the little bump just at the beginning of the cartilage. Her lips were wide and thick and permanently curved into her father's trickster's smile, which always fooled people into thinking she was amused by what they did or said.

Worse, she had John MacArthur's chin, broad and blunt; not the sweet pointed chin that made her mother's face so very pretty.

Cassie held her tongue until they reached the lower floor of the house. In the spacious hall, she blandly asked, ''Who's to supper then?''

''Och.'' Maggie preened in a conspiratorial voice, unable to withhold the importance of her visitors. ''The travelers, Cassie, the ones who saved ye. Euan told me they are the Marquis of Hamilton's surveyors, whom the king has commissioned to make a new map of Scotland.''

''Aye, I know,'' Cassie said lamentably.

Stunned, Maggie replied, ''You know that? And here, Millie told me you did not speak of anything with them save the direction of our farmhouse. Cassie? I don't understand.''

Cassie shrugged and looked away from her sister, at a loss to explain what she knew and hadn't mentioned in her month-long visit.

"Something is going on here, Cassandra MacArthur," Maggie demanded, as curious as a cat let loose in a basket of knitting yarn. "How is it that you know what a marquis and a king are a-plotting?"

"I dinna say I knew that." Cassie took a deep breath, not knowing where to start, exactly. "Would it suffice to say I guessed who they were by the way they were measuring MacDonald's high meadow?"

"No, it will not. Cassie, talk to me for heaven's sake. Here we are indebted to them for two lives, yours and Ian's. So they've earned the right to sit to our table as honored guests. For heaven's sake, talk to me!"

Cassie forced herself to look her sister in the eye and reluctantly began to tell her about the king's messenger who came to Castle MacArthur in early December. "He brought two letters from the king, one to MacArthur and one specifically to me, which I received into my hand directly. The seal had not been broken so I am assured that MacArthur does not know the contents of the letters."

"The king wrote to you?" Maggie did her best to keep her impatience under control. Cassie could be maddeningly secretive.

"Well, that's the thing, you see," Cassie murmured softly. "The king's letter was really addressed to Lady Quickfoot, but the messenger gave it to me as though it had said Cassandra MacArthur."

"And the contents...."

"Well, it was a royal command." Cassie sat on the long bench of the table. Maggie settled beside her and took hold of her hand. "King James commands Lady Quickfoot to put her 'services as a mountain guide at the disposal of his surveyors, Gordon and Hamilton, as they measure and survey Lochaber.' The king also requires that all the proprieties of the Highlands be met." Cassie stopped short of telling Maggie the worst codicil. *Should Lady Quickfoot be a femme sole, all proprieties would be satisfied by her marriage to one Robert Gordon, surveyor, upon his arrival in Lochaber.* The king was thorough, she'd give him that much.

Maggie went from shock to laughter. "King James wrote all of that to Lady Quickfoot, did he?"

"Aye," Cassie replied somberly. "'Twere it addressed to me, I would have told you straight away about it…but…it's such a conundrum!"

"Aye," Maggie said, her mouth having the same difficulty keeping the smiles at bay as Cassie was. Then the two of them burst into laughter.

"Oh, that's rich," Maggie laughed, wiping at the tears in her eyes. "To think our king doesna know a children's tale from reality… It's too funny for words. Why, imagine what you would do if he commanded Lady Quickfoot to come to court."

"Well, I guess I'd dress up Millie and her dolls and send them to court, wouldn't I?" Cassie broke up again, holding her sides to keep from hurting her tender ribs with laughter. "You know who's behind this, don't you?"

"No. Who?" Maggie asked, wiping her face with her apron.

"That devil, our dear brother Jamie." Cassie reverted to her normal solemnity easily enough. "I can just see him at court, spinning tales to the king that would make mine sound as tame as Ian's favorite pudding."

"Aye, it has Jamie's mark of deviltry to it. He's as glib as an English bard. Well, you never know, Cassie, perhaps some good would come of this. You could be invited to court. Imagine your chances for finding the richest husband inland, if that were to happen. You'd certainly no' have to settle for one of father's choices then, would you?"

Cassie remained firmly noncommittal on that subject, which made Maggie press her hand down upon Cassie's resting fingers. "Are you no' ready to be making yer own home somewhere, Cassie?" Maggie asked, saying what was on her mind.

"Aye, well, I am and I'm not." Cassie shrugged her shoulders rather helplessly. There wasn't an awful lot she seemed able to do about her situation either way.

"Has Father no' had offers for ye since Alastair was buried?"

Plain speaking seemed to be Maggie's forte inside these walls. Cassie wasn't particularly warm to the subject, but she couldn't see any route around the truth. After a moment of thought, her mouth deepened at the corners in that perpetual smile that graced her face. "Well, aye, one or two that made my hair turn white."

"Old men, then?" Maggie didn't quite frown over Cassie's less than forthright admission.

"Older than James and Lord Sinclair, none so old as MacArthur."

"He wouldn't marry you off to an old bounder, would he?"

"Not unless I make him mad again. This past May he swore he would hand me off to the next man that offered."

"What had you done?" Maggie laughed. Her littlest sister had been telling their father off from the time she started talking. Maggie had always counted that to the fact that redheads rubbed each other raw. So it had been for their elder brother, Jamie, too, as well as their oldest sister, Roslyn.

Cassie had taken the eternal battle for autonomy to a new height. At the age of ten she began speaking of their father only as "MacArthur" whenever she was forced to refer to him in passing speech. Maggie didn't know why Cassie did that, but she'd always been curious to discover the reason. In that regard, Cassie had been as closemouthed on the subject as their father had been.

Cassie's face scrunched up in a comical scowl. "It wasn't anything, really. MacArthur favors his newest confidant, Douglas Cameron. You know him, the Cameron with the black beard that struts about like he's the good Lord's gift to womankind."

"Aye, I ken who, sister. I've heard my serving girls call him Douglas the Darling, for he's bedded every serving wench in Lochaber. Let's see to the table while we're talking," Maggie urged, and the two of them got up and set to work taking out trestles to enlarge the table for supper. The corners of Maggie's mouth twitched. "Douglas Cameron's a verra comely man."

"I've seen handsomer." Cassie refused to be pinned on that point.

"He gets along verra well with Euan," Maggie added. "They arm-wrestled to see who was stronger, and damn me if it didn't turn out to be a draw."

To that Cassie said promptly, "Aye, well, he's a man's man, isn't he now?"

"Mumph." Maggie laughed. "So what did you do to poor Douglas the Darlin' that put you on the black side of Papa's temper? Stick a burr under his saddle or poison his brose?"

"Oh, I wouldn't do anything like that," Cassie said, with her blue eyes so wide and innocent she couldn't be speaking the truth. "He came courting Beltane night, the first of May, and asked me to walk out with him. I said no—I wasna going up to the revelry in the hills. I wanted no part of the fumbling in the bushes, though I did say I'd go to the May crowning and watch the games earlier in the day."

"Then what happened?"

"Well, he said I was being as prudish as a papist nun, and I pretended neatly not to know what exactly he meant by that. The poor vain soul was being sorely put upon to explain himself clearly, so he grabbed me and smacked me on my lips to diagram things more clearly, then groped at my breasts like he was milking a cow."

"Did you like it?" Maggie prodded, taking a cloth

from her pocket to buff down the long polished table-top.

Cassie looked horrified at the very thought. "Has breathing the air on a mountain farm robbed you of the last of your wits, Maggie MacArthur? No, I didn't like it at all! Douglas the Darling hasn't taken a bath since he sprouted the first whisker of that great black beard on his face. He smells like pig farts. After I clobbered him to bring him back to his senses, I told him that, too. You know what he did?"

Maggie shook her head, helpless to contain her laughter.

"He tried to put his hand under my skirts!" Cassie complained indignantly.

As straight-faced as she could, Maggie replied, "Well, Cassie, what else is a man with his reputation to do when you've likened his romantic efforts to pig farts?"

Cassie gave in to the need to laugh heartily. So did Maggie.

"Curiously enough, MacArthur laughed when I told him that, too." Cassie grinned.

"So how did you get out of randy Douglas's clutches and into our father's bad graces?"

"I pushed Douglas off the battery wall to get away from the bounder. He slid down the stable roof and then tumbled into the well. Douglas caught the ague from the dunking and couldn't drag his dirty hide off his cot for more than a month. That caused Mac-Arthur to miss the Glorious Twelfth and all the fair hunting days between."

"Now wait there." Maggie held up her hand. "The

Glorious Twelfth is in August. Douglas should have been up and running by August.''

"Och, did I forget to mention that when Douglas crawled out of the well he had a broken leg?''

"Cassie!''

Cassie shrugged. "Serves the great big oaf right. It didn't mend straight. He can't track boars anymore or keep up with the other hunters on foot. MacArthur is racking his wits trying to figure out what to do with the man now when he comes a-visiting. Douglas eats as much as a horse, and we don't even want to go into his other charming attributes. Mother has about had it with Douglas the Darling and told MacArthur not to invite him to Achanshiel anymore.''

"Ah, I get it now. So what you're really saying is that father's sleeping on the cold side of the master's bed and that's why he threatened to marry you off to the next man that asks, bounder or no'. Look at things this way, Cassie, you've got two new men to choose from now that surveyors have come from court.''

"One's a Gordon, the other is a Hamilton. They're dead men if they cross Glencoe into Lochaber. Besides, I wouldn't have either,'' Cassie replied, ignoring the niggling frisson under her skin that told her she'd definitely have one of them.

"I can tell you this—I'd likely run off to Wales if MacArthur tried to force me to marry a man I find disgusting.''

Maggie threw up her hands. "Well then, there's a whole countryside full of eligible of men. Didn't you like one of the young Maitlands that danced with you at Cathy's wedding?''

"I liked talking to him. Maggie, I don't like really big men—warriors."

"Och, don't tell me you want a farmer." Maggie groaned. "You've been cosseted and waited on hand and foot since the day you were born. A farmer's no good for you."

"I'm no more a princess than you were," Cassie said, justifying herself. "I've been thinking about marrying a vicar."

Maggie rolled her eyes at the ceiling. She probably couldn't get her Catholic husband to go to a Protestant wedding if her sister married a vicar, let alone allow the two of them to enter his house as a married couple. "A vicar, Cassie? Why a vicar?"

It wasn't easy for Cassie to explain, since she hadn't had much time to explore the fantasy completely herself. "What I mean is I like to read, and all the ministers I know are always reading."

"So...you want a learned and educated man."

"Aye, and one who isn't adverse to bathing," Cassie quipped with a flashing grin.

"They will all do that if you make it a requirement to touching you," Maggie assured her.

Men, in Maggie's estimation, were merely overgrown, hairy little boys, needing to be managed and nurtured very carefully by a wise woman who knew what she needed and he needed. Cassie clearly hadn't caught on to that fact. But then, her sister was very used to going about things her own way—and spent too much time in the hills reading and wandering, attended by no more than a couple of elderly gillies their father trusted with her safety.

Maggie came around the table and gave her sister a hug. "Oh, you mustn't worry, sweetling. There's the right man for you out there somewhere. All the good ones can't be taken. I must go and see how the cooks are doing. Set out the candles, will you please?"

"Of course I will." Cassie squeezed Maggie back, and only cast the smallest of envious glances at Maggie's smooth unblemished complexion as their quick embrace ended. "Why did I get all the freckles and you didn't get a one?"

"Because God always saves his best for last." Maggie kissed her cheek and left her with one final gem of sisterly advice. "After you've done the candles, do go an' rest awhile. You're not as strong as you think you are, and the bairns willna let you go to bed without another of your stories."

Cassie turned to the cupboards. She tucked her hand across her lips to cover a yawn, and the unconscious gesture brought to mind a stranger's fingers touching her mouth. An honorable stranger whose liberties had been performed in an heroic and generous manner. She was not going to think about that.

She was not going to think about King James's letter or demands either. It wasn't her wish to lead a Gordon around Lochaber, revealing to him where each of her kinsmens' fortresses and strongholds were situated in the hills. King James had the wrong idea of Cassandra and Lady Quickfoot.

Cassie only elaborated on older, more traditional MacArthur clan legends. The king thought he could marry off a woman who didn't exist. Lady Quickfoot was a character in oral stories that were over two hundred years old. She wasn't real. She wasn't Cassandra MacArthur!

Besides that, the last person in the world she would marry would be a Gordon. He could well be the very man responsible for killing her beloved Alastair. God might forgive the Gordons the men they killed in battle, but that didn't mean the Campbells or MacArthurs ever would. Not this MacArthur at least.

Did she have the king's letter in her hands this moment, Cassie would burn it. At least she was consoled by the fact that the letter commanding "Lady Quickfoot" to serve his royal interests in Lochaber was safely hidden where no one could ever find it— behind a loose panel in the headboard of Cassie's bed at Castle MacArthur. Furthermore, its obscure addendum to Cassandra MacArthur regarding an unacceptable marriage to a Gordon would remain hidden as well.

Instead, she turned her thoughts toward supper, hoping it wouldn't last too long tonight. She, for one, intended to go to bed as early as the children did.

Cassie took out Maggie's tall candelabrum. Beeswax candles were kept in the stillroom, where it was damp and cool all year long. She fetched her cloak and headed outside. The darkening sky above the faraway mountains took her breath away. Cassie stopped perfectly still in her tracks, absorbing all her eyes beheld.

To the west, the faintest glow of sunset still tinted the winter sky, but to the east it was dark enough for the stars to shine though the gloaming.

Cassie leaned on the fence, enjoying the quiet and the wind and the silence that settled so peacefully around this farm. If she stayed out long enough, the stars would become so bright and thick in the cold air that they looked like faint clouds racing and twirling in the heavens, heralds of Apollo's chariot. She had half a mind to go up in the hills to where she always felt secure and one with the elements. That would certainly solve her current dilemma.

Granted, this Robert Gordon had said nothing to her about Lady Quickfoot. But that didn't mean he was unaware of Lady Quickfoot's identity.

Something bothered Cassie more than it had earlier. Alone, she could feel Gordon's hand cupping her breast, touching her throat and chin and fluttering across cold, sodden cloth stuck at her waist.

Cassie shook her head, refusing to dwell on such memories. She needed to leave her sister's farm as soon as possible, by first light tomorrow, before the subject of Lady Quickfoot could ever be broached. Before that blasted letter from King James could ever be mentioned.

Chapter Four

A glaze of ice filmed over the water that Robert had planned to use for his ablutions before supper. One bucket was far too little if he was going to be presentable enough to sit down to the lady of the house's table. No matter how filthy he was, Robert drew the line at immersing himself in the nearest loch. He refused to suffer such frigid torment twice.

He was too damned civilized for that.

The last hot bath he'd taken had been at an inn in Glen Orchy. He consoled himself with the hope that there would be inns up the road in Lochaber, too. He wouldn't put the womenfolk of this house through the extra work of boiling water so he could shave or wash. They worked as hard in a day as he did. That mild consideration meant that those same ladies would have to suffer his presence at supper with a week's stubble of beard, packing creases in his spare shirt and a kilt that had received no more than serious brushing to free it of Glencoe's rich black mud.

He would wash anything he possessed in water

drawn from a good well and did so all the time on his travels. Hence he stripped down inside the barn to his kilt and bare feet for the second night in a row, grimly facing the task before him.

A yellowed cake of hard lye soap made a gray lather on his hands. The light in the barn was dim, only a punched tin lantern helped him with his difficult task.

Road dirt was one thing, but the dirt from the muck in the byre was of another class. Robert dunked his hands in the water to rinse them and revolted against using that soil to wash his face or other parts. He had to throw it out and fetch fresh.

He shook the excess from his hands, picked up the bucket and went out into the darkening night. He didn't really feel the snow under his bare feet. Experience on the march and through wintry mountains had hardened him to the point that he only felt the cold when he actually warmed up. There were some crofts that he couldn't remain long in now. Robert couldn't breathe when the air was close and overheated indoors, or so smoky it choked him.

Actually, he was most content to have a barn or a shed to pass a cold night in, sufficient harbor from the wind. Mostly he and Alex sheltered with crofters. Farmsteads like this were as rare as royal princes in Scotland. Wherever they were at suppertime, they were always invited to share what fare the family had. Glencoen Farm was a double boon. The food offered on this prosperous farm's table was filling and plentiful.

If there was one thing Robert missed on this mission to complete the first stage of his cartographer's work, it was hot food, served to him regularly. When this journey ended, he didn't think he would be able to look at a blackened coney on a spit with any sort of relish. But he did now. At this moment he'd have eaten a raw rabbit. That was how ravenous he always was at the end of every arduous day of hiking and measuring mountains.

Come June, the task would be over. Nothing was going to distract Robert from the goals he had so permanently fixed in his mind—nothing. Once all of Scotland was measured, they could sit down to the next task, that of compiling all the measurements, diagrams and drawings into a concise and perfect graphic rendering of Scotland as she really, truly was.

In Campbell country, King James's approval of their work carried about as much weight as the Marquis of Hamilton's endorsement—none. The coin of commerce in Glen Orchy and Lochaber was the bond and goodwill of the Earl of Argyll, Archibald Campbell. Even if Robert had garnered that august man's endorsement it wouldn't have mattered. He was a Gordon and Highland Campbells hated all Gordons. Their ill will came with the territory.

On the positive side, Robert and Alex knew more about Scotland than any other Scotsman alive. They had cataloged the elevation of nearly five hundred mountains, identified the longitude and latitude of each hamlet, village and township in the realm and measured the length and breadth of every lake, bay, inlet and peninsula in their convoluted, mountainous homeland.

All save what terrain lay in the shire of Lochaber.

Lochaber was the last. The only shire remaining on their list to be surveyed. Someday soon, the end result would be a map that was as precisely accurate as their mathematical brains could make it.

It was an occupation that would fill the best years of their lives and no small ambition. They were sworn on their scholars' vow before God Almighty to make their map the most accurate map ever made of their Scotland. A map that navigators could use for centuries to come with complete faith in its accuracy.

Since the age of ten and four Robert had been assigned to the George Gordon, the Earl of Huntly's vanguard, as a scout reconnoitering the terrain ahead of the earl's army. Robert had come to cherish accurate maps and guarded them with his life. It had paid in the end. He and his brothers and most of his kinsmen were all alive and for the most part, the victors in the recent civil wars.

Too many of Argyll's poorly prepared Campbells weren't.

Robert shook himself out of his reverie and stamped his way to the well. He hoped the day's luck held and MacGregor would crack open a bottle of his whiskey and invite them to share a wee dram or two of it.

The mud was more dense at the farm's well than anywhere else outside the pigs' byre. No matter where he'd traveled it never seemed to get cold enough to freeze the mud under a bunch of dirty pigs. He caught the rope and pulled down the well pole, dropping the bucket into the water below. The crackle of filmy ice snapped in the cold air, quite loud.

"Who's there?" a started voice asked.

Robert turned to find the speaker and found a woman at the fence gate of a shed. He raised his hand and called out, "Don't be alarmed. It's only me, Robert Gordon, the surveyor."

"Ah, the man who saved my life," replied the woman in a rueful voice.

He squinted across the increasing gloom and found the wry speaker. It was definitely the same young lady Robert had watched skate with the farmer's children—the redheaded maiden with freckles on her nose and lips set in a perpetual smile. The young woman whose life he'd saved and body he'd held and breath he'd shared. He'd wondered if she was avoiding him apurpose.

His Lady Quickfoot wore a most unlikely disguise—that of a simple hill farmer's sister.

It was dark. Not so very dark that he couldn't see her hair forming a river of captured fire against the deep darkness of her woolen cloak. Drat that, he thought. What was she doing out in the cold? She was standing still as the night air against the closed gate. Perhaps she'd only come outside to take some cooler air. He hoped that wasn't a sign that the farmhouse felt like Lord Hamilton's African hothouse.

Robert shook his head and told himself it was none of his business what she was doing outdoors. Did he have the good sense the Lord had blessed him with, he'd get his water and go back to the barn before his whole body turned into an icicle without his ever knowing it.

He could forget that he knew she was Lady Quickfoot and go on about his business. He didn't need a woman's help to complete one speck of his work. If the truth were told—which it never could be in Scotland when Campbell kinsmen were about—Robert had his own suspicions about King James's peculiar motives. Why the king would even want to pair another Campbell or Gordon together was beyond him. Robert needed nothing more than his own astute gifts of logic and scientific investigation to complete this mission of his in Lochaber. Yet the king thought otherwise.

Ignoring the beautiful woman, Robert tipped the dipper and poured its contents into his bucket. The excess splashed onto a layer of dirty straw. Cold water skittered across snow, ice, straw and black mud, soaking the toughened soles of his bare feet.

"There's a huge kettle full of heated water to bathe with in the shed behind the kitchens," Cassie said, reluctantly deducing his purpose for sojourning out into the elements in only his kilt.

It neither alarmed nor impressed her to see any man going about without his sark at this time of the day on the farm. Nor could she figure out why she was speaking to him. She might well owe him something for her life, but that debt ought to be well paid by Euan's offer of hospitality. Then she remembered, Gordon hadn't just saved her. He'd rescued Ian, too. So Cassie offered more…as an appeasement to her conscience. Maggie would expect that of her.

"Euan keeps soaps and razors and scrub brushes for all to use. You are welcome to help yourself. Your friend has already gone in to see to his toilette. You've time before supper. Do you want me to show you where to go?"

Robert looked down at the full bucket of cold water. She couldn't have tempted him more if she'd invited him to share her feather bed, provided the sheets were clean, and her body sweet and perfumed of lavender or roses.

He made a strangled sound inside the back of his throat that Cassie took to mean "give me a moment," about-faced and marched back into the barn. He came out moments later, his plaid swirled around his body, his feet stuffed in muddy boots, strutting stiff-legged like the soldier he really was straight to her.

She thanked the coming night for obscuring her reaction to his face and those eyes that had taken her breath away when she'd come out of her deep faint with his lips hovering over her freezing mouth. He'd been so warm and alive and concerned, she'd thought him an archangel. Thank God he didn't know who she was. No one at this farm would reavel her connection to Lady Quickfoot, either.

"The washhouse is this way." She gathered her cloak around her and picked up her hems, leading the surveyor to the back of the manse. There, the kitchens and laundry room became a tangled warren of additions, expanded the south wing of the house.

Cassie opened the door and peeked inside, then stood it ajar. Her quick glance confirmed that the other surveyor looked better for the washing he'd already done. He was about to shave as Cassie motioned Robert Gordon to pass inside.

She stared frankly at Robert Gordon and boldly wondered if his darkly handsome face would wash up as well as his companion's had. A bit shy of her own romantic thoughts and troubled by the memory of his life-restoring kiss, she wagged her hand in the general direction of tubs, soaps and huge black kettle steaming above the washhouse hearth.

"Euan and Old Angus have already gone in to the hall," she said in a husky voice. "Help yourself to what you need. Excuse me, I have to get candles for the table."

"Your servant, milady." Robert bowed precisely to her. She surprised the very devil out of him by dropping to a brief but very formal curtsy. Then she was gone from his sight, vanished beyond the closed door in a heartbeat.

That rattled Robert. The last deep curtsy to him personally had been given by the Duke of Atholl's youngest daughter. The silly twit had thought him some romantic knight errant, equivalent to the gallant-to-his-very-soul adventurer, Sir Walter Raleigh. Granted the setting had been Holyrood and Lord Hamilton had insisted Robert and Alex attend an audience with King James and explain their ambitious plan to the king and his full court. Both Robert and Alex had been flush with enthusiasm and idealism of the kind that belongs only to the very young and foolish.

As suited the king's pleasure, each had dressed in his foppish best to please the court. Robert Gordon had cut the best figure with his lean, athletic grace and inbred military bearing, and well he knew it. At twenty-one his young man's conceit had been without limit. The magical part of that affair was King James was not much older than he, Timothy or Alex, and was instantly caught up in the romance of their altruistic quest. Instead of being bored to tears by their pompous reasoning, James VI was delighted.

Had a bitterly contested civil war not interfered, their map would be complete today.

But war had interfered and could do so again before this new year was out. Robert accepted what he must. When a Gordon *cross truach,* a fiery cross, summoned the men of clan Gordon to their laird's aid, Robert answered duty's call. Today was another day of tenuous peace, forced upon the Campbells and Gordons by their king. Each day that the peace continued, Robert thanked God for it and best used the time to advance his work closer to completion.

Privately, he added his own prayers that the king's peace would continue into a second year with no renewed hostilities.

The young woman whose life he'd saved was a Campbell kinswoman, his clan's avowed enemy in every way, shape and form. He must never forget that fact when dealing with Cassandra MacArthur. Nor could he forget that he needed the king's peace to accomplish his goals of finishing his work. How much could Lady Quickfoot affect the uneasy peace? Would he be better off ignoring her identity and hillfolk title completely?

Robert snapped out of his reverie-induced thoughts as Alex snapped a razor blade against his face. He cut a crater through the thick lather coating his cheeks and hiked a fair eyebrow into the tangled elflocks dripping on his brow. He pointed the blade at the empty tub and full kettle, then spoke. "The water's still hot, Robbie."

When Alexander Hamilton deigned to speak at all, it was most commonly in the acquired brogue of the Lowlands. Alex's innate inclination to shy from conversation with most Highlanders had been honed to a finely measured reticence by their travels in Glenlyon and his reluctance to place any further claim on his Lowlander father's good graces. That they had funding to pursue their work was enough.

"Did you see that?" Robert asked in amazement.

"Eh, Robbie, what? No, I guess I didn't."

"That young woman curtsied to me. To me! For pity's sake, don't I look like something that just crawled out of a cave or washed up with a pile of wreckage from the Armada?"

Alex looked him up and down with a familiar jaundiced smirk, then said, "Oh, aye, laddie, you look all of that disreputable and then some—with your skinny arse barely keeping that kilt around your hips. Better ask MacGregor's goodwife if she can sew a few more pleats in that raggedy scrap before you put it back on."

"Shut yer face, ye half-wit." Robert flung his kilt onto a peg and folded into the steaming, soapy tub. He sat a while just enjoying the heat swirling around his feet and hips, the tub deep enough with him in it to cover his navel.

"Mayhap it wasn't so curious. You did save her life, Rob." Alex resumed his silent shaving, the understatement in his words reverberating against the low rafters.

Robert swatted that statement aside as he might an annoying horse fly, firmly and irrevocably. He wasn't going to launch himself on any young woman's heroic pedestal and remain there long enough to be snared romantically deep in Campbell territory. Not when his surname was Gordon and would stay Gordon all the rest of his days.

"What do you intend to do about your Lady Quickfoot?" Alex asked softly. As a spy this quiet man was always quick to draw the clearest deductions.

Robert's dark eyebrows narrowed in a concerned frown. "I haven't thought it through yet."

He didn't want to consider it now, either. He took a deep breath of the heavily scented air of this dark room and found it achingly aromatic. The sweet smells of soap and hair tonics competed with the overpowering aroma of the haunch of mutton sizzling in the kitchen next door.

One of the farm's servants came in from the kitchen and out though the door into the yard. Robert knew Alex would not say anything more for a good while, so he began to wash his head, soaking his long, tangled hair with hot water.

Lined up on a shelf at his elbow were soaps and sponges, back brushes and boar-bristle brushes to get the crusted soil off his elbows and knees and hands.

It was a while before he became conscious of Hamilton's chuckles behind him. Robert turned and glared at his friend. "Well, what?" he demanded.

"I think there must be a lot of Viking blood running in the veins of all you Gordons, Robbie."

"And what led you to that outlandish assumption?"

"Every last Gordon I've ever met takes more pleasure in a teacup full of hot water than they do in an entire loch. If you weren't so squeamish a line, you could get the same task done and over with as easily as any Hamilton does."

"And following on that erroneous pretense to logic, the first Hamiltons were great, fat, bloody seals, were they not?"

"At least we bathe whenever the mood strikes us, ice in the lake or no." Alex quipped, then ducked so the soapy sponge flying at him didn't stain his only clean shirt.

Cassie's brow puckered as she hurried back to the stillroom, her purpose high on her mind. She mustn't dawdle any longer. She didn't want Maggie sticking her head out one of the doors, hollering for her to come with candles before supper turned cold.

As she selected candles from the supply in the stillroom, she couldn't help wondering about the reticent young man. That bow of his had been delivered with what she knew to be military precision, modestly correct, elegant and brief. There was no artifice involved, no courtly posing or showing of the leg, which would have been ludicrous given his state of undress.

Twelve thick candles gathered in a fold of her cloak, Cassie shut the door of the stillroom firmly behind her and hurried back to the hall. She set each candelabrum on an imaginary line bisecting the long table. By then Sybil and Dorcas had come to put out the cold platters and tankards and silver.

Cassie hurried upstairs to see to her own toilette.

She unlaced her stays and shed her day dress, changed into a clean, ironed shift and scrubbed her face with mint water and coarse oatmeal to bleach her freckles. It never helped. Neither did vinegar nor great quantities of fresh cucumbers in season nor any of the exotic creams the Gypsies concocted or the tinkers sold. She powdered the worst of the spots and smoothed the rice powder onto her throat and shoulders with a soft puff of cotton lint.

She shook out her best gown and pulled it over her head, settling it down her chest and belly. Dorcas came to tie up her laces just as she picked up her new embroidered stomacher to put on over the gown.

"Is it time?" Cassie asked.

"Not yet," Dorcas said. She pulled the stomacher tight and threaded the laces with nimble fingers, drawing the corsetlike outer garment snug across Cassie's breasts and stomach.

The tight serge weave of the navy wool gown suited Cassie's coloring, darkening her pale eyes and making the pure white linen of her cuffs and shift look pristine and white. Cassie sat so that Dorcas could tuck her slippers over her heels and do up the laces. It wasn't possible to bend forward so much as an inch in the stiff stomacher when it was laced.

"Did ye hear that one of those surveyors is a Sassenach?"

"English, you say?" Cassie tilted her head, managing to feign surprise. "Which one?"

"'Tis the stout one, Hamilton. The handsome one is a Gordon, a Scot."

"Dorcas—" Cassie brought her head close to the woman's to whisper emphatically "—you dinna think they're here to forage out MacGregor's gold and slit our throats in the dark of night?"

"Och, Lady Cassandra." The elder clucked her tongue and shook her head. "Dinna be teasin' me like ye do the bairns. I'm too wise for yer tall tales. Here, let me put a brush to yer hair."

"I'm only teasing because you well know that Hamiltons have been notoriously breeding sons and daughters openly in Scotland since the Norman conquest, even if they do have the appalling habit of kidnapping rich English heiresses for brides."

"Humph," Dorcas grumbled. "Those that claim to be Scottish are Lowlanders."

"So now it's only Highlanders that deserve to be counted our countrymen?"

"There's no much difference between a Lowlander and an Englishman, is there?" Dorcas said firmly.

"Aye. I hear tell they both get in and out of bed the same way," Cassie agreed, but added a codicil in a delicious gossipy whisper. "One leg at a time."

"Lady Cassandra!" Dorcas tugged the brush against Cassie's scalp. "Ye shouldn't be talkin' of such scandalous things, or thinkin' them either. And mind that those bairns don't spill anythin' on this fine gown. 'Tis lovely enough to wear to the crowning of the king.''

Cassie didn't think so, but it was good that her abigail did. "Thank you, Dorcas, I'll do my best not to make a mess of it. You needn't bother with brushing my hair too much. I'll wear it braided tomorrow for the journey home. I want to get an early start, before the house has a chance to rouse, mind you, so pack tonight, please.''

"'Tis glad that I am to hear that,'' Dorcas declared. "And will ye be telling Lady Margaret that you're going?''

"Aye, I'll tell her at supper. See that you keep my plans secret from the surveyors,'' Cassie said unequivocally.

"So I will do,'' Dorcas snapped, giving her a puzzled look. "I'm glad of that.''

"Why's that? You never like going back to Castle MacArthur any more than I do usually.''

"Very well, if ye must know, Lady Cassandra, I don't want the responsibility of ye being in the company of a Sassenach.''

Cassie chuckled. Dorcas thought she wanted to escape poor Alexander Hamilton when nothing could be further from the truth. He wasn't the surveyor whose company would bother Cassandra at all. Robert Gordon, on the other hand, bothered her a great deal. She didn't understand why, not yet, at least. Nor did she want to stick around and find out. "Betwixt us at dinner, we'll probably scare the poor man back to London before the pudding is served,'' Cassie said, and gave her abigail's hand a squeeze.

Dressing and grooming done, Cassie went down to her sister's hall, wondering how this evening at Glencoe Farm would turn out. If Maggie sat poor Alex Hamilton anywhere near Dorcas, he'd likely not get through the meal without getting a dirk stuck in his heart.

To Cassie's great disappointment, supper turned into more of a trial than she'd bargained for.

Nothing had prepared her for Gordon's appearance in Euan MacGregor's hall. Granted the impact his eyes had made on her at first glance should have given her a clue, but eyes were only one of a dozen or more features that could attract a woman's heart.

From somewhere in that tinker's pack of overstuffed saddlebags, Robert Gordon had pulled out a spotless lace-edged cravat and tied it around his throat with continental flair that was more suited to the king's court than a hillside farm. Likewise, a set of beautiful cuffs spilled out of the sleeves of an elegantly cut black jacket. The knife-edge pleats of his kilt set off the lean lines of his tall form perfectly.

His beard-stubbled face had been scraped clean, his hair pulled back into a tightly bound queue. All in all, he quite took Cassie's breath away.

His hands elegantly punctuated his words every time he spoke. Swallowing food she never tasted, Cassie watched him as surreptitiously as she could, fascinated, but not wanting anyone at the table to guess how intrigued by this man she really was. Robert Gordon had transformed himself from a vagabond to a peer of the realm in the space of three quarters of an hour.

And he had kissed her.

Cassie found herself blushing to the roots of her hairline. Thank the Lord no one noticed. Even Maggie was much too entertained by the humorous anecdotes the surveyors told of their travels and travails while measuring Scotland.

Listening, Cassie realized very quickly that she was in the presence of a master in the art of dissembling. Robert Gordon never gave one hint why mapping the Highlands was so important to him any more than he missed savoring a heaping serving of the excellent foods put in front of him. Nor did conversation ever stray to what purpose their patron, the Marquess of Hamilton, had in mind for funding their audacious endeavor either.

"Why must ye make a new map of Scotland? What's wrong with the map we have?" Millie's clear soprano voice sang out, directly asking the question they all wanted answered.

Robert Gordon laid his hands flat on the table beside his empty plate, turned to Millie and answered her in a serious voice. "Because all maps of Scotland are wrong."

"How do ye know they're wrong?"

Children, Cassie knew, would do almost anything to escape being bored. She wanted to applaud her niece, but a quick check of Millie's parents' nettling brows kept Cassie silent.

"That's a very good question, Millicent." That he remembered her niece's name took Cassie aback.

"How do you usually know if something is wrong, Millie? May I call you Millie?"

Now he had Cassie's undivided attention. Men rarely took notice of curious little girls, let alone engaged in conversation with them.

Cassie watched his right hand unfasten a horn button on his coat, then settle contentedly on the warm bulge of his lean stomach. She saw that his tapered fingers and nails were as clean as her own and frowned privately because that was another mark in his favor. Drat the man! Why did she keep discovering new things about him she liked?

"Oh, aye," Millie chirped. "That's what everyone calls me. I know something's wrong because my da tells me so." Millie then thought about what she'd said and added, "Or I ask my mother."

"And if they can't tell you the answer?"

Undaunted, Millie responded, "I would go to the Bible."

"Have you seen any maps of Scotland in a Bible, Millie?" He sought clarity as subtly as an Edinburgh-trained tutor.

"No, they didn't know about Scotland in Our Lord's time. My grandfather, Laird MacArthur, has maps of Scotland. I've seen them, but he won't let me play with them because he says they're more precious than jewels."

"When I was a little older than you, I sailed as my uncle's cabin boy to the Orneys and learned to navigate the ship, chart the course it traveled each day at sea. I learned to use tools that correctly measure a ship's position. Let me give you an example. Do you know how far the pond you were skating at yesterday is from your home?''

Millie's face scrunched up in deep consideration of that question. She looked to her father, then without any prompting said proudly, ''A wee stretch of the legs is all.''

''Aye.'' Robert Gordon smiled at the little girl, lavishing the child with his undivided attention.

Cassie thought the smile very kind of him. He had a beautiful smile, white, even teeth and a well-formed head. His brown hair was thick and wavy, still damp and curly at the nape of his neck. She tried to imagine him in a court wig and couldn't.

She clapped her hand to her face and looked out upon the proceedings through widened fingers. Why was she was even trying to fit a vagabond wanderer into her imaginary daydreams?

''Three miles uphill is a wee stretch of any lassie's legs.'' Robert Gordon's voice interrupted her thoughts. ''Or more precisely, it is exactly fifteen thousand eight hundred forty feet or three miles.''

''Lordy! Do ye mean it for true?'' Millie quit staring at the mapmaker's clear blue eyes and looked at Cassie, exclaiming, ''Aunt Cassie, no wonder we dinna skate not nearly so much that day!''

''It's easier to come down than it is to go up,'' Cassie replied.

''Not with Ian dragging on yer skirts,'' Millie observed as she turned to her father to see if he had known that his wee stretch of the legs was now officially three long, measurable miles.

Robert Gordon looked over the platters of food to

Cassie, who was sitting at her sister's side. They were alike and they weren't alike. He'd never have picked them as sisters if the similarity of their blue eyes was not so pronounced. He spoke to them both, but his words rebutted Cassie's rather foolish observation.

"Up or down, it's the same true distance in miles, going and coming. That's the trouble with all previous maps of Scotland. None of them is accurate. She's a bigger country than we realize, with thousands of beautiful bays, rivers, inlets, lakes, islands and peninsulas. She's not a stubby thumb stuck on top of England as you may have seen drawn in most engravings."

Laird MacArthur did have some of those engravings in his study, maps of England and Spain and Ireland. Cassie had never spent much time looking at them beyond learning answers to her tutor's questions. And they weren't relevant to her interests as Lady Quickfoot either. What she relied upon in navigating Lochaber's mountains was her well-honed sense of direction and the well-worn trails of cattle, deer and other climbers.

Her brother James, however, had better maps— great sea charts that had to be carefully unrolled and needed a large trestle to inspect in any sort of understandable manner. Nonetheless, in most of them, Scotland was depicted as a sort of warty thumb stuck atop the better defined and more detailed maps of England, just as Robert had said.

Millie had exhausted her font of curiosity for the moment. Angus returned, having fetched Euan a cask of aged whiskey he'd requested to follow the meal. Cassie turned to Maggie and touched her sleeve.

"I thought to tell you tonight so you'll take the news in good stride. If the fair weather holds, I'll be going home tomorrow."

"You are not going home tomorrow," Maggie rebutted, in a voice that brooked no arguing.

"Nay, Maggie, tomorrow, it is," Cassie said just as firmly, then added her reason why in order to soften Maggie's disappointment. "I think it would be better if I arrive home before my birthday, else Mother will get her nose out of joint."

"And you think Father won't?"

"If you think he even notes my absences you're fooling yourself greatly."

"Och, Cassandra, when are you going to let the past go? I swear, you bear a grudge longer than a Campbell."

"I don't know what you're talking about."

"Oh, yes, you do, Cassandra MacArthur, do you but think about it." Maggie shook her head and repeated an old Scottish proverb. "'Woe to the child born the night no light will guide him to the truth.'"

"And what's that supposed to mean?" Cassie inquired, acting deliberately obtuse.

"You forget that you're winter's infant, born in the dark of the moon." Maggie crossed herself against old superstitions. "It's time you let go. Father's an old man now. He only wants peace in his family and prosperity on his land. What do you want from him that he hasn't given you already?"

"Nothing," Cassie said flatly. "Nothing at all."

Then she turned her attention back to Millie, who had climbed onto her father's knee and was patting his cheek with an adoring hand.

Euan caught the child's hand and brought it to his lips, put a kiss in Millie's palm and asked her to bide a while and in the crook of his arm.

It was a painfully intimate moment, one of unconditional love between father and daughter. Cassie, who had always looked for a hero, realized that her sister had found one in her Highland farmer with no ambitions to grandeur.

Sadly, Cassie had no memories of such intimacy or caring between Laird MacArthur and herself. She nudged her chin at the head of the table and asked Maggie, "Did you ever sit on MacArthur's lap like that?"

"Oh, aye." Maggie cast a fond gaze at her husband and eldest child. "A thousand times. Then along came Cathy—although Mother often had to hold her, because I wouldn't let her sit with Father and me."

Maggie grinned as she remembered more.

"I was a right terror at three, spoiled rotten, I suppose. By the time you were born, Cathy and I had paired off, amusing each other and watching out for each other. Father had you all to himself for a very long time, his baby and his pride and joy."

"I have no memory of that," Cassie said flatly.

"You don't?" Maggie frowned.

"No. My earliest memory is of the day the messenger came to tell us James was lost at sea during the Armada."

"Oh, Cassie, you were old then. Eight or nine at

least. I was past twelve. Don't you remember when James went away? Lord Almighty, the fights and arguments...I thought James and Father were going to murder each other.''

Cassie shook her head. ''The way I remember it Jamie was banished for good, never to be allowed to step foot in Achanshiel.''

''Och, we've always lived in a tempestuous house.'' Maggie took a sip of wine, then looked at Cassie concerned. ''The past was troubling, but Jamie came home, and Father forgave him, God be praised. It's the way of life. We make our own way in it, and find our own happiness.''

''I know that, Maggie. I'm not daft.'' Cassie cast a glance at the other diners, aware that her and Maggie's conversation excluded the menfolk. They didn't seem to mind, caught up in their own talk about cattle and crops. A definite sign that the meal was coming to an end.

''Of course you aren't. Speaking of Jamie, do you suppose he or Janet will come home for your feast day since you actually have a countable day this year?''

''I don't think so. Cathy might. She isn't so far away nor does she have any bairns to tie her and Georgie down,'' Cassie replied.

''Cathy owes me a letter,'' Maggie said. ''And Roslyn? She promised me in her last letter she'd come home if she had a wedding to attend.''

''She promised me the same thing.'' Cassie offered a wry consolation. ''But it hasn't brought me any luck.''

"Come, you can help me put my wee heathens to bed. You're verra good at making up stories, and Millie does love fairy tales."

Maggie rose and made their excuses to the men. Cassie followed, bringing along Millie, who, at the promise of a bedtime story, vacated her father's lap.

Beg the children might for a long story, but as tired as Cassie was, it had to be a short one tonight. On her next visit, Cassie promised, she would invent a new and exciting adventure for Lady Quickfoot to keep them dreaming a long while.

Chapter Five

Robert noted the ladies' departure with mixed emotions. He needed to speak to Cassandra MacArthur privately. She had caught him unawares on his way to the well earlier when he had not been dressed for a chat with a Highland lady. On reflection he admitted that it was her elegant mode of dress that had taken him by surprise. She was not a simple Highlander's daughter. No, that fine velvet cloak she'd worn belonged to a well-to-do lady, just as did the elegant gown she sat down to the table wearing. Her refined manners during the meal merely confirmed his belief.

Robert had also noted no one on this farm addressed Cassandra MacArthur as Lady Quickfoot.

She was simply Cassie to one and all. But then her sister claimed no title here either, other than wife of Euan MacGregor, though both were well-born daughters of a titled father and mother.

Neither Robert nor Alex lasted much past the ladies' departure. After the second cup of Mac-

Gregor's fine whiskey, they sought their beds in the barn.

The night air crackled with the frost inside the barn and out, which was fine with Robert. The sky remained clear, though there would surely be mist come morning. It was anyone's guess about how much of this second day of melting snow would freeze again by morning.

Alex was rolled in a woolen blanket in a haystack he'd stamped into suitable shape. Robert shed his jacket and waistcoat, rolled both neatly and tucked them into his saddlebags with fastidious care, then did the same exercise with a rough horse blanket as Alex had done. He shook out his plaid, preparing to wind it around his shoulders. A soft rapping on the barn door made him turn and look beyond the cone of flickering mellow light from their lantern.

Lady Quickfoot stood at the edge of available light, her dark gown blending deep into the night's shadows. Those wide lips curved into that perpetually enchanting smile and there was just the glimmer of white teeth as she spoke, but overall her expression proclaimed she was here to do a duty no one else would do.

"My sister suggested I bring extra quilts with her apologies for there not being a bedstead in the house you could occupy. Do you stay on, you'll find better accommodations on the morrow, for I'll be going home at first light."

Her arms encased a stack of patchwork quilts and feather pillows covered in ironed muslin. Robert blinked in surprise. He didn't want her to leave. Why that thought even came to mind troubled him. Alex snored softly from his bed of wool and hay.

"Angus says it's going to freeze the jams in the cellar." The merest hint of a true smile sent her enchanting freckles dancing.

At the sight of that reluctant yet mischievous grin, Robert felt his natural reserve melt into a responding grin of his own.

"We never expected our comfort to trouble either of you," he said politely.

He took the quilts from her arms and grazed her breast in the taking. They both froze, each very, very aware of the unintended touch.

"Your pardon." Robert recovered quickly, taking firm hold of the bundle and stepping back to give her room to maneuver in the stall.

"Oh!" Cassie mumbled, dismissing the accidental touch with a forgiving flutter of her hand and a self-conscious glance at Alex's recumbent form.

That scant and totally unplanned connection to her softly warm body made Robert much too conscious of her unspoiled beauty all over again. *Hold on there, Robbie,* he thought, tamping down the near-instant reaction of his nether region. *Watch your step with this lassie. She'll have you in over your head in a heartbeat, she will.*

"'Tis no trouble." Cassie deliberately ignored Robert's discomfort. "I was looking for an excuse to come speak to both of you. But I see your friend is already asleep."

"Aye, he is." Robert occupied himself with stacking the linen bounty on the clean straw. Finished, he turned back to the young woman. He regarded her more cautiously now that his body had shown serious interest in her. Lord above, but she was a pretty woman. Not that he dared forget he was in enemy territory, and she, in essence, was the enemy.

She hadn't stepped away.

Robert asked smoothly, "And what is it you wish to speak about?"

Her square chin thrust upward and she stood as tall as she could, shoulders square and bearing proud. Even so, the top of her head would have barely grazed his chin if he closed the distance between them to embrace her in his arms.

"I needed to thank you for what you did for Ian, saving his life. I'm very grateful that you came back to the pond and helped us. We would both surely be wound in our shrouds if you hadn't acted with such expedience to help us. I'm also certain that Laird MacArthur will want to reward you for your courage. He has a very special tenderness for Ian."

"And no similar regard for you, lady?" Robert asked, put a bit off center by her interpretation of his deed. The plain truth was, she'd rescued the boy. Robert had saved her life.

Her pale brows twitched, then quickly settled into a normal arch above her lovely expressive eyes. "It is not my place to speak to that subject. I am only one of several daughters, while Ian is the oldest of four cherished grandsons. Sons bear a different weight in the Highlands as well you know."

Robert started to speak but she held up a steady hand, begging him not to interrupt.

"Please, let me say what I must. The time has come to put gratitude aside and speak plainly. Euan feels too obligated to say what he should. You and your friend, Hamilton, are not welcome in Lochaber. If you insist on traveling here, something very unfortunate may happen to you. So please, take your rest for this night, then return whence you came and leave us be. Go back to Edinburgh and make your pretty drawings and be done with us. I will see that whatever reward due you for your heroics is promptly delivered to you there."

Cassie gulped, relieved that her message had been delivered with as little discourtesy as possible. She curtsied briefly and spun about to leave before that wild and unbelievable urge to kiss his breathtaking lips overwhelmed her. Surely she owed him nothing more than the polite, empty words she'd already uttered. She'd said what needed to be said.

"We canna leave." Robert responded before she could depart. "Unless you would have your famous Ben Nevis named as naught but a hill."

"A hill!" Cassie's eyes turned round as walnuts with her stunned declaration. "That's preposterous! Ben Nevis is the highest mountain in all of this isle!"

"Oh? Is that so? How tall is it?"

"Close to five thousand feet. I've climbed it myself!"

"Oh, I doubt that." Robert's challenge of her claim was seconded by an owl's startled fluttering. "And how many mountains have you climbed in England or Wales to use for comparison? What measuring stick did you use to count those thousands of feet?"

"Don't treat me like a fool. Everyone knows they haven't any real mountains in England. The whole country's flat as a Methodist's hat."

Robert loftily looked down the length of his nose at her smug expression. "And ye've been to Devonshire and Lancashire and seen this for yerself, ha' ye? Did ye pace off the whole bleeding English countryside on foot, then, milady? Use scope and scale and mathematics to calculate the depth of the Sassenachs' gullies and tops of their dales? Do ye know that to be scientific, a body of land's height above and depth below sea level must be measured accurately?"

"Saint Colum's toes, you've done it again!" Cassie caught herself staring too blessed deep into his compelling eyes. She shook her head and spoke more earnestly and urgently than before. "Hang your blithering double-talk! How much more plainspoken must I be? End your journey here at Glencoe. Can I no' get it through your thick head, you'll be killed if you venture into Lochaber? You're a Gordon!"

"That makes no difference," Robert said loftily.

"Oh? Go farther into Campbell land and see what difference it truly makes. This is madness! Go back to Edinburgh and the king's court and consider your surveying done. I wouldn't give a Scottish penny for your chances beyond this farm."

Again, Cassie turned to depart, angry that twice he'd taken her totally off the track of what she intended to say and do.

"I understand your feelings, but leaving is out of the question. We are on a sacred mission, fully endorsed by our king, Lady Quickfoot."

She froze. *He knew! Damn him! He knew.* She spun back to face him, her mobile face now clouded with alarm. "What did you call me?"

"Lady Quickfoot," Robert drawled, as possessed and cool as could be. "That is who you are."

"Nay, I am not!" Cassie hotly denied, her face and throat flushing anew with bright color.

Robert held up his hand for her silence. "Your fame throughout the great glen and the mountains of Lochaber long ago reached Edinburgh and the king's ears. I am certain you do not care to have further attention from the crown levied on your young head. Your forms of amusement have far outranked your fame."

"What's that supposed to mean?" Cassie's eyes narrowed. She prayed he was guessing, and refused to confirm his assumption. "I tell you I am not Lady Quickfoot! Why, she's naught more than..."

Robert had no idea why he reached out and put his fingers on her warm lips, softly squelching her words. The bold gesture was done in the span of a heartbeat. His direct touch made her inhale sharply and take a deep step back from him.

"Deny it all you like, but 'twill do you no good. The king is as well apprised of what goes on in this shire, as in others. Your identity has been kept no state secret," Robert reasoned. "Even your brother, James, boasts at court of your ambitious accomplishments. Why pretend it is not so now?"

"That answer should be obvious, sir. It smacks of a threat from a far court." Cassie gulped and swallowed, then bit her tongue. Lady Quickfoot was no more than an imaginary heroine, in an oral tradition of bedtime stories and tall tales repeated round clan MacArthur evening fires to soothe and entertain young children. Granted, Cassie contributed much to the legendary lady's spreading fame, but that didn't make her Lady Quickfoot in reality, because no one could ever really be Lady Quickfoot or do what that fabled heroine could do.

"What possible threat lies in the king's simple request, Cassie? He asks no more of you than what you have so often done, to act as a guide down the paths you already know so well." Robert shook his head, more than a little confused by her need to conceal her identity.

In truth, what confused him were his own actions. She'd given him the opportunity to tell the king he'd never come across Lady Quickfoot in his travels. What was he doing calling her out?

"What is it you want?" Cassie demanded, unimpressed by his pretended ignorance of the king's actual command. If King James only wanted her to be Robert Gordon's guide, it would be easy enough to accomplish. But the king had audaciously asked for much more than that. Much more than Cassie would ever give to a man named Gordon.

"My need is simple, Lady Cassandra. The king wishes you to assist Hamilton and me in completing our work—rather he *commanded* you to do so. I know that you received the king's notice. Do you refuse to obey our king?"

Robert knew not why he had swung about mentally and now actually asked for her aid. She would only slow his work, entangle him in a romantic dalliance that he truly did not have time for. Perhaps he was as mad as their king.

"It is one thing for James to command," Cassie argued. "It is another to see his command put into effect here in the Highlands. Lochaber is a great distance from Edinburgh."

"Are you refusing the king, milady?" Robert stated his question smoothly, even though everything inside him was screaming, *Accept her womanly refusal. James will understand. Surely the king does not realize how young she is, nor comprehend that she's yet a Highland maiden.*

"I am not *your* lady," Cassie snapped.

Her breath hissed through her teeth. She pulled her wits together, glaring at Robert with open hostility. She no longer cared that he'd saved her life. She clung to the fading image of fair Alastair Campbell, reminding herself that Alastair was the husband she would have had if a Gordon savage hadn't hacked him to pieces. Let the devil take this handsome traveler!

"It is the middle of winter, sir, with the worst weather still to come. All the mountain passes are full of ice and snow. I will not risk my life or my reputation on a ridiculous whim postulated by a distant court. If that isn't reason enough to deny you, then let me speak more bluntly.

"My father is John MacArthur. He will gullet you from end to end the moment he learns you're a Gordon. There isn't a man in his castle that feels any less than MacArthur does regarding all spawn of the Gordons. Even if my father let you live, because of what you did for wee Ian, he canna guarantee your life beyond his castle walls. Our nearest neighboring laird is married to my late betrothed's sister. Measure the Three Sisters, which are all within a day's walk from Euan's farmhouse, and have done with your quest. For you to attempt more than that is to sign your own death warrant.''

She'd spoken to the point exactly. Robert studied her womanly face, hardened now by stirred memories of the recent bitter losses. So she'd been betrothed, had she? And he could well deduce what had become of that nonexistent husband, dead in some nameless battle.

Now that he really looked at her, he could see that she wasn't in the sweetest bloom of youth—six and ten—as he had first supposed at the pond. She was definitely more mature. Perhaps she was even twenty or older.

Robert sobered considerably, because all she'd said and implied about her father, Laird John MacArthur, was true, and then some.

"I don't wish to be your enemy. We are under a king's bond, constrained to follow James's wishes regarding the peace treaty to which our lairds have affixed their signatures. Does your father or mine pick up arms and fight again, it will mean the immediate death of Gordon or Campbell hostages in Edinburgh. Worse, we force our own laird's hand, causing our very own downfall through arrest and judgment. I, for one, have no interest in distressing the innocents residing at court for my good behavior, nor, I think, will you. We must put aside our differences and work together for Scotland. We have no other choice.''

"This is preposterous!" Cassie wagged her hands in a gesture of frustration. "Of course there is another choice. Are you blind and stupid? Do you lack imagination? We can say we never crossed paths!''

"Had we not crossed paths, that could be done. I am not a man of devious means. I will attest to only the truth," Robert reasoned. "We have met, lady, and have no choice but to see this farce played through to the end.''

"You haven't listened to a word I've said. Do you realize what risk I would take unto myself, to act as your guide in my mountains? I may be able to charm MacArthurs and even a MacDonald or two, but how many Campbells do you think will allow a Gordon to be hidden by my skirts? All of us suspect the true purpose behind this mapping business. This is my clan's land, no one else's! You must go away!''

"The king wants this done," Robert resolutely declared.

"Aye, well, and kings come and go. So do their whims.''

"It is no whim to map this country. Every continent is being mapped and explored. There is a greater purpose here than you comprehend. No mere Highland laird can halt the advancement of knowledge in today's world.''

Cassie scoffed. Her lips compressed into a line of disapproval. "Next you'll tell me men will be exploring the moon!''

Robert's eyes twinkled as he replied pithily, ''To

every thing there is time and a purpose, Lady Quick-foot.''

"Have you given even a moment's thought to the uses men with naught but greed in their hearts will make of your vast compilation of knowledge about Scotland? The English would use maps of the Highlands to destroy us.''

Cassie put forth the most frequently used argument Robert had heard against the work. Every living Scot had long reasons for distrusting the English. But this work wasn't ordered for England's benefit, but for all of Scotland's enlightenment.

Robert shook his head, negating that statement. "Nay, they will not. You're clinging to the meanest reason for denying information. More good will come of it than evil. I cannot abide ignorance. How have *you* become so renowned for your guiding skills? Did not someone teach you all you learned about the mountains of Lochaber?''

"Well, now, what do you think? Of course I've been taught how to look for the trails even on stony ground.''

"Just so,'' Robert said in satisfaction. "Neither I nor the king ask you to give away your tracking secrets. We merely want your aid as a knowledgeable guide.''

"You refuse to see my point, sir.'' Cassie caught up her skirts, shaking her hem clean of the chaff that had collected on them from the thick layer of straw scattered on the barn floor. "I waste my breath discussing this. I have given you my best counsel, which you choose to ignore. I cannot help you. I would be ruined, a pariah in my shire for the rest of my life. We have nothing else to speak about. Good night, sir.''

Again she began to leave, and once more Robert played from the trump hand that the king had given him. ''Have you heard recently from your brother, milady?''

Chapter Six

Cassie's foot came down hard on a loose board at the door and she spun on that, making a floor joist squeak. Her eyes fairly gleamed when she found the mapmaker's bold and calculating stare had not wavered from her at all. "What exactly do you mean by that, sir?"

"Is it your brother's custom to remain in Edinburgh over Twelfth Night?" Robert asked, as bland as a vicar offering prayers at a funeral.

"Nay, it is his custom to return home as does every loyal Highland son," Cassie said, certain he was ignorant of her brother's movements.

"But he did not return this Twelfth Night past, did he?" Robert added, without bothering to say how he knew that was so.

"Nay, he did not," Cassie muttered, not at all pleased with the direction this conversation was taking.

What she'd heard from Jamie's latest letters had sounded dire, nigh onto desperate, but clearly her father hadn't shared with her or her mother the worst news. Instead, they'd quietly celebrated Advent, Christmas Day, Hogmanay and Twelfth Night without the cheerful company of Jamie, his wife and young sons. Cassie knew things were not as they should be in Edinburgh for her brother. But that did not bear discussion with a rank stranger.

Furious, yet hoping to keep her tongue under control, Cassie stalked out of the barn, letting the door bang behind her. The night air struck her flaming face with shocking force. The realization of how embarrassed she was drew her up tight, gathering her cloak as well as her wits.

Soundlessly, Robert slipped out the door to stand behind her as she took deep drafts of cold air to calm herself.

His voice cut like hot iron through water, robbing her of the calm she sought by setting her temper to sizzling again. "Have you considered the term 'house arrest'? Or the consequences to your family do you continue to ignore the king's command?"

Cassie spun around, facing the resolute, dark-haired man. Had she a blade on her, she'd certainly have run him through. Unarmed, she settled for jabbing a stiffened finger in the middle of his chest. "Stop mincing words and say what you mean, you blackguard, else I'll cut your heart out and make you eat it. Don't think I don't dare. You're beginning to make me very angry."

Robert caught her hand and restrained it, infuriating Cassie even more. Her already flushed face hovered just under his in a delicious temper. The urge to pull her into his arms and kiss her quivering lips was almost more than he could bear. He hesitated to be that imprudent.

"Let go of me!" Cassie tugged to get her hand free.

He didn't let go. "Och! You're a proud Highland maiden, full of temper and spirit and as hotheaded as your own fearless father." Robert laughed. "Listen to me, Cassandra! MacArthur of Achanshiel's reputation is one hundred times more fierce than that of his fair Lady Quickfoot. He is a brave, bonny man, untamed and wild in his hidden Highland abode, and thinks himself far removed from the long arm of the king's retribution. But your brother maintains a home in the shadow of Holyrood, and his wife and babes reside there, too. Whether you admit it or not, they serve as MacArthur hostages for the good behavior of the fierce clan in the hills, the same way my eldest brother Connor and his wife and children do.

"I visited Jamie this holiday past as a welcomed and invited guest, even though my surname is Gordon. Such courtesy reflects the hospitality I've encountered all over Scotland until I arrived here. What is the source of your animosity? I bear no grudge against you or your kin."

Cornered, held and trapped just as surely by the intensity of his eyes as by his urgent demand, Cassie resisted, relinquishing a little of the truth. "You're a bold man, Robert Gordon, and I do not like that one bit."

"Boldness is no cause to be despised, lady." He tugged on her wrists, shaking her gently. "Why do you hate me out of hand? I've harmed no MacArthur that I know of in my life.''

"How do you know that? Do you know the names of every man you killed?'' Cassie had a ready answer for that declaration.

"Since I have killed no men beyond those I faced on the battlefield, I know it well. And all the men on the battlefield were done in fair fight, with no quarter to be given the loser of the contests. Are you afraid to say to my face what you say to me only with your eyes?''

The night air crackled around them, charged with the energy of their two conflicting wills.

"I'm not afraid of you,'' Cassie said bravely, thrusting her chin upward. She realized then her words were true. She wasn't afraid of him. Far from that. She was excited by him, thrilled to be caught so in his grip, seemingly helpless and trapped. She could have freed her wrist at any time, but she made no move to do so.

Neither of them was trapped, but neither could they break loose from the emotional currents dragging them deeper beneath the other's polite veneer.

"Alastair Campbell died in the slaughter of Campbells at Glenlivet on the mountains of Strathavon,'' Cassie said. "We were to be married on the first of May, 1595. I would have been seven and ten, but only I lived to see that dreadful day come to pass with no wedding celebrated, for my husband-to-be lay dead and moldering in his grave a full year by then.''

Robert released her hands and stepped back. Five years ago he had been at Glenlivet and participated in a battle that had seen too many nameless Campbell warriors' deaths. Not nameless to their loved ones and kinsmen, only nameless in battle and unknown to the outnumbered and beleaguered Gordons.

"I see," he said solemnly.

"I don't think you really do," Cassandra responded, rubbing her left wrist, acutely aware of the loss of the warmth of his strong hand. She hadn't minded his restraint nearly as much as she should have.

"Do ye expect to hear me apologize for the slaughter that day or during any other battle, when I and the men I served with were outnumbered twenty to one? If ye must blame anyone for the carnage, blame our king, who did nothing to stop it beforehand, or the generals, Huntly and Argyll, who ordered boys into battle with naught but rusty claymores in their hands and only their wits to protect their lives."

"I do," Cassandra replied quietly, but with a vehemence that sounded everlasting.

Robert nodded as he dragged his hand through his hair. That motion freed it from the black ribbon that kept it back from his broad brow, and revealed how clearly agitated he was by their words. That he made no further rebuttal or denial of guilt set Cassandra back several paces mentally.

In her heart did she want to hear him deny being on that field that day? Aye, she did. For that might allow the smallest chink in her own cracking armor and justify the physical feelings assaulting her when she was in this particular man's presence. If she could not hate him out of hand, then she should be able to control her feelings and everything else. No, she couldn't hate him any more than she could have allowed Dorcas to deliver those quilts in her stead. She'd wanted just one more opportunity to see Robert Gordon before she took her leave for home in the morning.

Another thing that bothered her deeply was her rank openness to him. She'd actually blurted out her intention to leave in the morning at the beginning of this absurd conversation. She had no justification for doing that; it was so unlike her. She shared confidences with her sisters, not with untrustworthy men.

His fingers spread into the thick tangle of brown hair gathered at the nape of his neck as he tilted his head and stared up at the pale moon. She frowned, watching his expression harden into a Highlander's mask of forced calm. No telling what memories she'd awakened in him with her talk of battles that ought to be forgotten. "You were there?"

"Aye." He sighed and dropped both hands to his sides. He turned his face back to hers and his expression was deliberately blank. "I was there. Where else would a Gordon mapmaker be...but in our laird's vanguard, scouting out the terrain, alert and seeking each vantage place where men could best stand and fight?"

Cassie needed to hear nothing more to justify her aloofness, but something about the way he phrased that statement jarred her as wrong. She could not stop herself from asking for more. "How old were you, then?"

"Nine and ten, perhaps younger. I would have to

put pencil to dates that I have done my best to forget. The past isn't important to what I want out of life, so I push it out of my mind. I was younger than you are now, milady. That year and the two before it, each day was heavy and wet, full of fatigue and exhaustion. We fought often without stopping, day after day, taking this bridge or that hill, ever on to the next. There were times I thought the smell of brimstone and blood would haunt me till the end of my life, but I have my work to keep such memories at bay. War is gut-wrenching awful, milady, and I have learned that the beauty of peace is to be cherished and hoarded like the finest memories of childhood. I am sorry for your Alastair, and will add his name to my prayers.''

Cassie drew her cloak tighter across her shoulders, reacting to a chill that was more emotion than temperature. ''I thought Alastair invincible, for he had fostered with us from the time I came out of the nursery and we were friends long before our fathers decided we suited as bride and groom. The truth is he was wild and reckless. MacArthur called him Hotspur. He is a hard man to replace in these parts of the world.''

''As a hopeful bride's groom?''

''Nay, as a friend, for that is what I thought of him most, my best friend. You and I are not what I would ever call friends, but I entreat you to listen to my warnings. Gordons are not welcome in Lochaber and to go there is to risk your life. I want no more blood spilled.''

Robert nodded, as though acknowledging her last

statement for a shared sentiment. That nod was followed almost immediately by a resolute shake of his head. "Point taken and met with full agreement. I, too want the bloodletting at an end. Hence, I do note your concern. However, the feud is over, Lady Cassandra. It bodes neither of us well to bear grudges out of the past. All that matters to me is my map of Scotland. I will finish it, and that means I will survey Lochaber."

"My father isn't so ready to put aside his grievances as I. Nor will his Highlanders."

"It is *not your father* speaking so plainly this moment," Robert cautioned her.

Cassie grimly said, "As you like it. I do not forgive and forget ever. It isn't in the nature of this beast to do so!"

"Tell me, do you also engineer suspicious deaths by mischance of messengers from the court?" A dark brow hiked on Robert's expressive face. He looked so arrogant when he did that facial maneuver Cassie wanted to strike him. Did he stand but a breath away from laying a charge of outright murder at her feet?

"Nay, I do not!" She denied his charge. "The king's messenger left Castle MacArthur without a scratch laid upon him. A November rain caught the fool unawares in a Kinlochy flood. Mind you, the man was well warned not to travel due east. Rannoch Moor is no place to look for a shortcut to Edinburgh."

"Which a suitable MacArthur guide could have helped him avoid," Robert smoothly countered, determined to coerce her into cooperating with him. When had her assistance become so vital? Probably the very moment he'd risked his own life to retrieve hers from the water's depths.

Yesterday he wouldn't have pressed the issue. Tonight he could do naught but insist. The woman herself had become that important to him—a fascinating creature. She was like a firefly trapped in a bottle—alive and full of exciting vigor. He was bound to her now, from the simple binding of giving her his own life force until she could breathe on her own again. The unseen bindings caused by that act were nigh onto impossible for him to sever.

How much easier this would be if she would simply react with the healthy attraction most young women showed him. He wasn't an ugly, disagreeable man. She acted as if he were detestable.

"I do not care to imagine the fate of your father's only son if an untimely accident should befall Alex Hamilton or me. One accidental death can be explained, but two and three? I think not."

"You are threatening me." Cassie's fair blue eyes opened very wide. She wasn't surprised he'd stooped so low. He was a Gordon after all. "I don't like that one bit."

"Your satisfaction isn't the issue. Your assistance is. I assure you that if Alex and I do not return in good time to the king's presence, whole and intact from our venture in Lochaber, your kinsmen will bear the brunt of the king's wrath."

Hold on here! Cassie thought, glaring into brown eyes she'd once thought so gentle and mild. This Gordon could be as ruthless and implacable as her own father. To that she said only, "I do not care for your implication."

Robert watched her nostrils flare in anger all the while those lovely lips of hers trembled. He was never more acutely aware of her womanly beauty than he was that very moment, when she demanded, "What is it you truly want of me?"

There was a question that arrested his heart's beating and sent him drifting into dangerous waters of pure imagination. What would he give to bury his face between her warm breasts and feel her legs tighten around his waist as they fell to the fragrant hay-strewn floor, making wild and passionate love? His future, his life, his soul? She'd make any man a bonny wife.

He shook his head to clear it of such premature notions and stayed on the firm footing of the here and now.

He stole a gallant's trick from Alex and bowed from the waist to her. "I want your guidance from Glencoe as far north as the River Spean. I want the names of each mountain crest, river and stream and land formation, to the best of your knowledge. A simple request for any native of these parts, nothing more, Lady Quickfoot."

Cassie's eyes narrowed in outright displeasure. Her foot tapped in agitation and she toyed with the idea of giving him the bold truth, that Lady Quickfoot was nothing more than a figment of the MacArthur clan's fertile oral tradition. But she said nothing, letting the ruse lie, playing him for the fool that he was. "Very well, sir. Have it your way. I leave at dawn. See that you and your silent companion are ready to travel. *Guid nicht!*''

That said, she whirled about, snatching up her skirts, and ran from him without allowing him the chance to make another successful rebuttal.

Robert returned to the barn and shut the door firmly against the night wind. The connection of solid wood echoed into the rafters, disturbing nesting creatures. A small cloud of white owl feathers showered down onto his head and shoulders like a blessing—powerful omens of good fortune.

Robert stood perfectly still, savoring the repercussions of Lady Quickfoot's retreat. Only now, in her absence, could he detect the potency of her lavender perfume. Its sweetness lingered in his nose, overriding the smell of animals and straw. He wondered what would have happened if he'd pulled her into his arms and kissed her perpetually smiling lips.

Then he grinned, knowing he'd savor that treat on another night to come very, very soon.

Several minutes wore on before Robert's wool-gathering passed and he focused on his traveling companion. Alex sprawled comfortably upon the straw, elbows splayed and hands clasped behind his neck, grinning like an idiot.

"You bungled that tête-à-tête rather badly, eh, Robbie?" Alex scolded.

"You think so?" Robert strolled to the haystacks and picked up a folded quilt. He shook it out and spread it upon the woolen blanket he'd already laid out, then settled on the fragrant bed, mirroring Alex's contented position.

"Were I you, I'd keep sharp watch for dirks pointed at my heart. That lady would gladly see you skewered through."

"Aye, I noticed that." Robert closed his eyes and a yawn stretched his grin. "Feisty wee creature, is she no'?"

"Not dangerous though, eh?" Alex surmised from Robert's lack of concern.

"No. No' dangerous, save to a man's heart," Robert concurred. His heart, he feared, wasn't going to survive this journey into Lochaber, no matter what happened now.

The short run from the barn to the house wasn't nearly enough of a release to suit Cassandra. Heavens above, but that Gordon bastard was bullheaded—born without a speck of common sense in his educated head! Edinburgh-schooled indeed! Cassie kicked a slat in the fence enclosing the pigs. An old boar grunted contrarily from the mire, disturbed in his rooting for more table scraps.

"Och, bugger off!" Cassie told him, and didn't blush a bit for the use of such foul language. It was certainly called for at this moment. She'd been pressed to the limit by Gordon's arrogance.

Her brother-in-law was out behind the house, feeding his dogs and seeing to their bedding for this cold night. He looked up as Cassie stalked up the path from the barn.

"Trouble?" Euan inquired. His voice rumbled from the deepest portion of his chest. Cassie flashed a cautious look his way and fiercely shook her head, thankful Euan hadn't heard her swear at the pigs for the racket his hungry hounds made.

She knew exactly where her sister and her brother-in-law's sympathies lay at this very moment. Young Ian held more value to them than anything else in this world. They were beholden to Robert Gordon for saving him. Cassie wasn't so certain she could or should feel the same measure of gratitude for her own life. Not when she had the most horrible feeling that she would be better off dead before this venture to appease their king was over.

"Dinna tell me those bounders insulted ye?" Euan glowered, his brow roughening as he caught clear sight of Cassie's face.

"Nay. They were civil enough," Cassie replied as she passed Euan. Inside the house she closed the door carefully and leaned against it. Her heart raced inside her chest—and not from the short sprint either.

Robbie Gordon had her more upset than he deserved.

She'd been snared as neatly as a hart in a crafty stalker's trap. The blasted man! Well, she wouldn't do it! She would see Robert Gordon tumble head over heels down a cliff as steep as Arthur's Drop and damned if she'd toss a rope to him. Accidents happened. Who could point a finger at her if something befell the blasted pig?

And just how could she do that, she wondered, and hope to get away with it? She couldn't. He had already pointed out the worst possible repercussions. The king's implied threat to Jamie was real, and Cassie was too smart to doubt it.

So the king and his so-called *educated* court believed Lady Quickfoot a living and breathing woman? That was a fine piece of mischief. She wondered if she had her own brother Jamie to blame for that fact? Hadn't he asked her to write down the Lady Quickfoot stories so he could recite them to his own bairns? Aye, Jamie had, and so she had done, and sent all of the ones she could remember to him well before the holidays so he could begin teaching his boys about their clan. Well, what could she do about that now? Nothing at all.

She was caught, betwixt and between a legend and reality. Yes, she knew the hills better than most men of her clan, but only because she had spent all of her days chasing after Alastair as Angus taught him everything he knew.

In the beginning they'd always tried to scare her into going back to the castle. Her father had also come up into the hills to find her and bring her home. It had never mattered to her how dire MacArthur's punishments were. She couldn't abide sitting still at her mother's side or the looms, making worsted wool and sewing samplers of stitches. The ladies' lot wasn't for Cassie. She wanted to be out-of-doors with Alastair, roaming the hills, learning all the trails, watching the birds and climbing the rocks, just like the legendary Lady Quickfoot she heard about all of her life.

Angus had aged much since Alastair's death and really couldn't keep up with her anymore. He was getting old and Cassie often wished there was someone trustworthy to replace him, because there were times in the mountains that she needed the help of a strong, fearless man.

Robert looked to be such a man. The kind of man who knew no fear, just like Alastair. Neither would bat an eye if challenged to scale a vertical as dangerous as Arthur's Drop. Both had been blessed with the lean, whipcord strength, the quick eyes and certain judgment so necessary to manhandle rocky crevices and cling like spiders to cold stone walls.

Damn, damn, double damn, she swore under her breath. How dare God send her a man with eyes like that in his head and name him a Gordon!

Cassie wiped her face and groaned. Why, she was wringing wet under her *cutty sark* and her stomach was churning as if she'd not eaten in days?

"I will not allow him to get under my skin!" Cassie vowed aloud. "He's a bloody Gordon!"

Cassie woke to find the sheets and the eiderdown twisted and tumbled in a stranglehold about her. Dorcas set a pitcher of steaming water on the stand beside a morning candle. She looked at her, shook her head and clucked her tongue as Cassie unwound from the tangle and stood shivering on the cold floor, shaking her nightgown back down to her toes.

"'Tis a good thing ye sleep alone," Dorcas observed. "Ye'd bludgeon a husband t' death t' be sure."

"I shall make certain I pray for a rich man, then, one who provides me my own chamber and bed to sleep 'n," Cassie replied snappishly. She felt in no better humor this morning than she had the night before. So much for feeling rested. She was anything but rested.

"Oh, aye, and while y'er on yer knees pray for a fine coach and six," Dorcas added, moving into pre-dawn shadows. "Make sure ye ask the good Lord for paved roads lined with gold across the Highlands, too."

"Oh, aye," Cassie called after her. "It never hurts to ask the impossible."

She dressed for winter travel. In one way the cat was out of the bag. The mapmakers knew one truth about her. There was no better guide in Lochaber than she. Cassie saw no need to put on airs wearing a gown that would only hamper her nimble feet in shrouds of petticoats and skirting. She donned her warmest trews, leggings and cross-gartered boots. Wrapping her chest well in wool sark and fleeced vest she settled her plaid firmly at her shoulders with her brooch, and buckled on a wide belt bearing her dirk.

She fastened her hair in a firm, but partial braid at the nape of her neck, allowing it to lie free on her shoulders and back. That kept it out of her way in the only restraint allowed her, considering her unmarried status. She found it ironic that she could wander all over the mountains garbed thus in the clothing of a youth, armed with her own hunting knife, bow and arrows if she liked, but she could not wind her hair in utilitarian braids close about her head. Not until after she was married! Her people had peculiar rules. But she got away with her boyish clothing on the trails, so long as all the men and women she met could identify her as a young woman. Some things about the Highland folk simply didn't make sense.

Sometimes, she thought the solution would be to handfast herself to some buck from her father's tail and be done with this marriage thing. It would almost be worth a small scandal at Castle MacArthur to have the privilege of putting her hair up and out of her way. Yes, her mother would have a fit if she did something that radical. God knew her father would strangle her for marrying beneath her right without permission. He hoped to gain prestige by her marriage, which was why he pressed the Cameron—Douglas the Darling's—suit. The less she annoyed her father the better.

Downstairs in the warm kitchen, there was porridge ready on the hob. Angus was gathering their little gear and packing the luncheon Maggie insisted on providing in their saddlebags. Euan and Angus had decided they should take horses. Cassie thought that a poor idea considering the condition of the hills and the ice that had formed during the night. Euan argued horses would make up for any time lost due to the ice.

As always, Euan had his way. Cassie was no match against her brother-in-law and her gillie together.

Actual dawn was held at bay by a dense mist that had formed over Euan's small valley, making night linger. The children had yet to rise from their beds.

At first light the mapmakers came to the kitchen and enjoyed another sampling of Euan and Maggie's too generous hospitality. But Cassie could say one thing in the mapmakers' favor—they were exceedingly polite and graciously gave thanks to Maggie for their accommodations.

Cassie finished her porridge quickly, gave Maggie a hug and saluted Euan as she went out the door.

"When will you be coming back, Cass?" Maggie wanted to know.

"Soon," Cassie answered. "Or whenever Father tries my patience again. Give the babes my kisses. I'm going to miss them." She kissed Maggie farewell, mounted her pony and settled in the saddle to adjust her plaid against the mist.

Angus boosted Dorcas onto her seat and then bounded onto his own saddle with an agility that defied his three score years. His weathered eyes scanned the faded and dismal sky, then he grunted deeply, turned to Cassie and pointed at the far northwest and the crown of dark clouds clinging to the snowy cap on Ben Nevis.

"Storm, you ken?" Cassie asked.

"Aye-ah," he responded, flicking the tail of his plaid round his shoulders. "We'd best move and keep a lively pace. MacArthur won't like it if ye sleep this night in the hills."

It went without being said that Cassie wouldn't like that either.

The mapmakers' horses looked no better beneath a man's weight than they had bearing an overload of baggage. The tools of their trade were now borne by two sure footed mountain ponies Euan had gifted them.

Cassie gave her kinfolk one last farewell, then clicked her tongue and set her mare to a steady trot, leading the way through Glencoe to the hidden glen of Achanshiel. She'd be home by dusk, God willing.

Chapter Seven

Robert detected one patent certainty within the first moments of departing MacGregor's Farm; Lady Quickfoot, her gillie and abigail had all resolved to be silent traveling companions. Not a word was exchanged as they set off during the first good hour of travel. A second certainty became evident as the weak winter sunlight began to lessen dawn's shadows—the farther north they traveled, the starker the land became, the more profound the quality of the silence.

Silence befit the rugged, rockbound, barren passage above the twisted River Coe.

There were no stalker's houses. Even the occasional stone shelter where a lone hunter could wait out a bad storm, was covered under a tumble of rocks telling of recent avalanches. Civilization seemed to have given up on these stark hills and this desolate range.

No wild animals came out to challenge their passage. Throughout the early morning, only an occasional eagle ventured into the cold, changeable sky.

The upward path allowed only single file traffic. The glazing of new ice made it dangerous to stray off it or venture to ride at anyone's side.

If he tried, Robert could have imagined he and Alex were traveling alone. Or rather, he could have done that until Cassandra's red braid swung across her back a few yards ahead of him. When the track widened in the hollows to allow two horses passage side by side, the abigail inevitably pressed her mount close to Robert's horse's flank. Though she said nothing, the frequent soft clearing of her throat against the prevailing wind declared the abigail's presence and ill humor spoke more eloquently than shouted words. An hour into the ride, Robert found his situation laughable. Even Alex talked more than these two women did.

A good two hours after sunrise they reached the bottom of a narrow gorge. The day's miserable sunlight made little dent in the prevailing mist clinging to the bottom of each valley. By midmorning they were again tackling a steeply rising incline. The dense fog began to lighten, and briefly, at the highest point, a panoramic view opened to Robert's eyes that was utterly breathtaking in its unique beauty.

A rolling sea of moist clouds blanketed all the visible glens, enhancing the sensation of having come to the very top of the world. A cold wind, sharp and driven, flattened the folds of Robert's plaid across his chest and shoulders and rattled in his muffled ears like corn in last year's crib. Jutting from the roiling sea of clouds like islands in the ocean were the jagged peaks of the adjacent mountain ridge and distant pinnacles. He urged his mount forward across the sharp shale, reining in beside Cassandra.

"Where are we?" he shouted above the roar of the wild wind. "What loch is that at the bottom of the glen?"

"That—" Cassie pointed through a break in the clouds below them "—is Loch Leven. Bidean nam Bian is here to your right, the ridge of Aonach Eagach to your left. Ahead, there is the mist lies Buchaille Etive Mor."

Robert nodded, making a mental note of the names and positions of the mountains known as the Three Sisters. The day's weather was no good for taking measurements. "Why come this way? Isn't there a better route below?"

Cassie shrugged. If she was cold she gave no sign of it, though her lips were chapped and her cheeks looked stung by the force of the wind. "The Devil's Backbone is the most direct route into Lochaber, no matter the weather or season."

Robert frowned and looked back at the steep climb they'd just mounted. On horseback it looked like an impossible climb, but they'd zigzagged up it without a single horse stumbling. He shook his head and took out his small logbook, jotting down notations.

Sheltering the book in the crook of his arm, he wet his pencil stub on his tongue, and scratched his remarks onto the fluttering parchment leaf. Cassie watched him concentrate, astonished at how oblivious he was of the wind stinging his ears. His raw, red fingers gripped the stub so firmly his knuckles lost their chapped color. He was efficient at the task, taking no more than a moment to complete a drawing with strange markings. Finished, he tucked his tools safely away inside jerkin and sporran.

She looked back to find Angus. He brought up the rear, following Lord Hamilton. Euan's shaggy ponies trudged along, staying close together, more used to this uneven trail than the mapmaker's larger horses.

"I'll want to travel this pass again to make accurate measurements of the peaks," Robert told her. "In better weather."

Cassie couldn't stop a wry grin from creeping onto her lips. "Better weather is hard to find. 'Tis a rare day, mapmaker," she remarked offhandedly. "Rare indeed when the Coe River turns sluggish, otherwise she's fit only for the salmon to run. You'll see proof of that soon enough."

He was as aware of that as she was. The narrow gorge they traveled was too steep and treacherous for placid waters ever to move below.

"I've set one goal for this journey. To be home by nightfall, safe and secure in MacArthur's castle. Let's move on."

Robert followed her down the north side of the peak. "We needn't treat each other as rank strangers," he said next, having had the best portion of the morning to consider how best to call a truce between them.

Cassie cast a sloe-eyed glance back at him, her mobile mouth making an effort to look displeased. "I'd rather we were."

"Aye, but you have no idea how I passed the night."

"That you lived to wake up, says enough."

She cut off him off very effectively. This would never do, Robert decided, studying the determined jut of her chin. She thrust it arrogantly forward, though her head itself bobbed in accord with the uneven gait of her shaggy pony. They descended another steeply zigzagged flank, where there were no signs of melted ice from the day before. Like the ice underfoot he wanted to rattle her composure, as payback possibly for the stirring dreams that had rattled him during the night.

Twice he'd woken, jerking out of a deep sleep with a clear picture in his mind—a weightless cloud of red and gold hair swirling about her in a halo of watery sunbeams. Her pinched features breaking into a startled smile as she'd realized he was real and swimming to her. From then on, through the rest of the night, the feel of her cold lips warming under his as he'd given her back her life wouldn't leave him. Now he wanted to kiss and taste her for true.

"I have decided we are bound and beholden together, milady. Kismet, the Easterners call it. Besides, our king is right. The only way to satisfactorily end the conflicts of the clans is to breed them out."

"Breed them out?" Cassie sputtered. "I don't think I like the sound of that at all, sir."

"Aye, breed them out," Robert repeated. "Our king believes he can resolve all clan frictions by marrying each warring clan to the other. For example, he could very well do exactly that, say, to you and me."

"What?" Cassie yanked on her pony's bridle, startling the beast. Robert put out a quick hand to catch the animal and steady it.

"Aye. You needn't act so surprised. He's already begun doing that and discovered 'tis a true and certain way to end a feud forevermore. I mention you and me because we are each of age and thus far unattached. His experiments in this endeavor in the past have only been worked on babes in the nursery, but I see the way King James's mind works. Dinna look so surprised."

"Don't patronize me. I don't like it, and take your hand off my horse."

"I've startled you with the suddenness of my thoughts, I know. But it makes excellent sense when you look at the facts. With your skills and abilities as a Highland guide, you'd be well suited to be a mapmaker's wife."

"You're being absurd, Gordon. I don't even like you. I would never marry anyone I do not like."

"I'll grow on you," Robert bantered rakishly. He was flirting with her, and having voiced the thought he found he liked it—enough to imagine exploring it over the next five to six decades.

"Don't be a fool. This track is too tricky to ride side by side. Fall back and allow me to continue in the lead and do stop talking. Your mindless jabbering makes me think the thin air of the mountains is going to your head."

Robert laughed heartily at that pronouncement. Then he deliberately confounded her current confusion. "I dreamed of you last night, Lady Cassandra."

Cassandra's eyes jerked away from her horse's

path, but this time she did not drag her pony's attention off the trail.

"I've done nothing to merit inclusion in your dreams," she shot back rather too quickly.

"Save sink like a stone in the coldest pool of water I've ever jumped willingly into in my life," Robert responded, just as bewildered by his own recklessness as she probably was. He wasn't sure why he was doing this. He didn't have to bring up his rescue. But there it was, torn up from the depths and brought to the surface just as surely as he'd forced their heads to break through the surface of that pond.

"I'm sorry," she said hastily. A rush of color mounted her already wind-stung cheeks and swept upward to highlight her high forehead. "I never meant to invade your rest or give you a troubled night."

"Nor did I. I canna seem to erase from my mind the vision of your hair floating round you in that shaft of sunlight. You were so exquisitely peaceful—a naiad—fair enough to grace King Neptune's court. Too beautiful to die so young."

Cassie stopped her mare on safe footing and glared at the mapmaker. He insisted upon reminding her of that intimacy she'd rather forget. Not only that, he brought up her moment of direst distress. That wasn't well done of him. "Is it too much to ask that you be as silent as your partner?"

Robert grinned. He liked her saucy temper. "Alex isn't at all quiet once you get to know him. You aren't either. You're too flamboyant to blend into the scenery. It's lovely here, isn't it? I can well understand

why you wouldn't want to share this with the rest of
the world. 'Tis a very special place.''

The corners of Cassie's mouth twitched, but she
managed to withhold a more generous smile. The
damned fool was flirting with her. She couldn't think
of anyone who'd done that so well in a long, long
time. ''The ice is too thick. We'd best walk the horses
down for safety's sake.'' She dismounted and called
out the same to Angus, Dorcas and Hamilton, who
were three hundred yards or so back, battling the wind
at the crest of Aonach Eagach ridge.

Robert bounded out of his saddle, glad to set to
leading his horse rather than trusting the beast on this
incline. With reins in hand, he fell into step beside
Cassie.

''I gather you're more comfortable on foot than in
the saddle?''

Sparing words, Cassie nodded. Her mare followed
easily on the tether of the reins, picking her footing
as carefully as Cassie did. ''I like to know what's
underfoot all the time.''

''Does no one in these hills object to your habit of
dressing like a boy?'' Robert blurted out the one
question that had bothered him since he'd first laid
eyes on the lady that morning.

''Who is to object?'' Cassie asked him. Her free
hand waved at the stark crags surrounding them. If
there were others anywhere on these vistas, they were
totally lost from their sight. Not even the red deer or
eagles braved the raw winds yet. Later, when the day
had warmed some, they'd see plenty of deer foraging

for what they could find in the bracken and ice on the hills.

"I see what you mean, but I assume we will eventually come across others," Robert murmured.

"I don't think so. Is it you who object?" Cassie asked point-blank. "Or your friend, Lord Hamilton?"

Her long-legged stride matched Robert's step for step along the ice-covered rocky path.

"I haven't decided. I admired your gown last eve. You looked lovely."

"Do you advise ruining such a gown traveling these hills? Tearing yards of hems and a ransom's worth of lace upon the rocks and mud?"

"Nay, you're a sensible lass, I see that, though I didn't think I like seeing you look like one of my wee brothers."

"And how many wee brothers do ye have, Robert Gordon?"

"Two if the truth be known. And wicked brats they are—twins, and my mother's favorites since they're her youngest. Douglas and Donald and I heard tell they scraped the bottom of the family barrel for names for the wee devils. If I calculate right, they'll be twelve this coming Dark Night. Changelings they both are, full of mischief and bad to the bone, to hear the antics told round holiday fires."

Cassie jerked her gaze back to him at the mention of the same night that she'd been born on. "Och, so you're familiar with old wives' tales, I see. It so happens I was born on the Dark Night as well."

"Truly?" Robert met her inscrutable expression head-on.

"Aye, no one would joke about that, I should hope. There's enough superstition accompanying that night to fill a book. God's truth, every foible I could claim is laid upon my shoulders sometimes and all accounted for being born on the 29th of February."

"Ye'll be twenty or twenty-four, mistress?"

"I could be sixteen," Cassie answered solemnly, not committing to any age.

"Aye." Robert chuckled. "And going on four by the way your lips pout now."

Cassie tried not to laugh, but she couldn't stop the sound from escaping her lips and echoing across the stark hills. "Have ye no sisters, or do ye Gordons just breed fighting men?"

"Och, nay, I've two sisters, married with bairns of their own, and three older brothers in the king's service, all married save me and the young rascals, Dougie and Donnie. And you?"

"Four sisters and Jamie, all married and raising fine families of their own, save for Roslyn and Kathy, who prefer to torment their husbands with the labors of making their heirs."

At that mildly spoken statement Robert burst out laughing. "'Tis no torment there, my lady. I do believe you have the gist of the word 'labor' wrong to have stated it so."

Cassie tucked her nose in the cold air. "I have no need to justify my meaning of the word. That would be an even bigger conundrum than your original request."

Cassie smiled abruptly over her private joke, then leaped over a fast-running freshet. Robert took a more circuitous path, skirting the rocks the stream splashed freely over.

"I was not making a judgment in either direction, milady," he replied evenly, refusing to be baited into an argument—especially not one based on her maiden's innocence.

"Good." Cassie's smile returned. "I have been giving this dilemma of ours some serious thought this morning and I think I have landed upon a better solution than yours."

"Oh? What would that be?" Robert inquired. He took the time to pat his mount, to give it a bit of encouragement for having trod through the icy bath without bolting.

"I shall write the king a letter." Cassie offered her simplistic answer with a bright smile.

"You shall? Pray do tell me what this letter of yours will accomplish."

"Certainly." Cassie gladly enlightened him, since it would put an end to her need to do anything more for him.

"I will explain to King James that my Lady Quickfoot name is nothing more than a family joke. Jamie started it years ago. I liked to run when I was a child. In fact, I was quite fast and could beat anyone in a footrace. Jamie called me Quickfoot, and the name stuck."

"Och, well, that explains it all." Robert turned his eyes to the tricky path ahead—a descent as dangerous as any he'd ever ventured with a horse trailing behind him.

"I'm not really a Highland guide, you ken." She

put out her hand, staying him from stepping on a moss-covered boulder. She pointed to the frozen shale path that went around it and carefully led her horse around the natural barricade, then waited to go on till he caught up with her again.

Robert managed not to laugh outright at her bold disclaimer, which was totally absurd all things considered, beginning with her mode of dress. She looked prepared to scale the crest of Aonach Eagach without batting one of her very pretty, pale eyelashes. Nor had she once turned to Angus and inquired any direction of him. She knew these hills the way he knew the creases and calluses of his right hand.

"Well?" Cassie demanded after the silence between them lengthened ominously. "I think that should do the trick, don't you?"

"No," Robert said flatly. "It's rather too late for a letter of denial to do the trick. I'm here and the king's expecting results. You're dissembling."

"I'm doin' no such thing." Cassie insisted.

"Honesty rarely exists in the same category as diplomacy, milady. I'm being brutally honest. His Majesty awaits the first sign of trouble to send his army swarming into Lochaber to destroy Achanshiel, and Laird John James MacArthur specifically.

"Your father has meddled with the king's peace too often. It won't help to remind you that my own clan would rise most viciously if your MacArthurs were to wipe me from the face of the earth."

"No," Cassie managed to mutter.

Robert shrugged. "Aye, and I did say it would do me no good to bring that to the fore, because one

Gordon more or less to you is nothing. But to me, it means a great deal. It willna take more than the spilling of one dram of my blood to bring the laird of the Gordons hying across the water, and a hue and cry will go out for vengeance before the Gordons fiery cross summoning the clan to war burns to gray ashes. Then, my fair lassie, MacArthur blood will run through the Highlands like rivers at full flood.''

''That's preposterous.'' Cassie stood her ground in the debate, refusing to give an inch. They were at peace, agreed so by all the clans. ''As many Gordons would die as would MacArthurs if war came again. We've lost enough!''

''Exactly so.'' Robert pounced quickly upon her verbal admission. ''So why should Gordons be blamed for instigating your destruction?''

Cassie snorted in disbelief.

Determined to paint a clearer picture to her of what the king had in mind, Robert continued. ''In short, our entire way of life will be done away with, lassie. Ye dinna understand politics the way it truly is. It's the clans James of Scotland wants destroyed—your clan and mine—and every tribal family alive in these hills. When that is accomplished, the king's peace will settle on the Highlands as smoothly as his silk stockings fit his legs. There'll be naught here but roe deer and sheep and the wolves that feed upon them.''

Cassie kept her silence for a long moment, considering things the way he painted them. Not that she believed him. She had no better rebuttal so she kept quiet. She looked back over her shoulder to see where her abigail and Angus were, and found them following on foot, a bit of a distance behind. The wind at her back kept her words and Robert's from being overheard by them. Even so, she needed to gather her thoughts if she was to continue with this useless argument that she knew she couldn't win.

The king's peace was in effect. Valuable hostages from each clan that had participated in the great civil war were held in Edinburgh seeing that the peace remained. Cassie turned to look at the gully trenches before them.

"You paint a rather harsh reaction for a simple explanatory letter, don't you?" Cassie remained where she was. The ice-crusted path before them would become more of a mud track. She gathered her pony's reins to remount, but made no further move to do so, letting their talk linger, while the rest of their party advanced down the steep incline.

"It's the truth, unvarnished and raw as green cut wood, but the truth, every word."

"And you know this truth. Young as you are, you have the ear of the king and the gift to see inside his very soul?" Cassie's voice was as scalding as her metaphor. Then she laughed, but it was a hollow sound. "You would rival Countess Seaforth's seer for prognosticating dire futures for us all."

Just as determined, Robert stood his own moral ground, planted right in front of her, blocking her from taking her seat on her horse. "Nay, lassie, no seer need show me the way of kings in the future. I have learned all that I know as truth from history and the world as it is today.

"Times are a'changing, Cassandra MacArthur. If

you want to live t' see the future, you adapt. Elizabeth of England wields power and James of Scotland craves his own hand on the sword of the ship of state. All of the Gordons willna keep him from it, nor will the earl of Argyll, nor the petty despots in hidden glens like Achanshiel, nor every Highlander alive in this stark and beautiful land. Change with the times or be swept under by them, lady.''

Alex, Dorcas and Angus and the rest of the horses rattled the stones on the flat rise above the deep gully where they soon stopped and stood waiting.

Robert offered Cassie his cradled hands as a boost to the saddle. Cassie paused at his unexpected and definitely chivalrous though unspoken gesture. ''I'm quite capable of mounting unaided, sir.''

''No doubt you are.'' His expression remained fixed as did the cradle of his laced fingers.

''As you like it then. Mount up, everyone. We ride from here.'' Cassie accepted the offer and put her muddy boot in his palm and took the boost onto her pony's back.

Seated, she looked down at Robert Gordon. She wanted the last word, even if she hadn't won the debate. She tossed her head and galloped ahead, leaving the mapmaker to clean his hands before he mounted and caught up.

Chapter Eight

It wasn't Robert Gordon who clattered down the ridge, riding hotspur to stop Cassie's wild race down the gully's ridge. It was Angus. "Cut out yer prancing around the peaks, milady. The snow's melting too fast this side of Aonach Eagach. Tha's no good for us. Y'er taking us down t' cross wicked water. Kindly cease palavering with that bonnie mon, and think about how to get cross yon Twisted Gully and get us home safe before darkfall."

Cassie nodded, acknowledging his half-scolding advice.

Robert hung back, waiting for Alex and the abigail to catch up. Dorcas urged her mount past them both, and solidly insinuated herself at her young mistress's side. The dour chaperon's presence was sufficient impediment to further discourse with Lady Quickfoot. Robert wasn't surprised. Dorcas clearly thought little of him.

At the timberline he caught his first clear sight of Loch Leven, filling the bottom of the glen edging the mountain. The number of rushing streams and water-falls feeding it was a daunting sight.

While the lake stretched east and west, flanking the mountain base, primordial forests rose off its banks for countless miles as far as the eye could see. No welcoming castles guarded either shore. In fact, Robert's sharp eyes detected no crofts, kirks or villages either. He couldn't figure out why there were no signs of human habitation in this glen until Cassie turned east along a high trail circumnavigating the long loch. The explanation came with her first conversational bid in more than an hour's tedious ride.

"We're at the southernmost edge of my father's hunting lands, Glenedon. We'll stay to the hills, though," she told both him and Alex. "Wolves have the rule of that timber."

They stopped at a multitiered waterfall to rest the horses and sample the lunch packed by Maggie MacGregor. The wind howled hard over the stony ridges. Huge mounds of ice-bearded mists had frozen solid. Beneath the pinnacles of the rising Mamores Mountains to the north, black clouds ran faster than Robert had ever seen clouds move, even at sea during gales.

In contrast, the air where they rested held an odd, unseasonable warmth. Robert shed his plaid for shirt-sleeves and even thought about removing his leather jerkin for the time being.

"What do you make of these clouds?" Robert had crossed the rocky clearing to speak to Angus. The old gillie tucked his whiskey flask into his sark and wiped his mouth with the back of his grizzled hand.

"Bah. Naught but a storm stuck over Ben Nevis," Angus replied calmly. "Ye ken it's flooding below so all paths down are out. We must stay high in the hills a while yet."

"How much farther to Castle MacArthur?"

"Four hours the hard way…no more." Angus efficiently spread a sack of grain on the ground for the hobbled horses. "Those who want to live to see the end of the trip go roundabout Arthur's cliff. 'Tis not far as the crow flies. Aye, ye'd be there now if ye could fly, wouldn't ye?"

With such encouragement from the gillie, Robert decided against eating another of the crunchy rolls stuffed with cheese and sausage. Better that they save some sustenance for later—in case the weather worsened and they had to hole up for the night.

"Dinna fash yersel', Gordon," Angus said. "Storms always blow out on the north face of Ben Nevis." The gillie coughed deeply, then settled comfortably between a pair of rocks, two toil-worn hands flattened over his chest, his chin a gnarled nub just to the top of them. A moment later the odd little man snored, sound asleep.

Angus had a certain grayness when he coughed that made Robert think he wasn't in the best of health. Consumption wasn't reserved only for the stews of Edinburgh. It took its fair share of victims in the Highlands, too.

Angus's coughing spell eased, no doubt assuaged by the liberal doses of whiskey the gillie fed it. Robert decided Angus's value as a protector of Lady Cassandra was as questionable as his sobriety. The old gillie certainly wasn't her *guide*. He wasn't asleep long before Cassie came and tucked a corner of his plaid over his gnarled arthritic hands.

Robert determined it was time to get some work done. He took out his ledger and rapidly began expanding his notes of the morning's travels. During his earlier survey of Morvern, the shire to the west, he'd been told that the castle of MacArthur of Achanshiel lay in a protected glen on the western slope of Ben Nevis. Hopefully, that glen was less than five nautical miles away. Miles that could see increasingly bad weather scuttle even the gentlest track. Thus far this passage through Glencoe had shown him everything but mild terrain.

They shouldn't waste daylight here under the pretense of allowing for a leisurely luncheon. In truth, they shouldn't have traveled with the horses because all horses were a liability in these mountains. Even packhorses. It would only take a small accident or injury for the animals and the gillie and not so agile abigail to become a liability, too.

He joined Alex at their impromptu camp toward the high ridge of the waterfall. Alex stood with his head back, staring in rapt fascination skyward, eyes fixed on the unusual clouds spilling over and engulfing the long mountain crest and a parchment drawing of the course of the twisting falls in his hand.

"That...sky advises finding shelter, Rob." He shouted to be heard above the wild roar of the waterfall, gesturing with a shaved stick of charcoal. "We can't cross any of these streams, either."

"Aye," Robert agreed, wishing there could be time

to paint any of these wonders. Hasty sketches would be all they could rely upon to capture this scene for the treatise that would accompany their final map.

Fast-moving, purple-bruised clouds did not bode well for travelers in any clime, and God only knew where a man would wind up if he braved wading through any of the racing white-water flows. Experience had taught them both to trust their instincts in freakish weather climes. Better safe than sorry.

"Let's see if we can get the ladies moving."

"'Tis her gillie's peckish ways that have the lass cooling her heels. I said last night we should press on alone," Alex added rather mournfully.

"And I thank ye for not saying I told ye so," Robert added with a wry smile for his own idiocy. He was stung hard and knew it. He couldn't take his blasted eyes off the girl.

"Dinna be so hard on yourself, Robbie." Alex clapped him on the back. "Personally, I think Angus sips a bit much of MacGregor's whiskey. He's kept the cork off that bottomless flask all morning."

Robert grinned, not at all sorry that Angus's complaints had fallen on Alex's stoic ears rather than his own.

Alex wagged his hand at the threatening sky. "I mark it two hours till the snow flies, hard as rocks."

"So it's snow hard as rocks, is it?" Robert asked. "You're certain?"

"Dead certain. Care to wager who collects the kindling when we camp for the night?"

Robert laughed. "Though I'm not a wagering man most days, you're on."

He left Alex to pack up and caught up with Cassie and her abigail, washing at a quieter pool sheltered by wind-twisted pines.

"Your gillie seems to be in dire need of a wee kip, but I think we'd best move on," Robert said without preamble. "The weather's disintegrating."

"Angus always takes up glorious at midday." Dorcas handed Cassie a linen towel with her dour pronouncement.

"Aye, and those wee nips of whiskey makes him sleep longer, too." Cassie patted her face and hands dry.

They looked incongruous together, the scowling abigail in her fine, braid-trimmed traveling cloak and the lady in her dun-colored hunting plaid, cross garters and boots. To Robert's view the finer clothes should have been on the younger woman. But Cassandra MacArthur looked beautifully alive and vivid just the way she was.

She certainly garnered his attention with every move she made. She gave a last pass of her hand to her secured hair, making certain her lone braid had not frayed overmuch in the morning's ride. It had, but her fingers were probably too numb from the cold washing to tell that, for she made no further adjustments to bring an aura of endearing curly red tendrils under control.

"Gordon's right. Rouse Angus, Dorcas. The clouds draw low."

"It's probably not my concern, but isn't Angus a bit old for trekking about these mountains?" Robert suggested.

"According to Angus he'll never get too old."
Cassie managed an easy smile in response. "Did you
have enough to eat?"

"For the now," Robert answered. "We're in for a
storm before day's end."

"Have no fear. This side of Nevis never gets the
worst of a blow," Cassie assured him.

Nice, Robert thought, maddened momentarily by
the inane platitude she had offered him. He stalked to
his horse to remove its hobble and tightened the saddle girth.

"I have been thinking about protocol," Cassie
said, her energetic step apace with his. "When we
reach Achanshiel, it would be best if you allow me
some time to introduce you to my father. I must explain to him fully how we MacArthurs are indebted
to both you and Hamilton for Ian's continuing good
health, as well as my own."

Robert glanced over his shoulder at her and
watched her fight the wind to subdue a handful of
hair that flew into her face. "Sometimes it helps if I
gain my mother's goodwill before my father has a
chance to broadcast his opinion. What I'm saying
is…I'd prefer you didn't broadcast your surnames at
the gate. Is that agreeable to you?"

Robert got to his feet, caught the offending tendrils
of hair and drew them out of her eyes. Then, because
there was no place to smooth them, he stood there
holding them.

"We have ample endorsements and credentials
with us," Robert said as he opened his sporran and

drew out the length of black ribbon he oftentimes used to tie back his own hair. "Turn around, please."

Cassie did as he requested, glad for the moment to face the wind. It felt odd to have a man's fingers raking through her hair, catching it all together at the nape of her neck.

"Granted, you will present those to my father just as you gave your recommendation from the Mac-Gregor of Balquihidder to Euan. All I'm requesting is that you let me decide when that presentation should occur. I think things will go easier that way. MacArthur could be rather difficult otherwise."

"You truly anticipate trouble?" He thought that was absurd. MacArthur would not be able to deny that Cassie owed her life to his rescue. He pulled the ribbon tight and fastened it securely.

"Not exactly." Cassie spun to face him and completely misjudged her footing and his proximity. Their shoulders collided, knocking them both off balance.

Robert's hands were quick to steady her. They each froze for a second in time—he with his hands on her shoulders, she with her forehead pressed against his cheek. For the space of a magical heartbeat neither of them moved.

Then Robert dropped his hands and she stepped back, murmuring, "Oh! Sorry about that."

"No trouble at all." Robert added hastily, forcing his electrified hands to remain perfectly still. They tingled, and the urge to catch and pull her to his chest and kiss her full on her lips made his brain spin.

Cassie cleared her throat and turned to look for Dorcas. Her abigail was bent over Angus at his rocky perch, shaking his shoulder. Her billowing cloak blocked any view they had back to Cassie and Robert. Coloring deeply, Cassie pressed her hand over her smoothed-back hair and said softly, "Thank you. That will help in this wind."

"Aye." Robert smiled. "I like your hair flying in the wind, but it can prove difficult, I imagine. And you may be sure I will make no mention of my assistance to anyone."

"You are too kind."

"Only to you," Robert replied, presenting to her a short, eloquent bow.

Cassie took a deep breath, more to gather her courage than to stall for a lack of words. She knew what she wanted to say. "I'm resigned to playing my part in this farce of acting as your guide as the king commands, but I don't want to be taken unawares by some unexpected countermeasure made by my father. He's a grand master at sabotaging the most carefully constructed plans."

"I've heard tell of some of his more outlandish ones," Robert added tongue in cheek.

"Aye, well, I could arrive home to discover I'm being married off to the devil under the bridge at Glen Orchy. And dinna think something that bizarre is past MacArthur. His idea of suitable marriage material extends to trolls. When I left the castle he was on one of his rants to secure my future with all due haste, which he thinks is the best solution to every problem a young woman has. Since I have no interest in marrying a troll, I left him to his devices. We may arrive and interrupt some diversion. One never knows with MacArthur.''

Robert wasn't exactly convinced, although he was fully aware of her father's reputation. MacArthur was a troublemaker from the day he came to lead his band of clansmen. ''I agree to play this by ear once we get there. Right now, we'd best get back in the saddle and move on, else this discussion will be moot, for we'll be spending the night right here.''

''Trust me, we won't spend the night in the hills. I don't care for sleeping in soggy snowbanks.'' Cassie stepped up to her horse and nudged her pony away from the hulls of grain scattered on the ground.

The mare lifted her head, accepting the bit back in her gentle mouth. Bridle in place, Cassie checked her cinches and tightened them, then called to Angus. ''Are ye movin', mon?''

''Aye-ah.'' Angus slowly shambled to his mount. He yawned, coughed, then set to work saddling up. They set off shortly after, circumventing the snow-capped craggy peak of Ben Nevis.

They weren't in the saddle more than an hour before the first flakes of snow began falling. The flakes were big and stuck to their clothing and saddle gear, and covered the ground.

Cassie gave a dismayed look skyward on the advent of the first snow, but she didn't remark about misjudging the weather. The mountain was quickly becoming invisible as the blanket of foul weather sank down over it. Robert pulled his plaid closer around his chest as the temperature plunged just as rapidly as they descended into the next gully.

Due south of Five Finger Gully, the track they were following dipped into the pines and broken boulders that marked the edge of what Cassie called the Red Burn.

For Robert's notes, she paused long enough to point out the prominent rock formations and a ring of ancient standing stones, which was all but becoming invisible. Their world shrank with the dropping of the gray winter storm. Robert scribbled in his ledger, trying to get it all down, although he was more entranced by the sight of her eyelashes and brows spiked with flakes of snow under the bright cowl of her plaid over her head.

Despite the increasing danger of the coming storm, rising wind and Angus's irritated grumbling to move faster, Cassie held him so enthralled with her near poetic attention to minute details of rock and stone, Robert rode them all straight into disaster.

Angus gargled out a strangled sound, clutched his chest and toppled headfirst from his saddle onto the stones beside Dorcas's horse.

"Milady!" Dorcas shrieked.

Cassie whirled in her saddle to look back, then screamed and wheeled her horse about, galloping to her fallen gillie.

"Angus!" Cassie cried out. She bounded out of her saddle and was the first to kneel at the elder's side, grabbing fistfuls of his plaid and shaking him. "What's happened?"

Chapter Nine

Angus's eyes bulged in their sockets. He gripped his chest fiercely and writhed in anguish. His mouth worked like that of a landed fish, but no words explaining his condition became audible. One thing was clear, he was choking and in grievous pain.

Cassie tugged his muffler loose from his throat and felt the throbbing pulse in his neck. Every vein in his face stood out as though about to burst. "Are you hurt, mon?"

"Aye." Angus choked out that one word, then gazed helplessly at her face as she dabbed the tail of her plaid across his brow. He lifted intensely blue fingertips to her face, then his hands fell suddenly as he fainted dead away.

"Sweet Mother of us all, Angus is dying!" Cassie wailed. "Damn you, Angus Christianson Campbell, don't you dare die on me!"

Unnoticed, Robert dismounted, moving immediately to Cassie's side. "What's wrong with him?" he asked Dorcas.

"He's got apoplexy!" Dorcas dismounted unaided and began frantically tearing open a bag on her saddle, all the while repeating, "Oh dear, oh dear."

Robert could see that the gillie's lips and tongue were as blue as his fingertips, as though the old man were choking. He lifted the elder's shoulders, giving Angus ease from the stony ground so Cassie could tend him better.

"Can the poor mon no' breathe?" Dorcas demanded, as she set herself strategically to Cassie's other side.

Alex Hamilton shrugged off his fine plaid and laid it over Angus.

"Perhaps a wee dram of would help." Alex offered his own flask of whiskey, warmed from being inside his coat. Dorcas gave him such a scathing look, his hair should have been singed.

Angus roused when Cassie rubbed a handful of snow over his face and throat. That started him coughing—coughing so deeply it turned into a spasm. He was alert enough to clutch Robert's hand as Robert unfastened the cinch of Angus's belt and removed his stash of whiskey from inside the warm confines of his jerkin.

"Whiskey!" Cassie cried out. "That's what's made him this way in the first place!"

"Shush, milady. 'Tis his age and his heart, no' the drink," Dorcas said more calmly than Robert would have imagined she could ever be in this situation. She produced a leather pouch that contained willow bark, ground to a fine powder. She mixed powder and snow together making a paste in a small silver cup to which she added several drops of whiskey. "This will soothe his pains. Sip this, Angus."

She held the cup to his lips. Angus grimaced at the bitter taste. The pain assaulting his chest left him no choice but to accept whatever aid anyone thought might ease his misery. Had Dorcas suggested burning eagle feathers tied to his beard, he would had suffered it because he implicitly trusted both her and Cassie to care for him the best they could.

"We'll have to make camp," Robert said to Alex. "Get fires started. We'll need shelter for the night."

"Here?" Alex frowned.

Cassie spoke coherently for the first time since Angus had taken ill. "We can't make camp below Five Finger Gully, not when a storm blows from the west. We'd all be dead by morn. We'll have to move Angus to Chattering Otters Cave. 'Tis not far. We'll be safe from the storm there, and I'll have time to figure out what to do. I don't like this one bit. I canna have my gillie dying while I'm in his custody."

"Harrumph!" Dorcas snorted before anyone could utter a word to the otherwise. "Ye'll not be spending the night in any cave on this mountain hills with these two men so long as I'm yer abigail, milady. I forbid it. Laird MacArthur forbids it. No. Angus will be fine in a moment or two." She made her position as chaperon perfectly clear.

At that disparaging remark from the abigail, Alex looked harder at Robert for direction.

"Beggin' yer abigail's pardon, Cassandra, but the snow grows thicker by the moment." Robert sided with Cassie's first prudent suggestion. "Angus needs shelter now. How far exactly is Castle MacArthur and how close is Chattering Otters Cave?''

Cassie sat back on her heel, shielding her eyes to look ahead through the storm. "Six, seven miles to the castle at best. The cave's five, maybe six hundred feet below the first gully."

"Then the cave it is till Angus recovers," Robert decided.

"I say, no!" Dorcas's voice rose. "MacArthur will lock the gel and me in chains and leave us to rot the rest of our miserable lives were that t' happen."

"Hold on here, woman," Robert interjected more forcefully than necessary. "You voiced no objections to our riding out with your lady this morning. Why the ruckus now?"

"I had my objections!" Dorcas answered, undaunted by his flash of temper.

Angus roused that moment, glaring at them all crankily through one squinting eye. "What's all the bleating for? Y'er making a din to wreck me ears. Cassie, take me to Otters Cave. I'm colder than the grave."

Cassie gripped his hand. "Angus, I'm afraid for you."

He coughed, then settled again, resting. "I'll keep. This wind is about t' kill me, though."

"The cave it is, then." Cassie nodded at Robert, agreeing to move out of the elements there. "It's for the best," she said by way of appeasement to Dorcas.

"Maybe," the abigail admitted, grim-lipped. She gathered up her medicines and cup, stuffing them back inside the cloth sack from which she'd taken them.

"Be careful with him," Cassie admonished them as they helped Angus to his feet. "He's more a father to me than my own has ever been."

"Of course." Robert nodded crisply. He wrapped Angus more securely in Alex's plaid to keep him warm. Alex's horse was the largest of the lot. He mounted and Robert hoisted Angus up before Alex on the saddle. "Show us the way, Cassie." Robert stayed at Alex's side, to lead the horse down the trail and assist if anything further happened.

Cassie gathered up their horses and waited for Dorcas to mount before she led them off to the main path, down into the steep-sided gully. The walls of the crevice protected them from the brunt of the wind on the stark hill and it wasn't long before they came to the cave. As promising as it appeared, there would be no fire available inside unless one of them went back out foraging for wood.

Once Angus was settled, his teeth chattering in spite of the wrapping of every spare cloth both Robert and Alex carried in their pack, Alex volunteered to go and find firewood.

After a quick inspection, the cave proved more suitable than Robert had imagined it could be. No bats or animal carcasses or scattered bones revealed it to be the home of a predator. The main cavern broke off almost immediately into four chambers. One they set aside for the animals, and Robert busied himself there, unsaddling the mounts and relieving the ponies of their burdens.

He found signs of recent use, most likely from reivers, men who came to steal cattle from other clans and retreated back their own lands with the stolen booty. One of his measuring ropes came into use, strung from rock to rock forming a temporary enclosure to keep the animals from wandering free. A clear spring offered ample water, and the pool was shallow.

Alex returned shortly with wood to start a fire in the main chamber. Once that was crackling into life, and the smoke from it rising to the high ceiling of the cave, Robert returned to the entrance to take new measure of the storm. He found Cassie there, her arms folded tight against her chest. Her hands were hidden under a thick shawl thrown over her plaid.

Robert put his hand on the rock wall above her head and looked out into the stark gully, as silent as she was for the moment in contemplation of the white wall of swirling snow.

"We'd best thank the Almighty that he made it cold enough to snow," Cassie said by way of greeting. "Rather than rain."

"Why?" Robert stared into the dizzying white that seemed to possess no true direction beyond the stones.

"Because rain would mean flash floods and water rising above our heads, why else?" Cassie answered in puffs of frosted breath. She sighed and Robert thought he saw a small shiver shake her shoulders.

"Angus has taken a bad turn," she said. "Dorcas told me she thinks he's had a stroke. He canna move his left leg or hand. I must go to my father. Angus needs MacArthur's physician, medicines and more care than we can provide him here.''

"You canna strike out with a gale about to blow," Robert declared. "Six miles could be half a day's ride in this weather."

"I have no choice but to go down Arthur's Drop." Cassie pivoted, facing him. "Help would be back here before dusk, do I go now. It's an hour journey on foot, two hours at the most, even in this."

"If it worsens you could get lost."

"Nay, I know the mountain too well."

She looked up at the rock where Robert's hand rested in lieu of being wrapped around her shoulder. Robert dropped his hand to her shoulders and drew her back from the opening. "Nay, lass. You'll not set out from here alone in this. I forbid it."

Instead of twisting away or arguing, Cassie stood perfectly still, gazing up at his face. "Do you doubt that Dorcas believes I should go now?"

"I would hear it from her own lips, and have another look at Angus to judge his condition for myself, before I would agree. Come, we'll do that."

"Not yet." Cassie untucked one of her hidden hands and laid it on Robert's chest. "It's quiet here and I was taking a moment just to gather my thoughts and my strength before I fly into the storm. I need a bit more time before I'm ready."

Cassie turned back to face the wall of white, and fixed her eyes on some sight she imagined beyond the blinding swirl. Her shoulder pressed into Robert's side.

"I like snow," she said several minutes later, sounding calm and certain.

"Aye." Robert did as well. He could have stood there much longer, watching the storm, holding her gently against his side becoming more and more aware of her womanliness. The scent of her hair and her clean shawl filled his chest and he wanted so badly to kiss her warm lips. But this wasn't the place or the time.

Soft footsteps alerted them both to someone's approach from the rear of the cave. "Ye havena left, milady?" Dorcas came to a startled stop in the narrow opening, the small lantern in her hand guttering in the gusts entering the mouth of the cave.

"No." Cassie moved slightly away from Robert and his right arm returned to his side. "Mr. Gordon had reservations about my leaving alone."

"And well he should," Dorcas agreed, shaking her head at the look of the snow falling. "But ye must. Angus has fallen into sleep and I canna rouse him."

"I'll have a look at him." Robert caught Cassie's arm, drawing her into the cavern alongside of him.

Dorcas clucked her tongue and shook her head, leading the way with her lantern raised high. The open fire cast eerie lights on the uneven walls. Alex had fashioned a support from their packs to prop Angus up in a somewhat inclined, half-sitting position, which they all believed was better for his ailing heart. The gillie leaned to the left, as though he couldn't support his body, and his mouth and left arm drooped oddly. His foot fell inward at the arch. That was all Robert needed to see to know the truth. He'd had a stroke or some sort of major attack involving his heart or his brain.

"I've given him another dose of willow, but I havena enough to last the night," Dorcas said quietly.

"We've no food save the slim pickings from our luncheon," Alex said, and waved at the open basket covered with a single cloth to keep the foods fresh. "And it's a bit late to think about laying traps or fishing up a bounty to tide us all over."

Cassie knelt beside Angus and tried to wake him. Her shaking of his right shoulder only caused him to sink more onto the stack of packs supporting him on the left. His mouth hung slack and his breath appeared labored at best.

She kissed his cheek, then stood and removed her rucksack from the pile at Angus's side. She swung that onto her back and looked at Robert. "I'm going, mapmaker. I'll not let him die up here unshriven. My father will know how to get him down safely, even if it snows from now until Judgment Day."

"I'm going with you," Robert responded.

"You don't know the mountain. I'm two hours from home at the most. Stay here and don't jeopardize your mission. Help will be here by nightfall."

"I'm going." Robert stuffed a rucksack with provisions that even the wildest climb through the mountains would require and slung that over his shoulder. "Alex, keep the old man alive. He means more to Lady Quickfoot than she's willing to say."

"Aye, he does." Cassie nodded briskly. She cast a troubled look back to Angus. Her words, though, were only for Robert Gordon. "Dinna blame me if you lose your nerve. I won't delay my descent to guide you safely back here.''

Robert didn't particularly like hearing such a comment from her. It sounded too much like a threat. That made him wonder just what kind of reckless path she intended to take to reach Castle MacArthur in two hours' time.

Dorcas and Alex accompanied them to the mouth of the cave and stopped there. Both stared dubiously into what were fast becoming impossible conditions.

''Ye won't have much time before the ice and snow drifts over this cave's entrance.'' Alex remarked astutely. ''You might not find this cave if you try to come back here.''

''Aye. That's one chance I'll have to take.'' Robert fixed Lady Quickfoot with a penetrating stare.

Could he—a Gordon—trust her with his life? Did she have murder in her heart? Could she have a thirst for revenge running deep and have kept it hidden from his detection? He didn't know the answer to those questions. There was something about Lady Quickfoot he couldn't seem to uncover. Perhaps he just needed more answers for his sudden obsession with her to end. ''Are you absolutely positive this is necessary, lass?''

''Aye.'' Cassie wasted no words. ''The cave's easy to find in this gully. Every man at Castle MacArthur could find it in his sleep.''

''Take care, milady,'' Dorcas urged, stepping aside so Cassie could go out the narrow entrance.

''I'll put a flag up in the wind,'' Alex said as his farewell.

''Do that,'' Robert decreed.

Chapter Ten

It was clear they both thought she was being reckless. Cassie grimly shook her head. "I dinna give a damn what either of you think at this point. Angus's breathing and useless left hand frighten me to death. He's dearer to me than anyone, save my mother. And dinna tell me he can't live forever."

"I wasn't going to," Robert said as he settled his rucksack on his back and pulled on his worn leather gloves to protect his hands.

Cassie took a moment to compose herself and followed his lead, pulling on gloves and making certain her pack was closed and secure on her own back. Then with a quick nod of farewell to Dorcas and Alex, she faced the white peril. Robert joined her at the mouth of the cave.

"It won't be so bad at the top of the gully. Storms wash across Ben Nevis in waves, but right here there are updrafts compounding it."

"Aye, I see that." Robert stepped forward first. The sky was white and low, but so far the snow was still falling thickest at the crest of the mountain. It was a rare storm that did that.

Cassie gave herself an hour's time to reach Arthur's Drop, overlooking her father's castle, and from there it was a straight shoot down the glen.

Cassie had shaken off her fears the moment she emerged from the shelter, before they had a chance to sink in and cripple her resolve. But they came back again at the unbidden memory of Arthur's Drop. A more sheer vertical face on Ben Nevis was hard to find.

That cave offered safety from the elements but nothing for Angus's heart. She must go home. There medicines aplenty stored in her mother's herbal larder and the capable assistance of her father's physician could be obtained. McRayburn had brought Angus through terrible bouts of apoplexy before.

She turned to Robert. "Can you give me a boost onto that rock?"

"I'll do my best." Robert made another cradle with his hands and she scrambled over the stone to a ridge that ran along in a fairly decent track. Taller and blessed with stronger arms and a better reach than hers, he needed no boost to raise himself.

"Thank you." Cassie dusted the snow from her hands. "Do you have a grandfather?" she asked, beginning the forward march to the west.

"Aye, two of them, both still alive and kicking. Grand old men they are, too." Robert stayed close to her back, regretting only the narrowness of the running ledge of stone that wasn't wide enough to allow them to press forward at each other's side.

"Well, mine were both gone by the time I was born. Angus is the closest thing I ever had to a grandfather. I couldna love him more."

"Watch where you step," Robert cautioned as he fastened the throat of his sheepskin jerkin. Cassie kicked a small drift of snow off the stone and continued, her step sure and true.

They caught the brunt of the wind at the bottom of the gully and it sliced right through them. An hour hadn't passed since they'd come inside from the wind. Returning made it feel twice as cold and wicked to the bone.

Cassandra was the first to bring her plaid over her head, cowl-like, to keep what warmth she could inside her body. Robert soon followed suit, thinking to himself this was insanity to race straight into the bitter wind when it took his breath away.

It was doubly maddening not to know where they were going or what trail this woman followed. Cassandra didn't allow time to discuss it. She set out the way she intended to go, at a near run, no longer lazily zigzagging down the mountain as she had done on horseback. She headed straight down, over the rocks and boulders that presented themselves in her way.

Only once in the first quarter hour did she change her direction and that was because the crust of ice forming over a quick running spring could not be trusted. Otherwise, in that half-hour descent, they passed once more directly below the hidden mouth of Chattering Otters Cave by nearly a thousand feet, traveling on a steeply cut, single-file ledge that turned them fully into the force of the buffeting wind and oncoming storm.

Traveling the entire length of that ledge took another quarter hour. In all, Robert estimated it had added no more than a mere twenty-foot drop to their descent.

The ledge came to an end at a deep crag in the rocky face of the mountain, where the previous fissure had broken free ages ago and tumbled into the glen below. The remaining rock formed a tor jutting free of the mountain itself. The huge tor provided shelter from the sting of the wind. Cassie leaned against the cliff, resting her legs, removing the rope she'd carried over her shoulder.

Robert quirked a brow, questioning what she was preparing to do. His cold expression said clearly he thought they both were daft for risking the storm. "What now, Quickfoot?"

Cassie looked up from the knot she was unfastening before she could uncoil her rope. "Your voice sounds rusty."

"Well, it should. You don't believe in using your own."

"Chatter is useless in these conditions." The sheerness of the cliff was dizzying. She stepped back, connecting with her companion's body. His backside seemed frozen to the stone wall at their backs with good reason. The ledge had narrowed to just a single foot's width underneath them. Fortunately, the wind flattened them so resolutely they didn't have to worry much about falling.

"Aye." Robert shook his head. She was an uncommon woman to be sure. He knew of none other that would do what she did or be as ready as any stalker on the hunt of a worthy prey. "Do tell me, though, now that you've run out of road for this hike, where to from here?"

Cassie made a loop in the rope and stepped forward, fearlessly embracing the jutting tor. The wind ripped her shawl and plaid off her head and sent both snapping hard against Robert's chest. It made as much noise as a sail sprung loose from its sheeting in a gale.

"Isn't it obvious?" Cassie grinned back at him, her cheek plastered to the icy tor. "I'm going down the easy way."

She embraced the tor, then drew the rope tight around the tor. As she moved back her flattened palms pushed off the tor and she fell back against the rock wall of the mountain next to Robert. He threw out his hand to catch the ropes, which weren't knotted in any way.

Other than reacting to that, he was of no use to her, being too concerned about his precarious position on the vertical. Then he saw that she had had the sense to wind the rope around her wrist so it wouldn't be lost by the wind.

Cassie leaned as far out of the wind as possible, which meant crowding Robert badly. It couldn't be helped. "I don't think I can tie a secure knot."

"Aye, I noticed ye dinna bring suitable gloves for this, Quickfoot." Robert grasped the ropes and held on to them firmly.

"Lost them," Cassie admitted. "These were the best I could do."

She gave up resisting her urges and moved closer to Robert, drawing in his warmth. "You feel warm. I'm fair frozen. Knot it well, Gordon. 'Tis an awesome drop straight into the river below."

"I wondered if you'd even noticed." Robert took his time making certain the knots were well done and fast. When the task was done he held the length of tied rope in hand and said, "One thing more, milady?"

"What's that?" Cassie allowed herself the liberty of gazing into those wonderful blue eyes of his.

"Where the hell is that rope going to take us?"

Cassie blinked in surprise at that question. With her face turned to his and her back to the wall she didn't feel as if she was on a mountain at all. His eyes made her think of summer days and clear skies and heather blooming in the glen. His eyes made her think of kisses she'd never tasted.

"You don't know? You can't see it?"

"See what, for the love of Christ?" Robert looked up into the angry clouds instead of looking down into the rock-strewn valley below.

"Achanshiel...Castle MacArthur. It's right there, below us." Cassie pointed to the spires and stone walls that were barely visible in the swirling mists of increasing snow. With its cloak of snow, it looked like a castle in a fairy tale.

Robert took a deep breath, then turned his gaze from her face and followed the downward point of her right hand. His gorge rose in his throat at the dizzying sight of snow rising on the wind. Odd that, and here he was sweating as if he'd run twenty miles on a summer's day.

Castle MacArthur was right there, a mile, maybe a mile and a half west of the cliff's bottom. To reach it one only needed to be able to fly like a bird. "I see."

Robert shut his eyes and opened them in another less daunting direction. The descending gray clouds and onrushing blizzard was infinitely more reassuring than the sheer drop at his feet. He had to force himself to return his gaze to Lady Quickfoot. "One more question. Have ye done this before?"

Cassie thought about exaggerating and boasting that she'd done it a hundred times. She couldn't be that callow. She'd seen it done. Her brother, James, had done the trick one summer's day ages and ages ago and caused Angus's first onset of apoplexy in the doing. And she'd been made to witness, along with every other inhabitant of Castle MacArthur, the justified skelping Jamie received as payment for his recklessness.

This, of course, wasn't summer. She was fairly certain no one at the castle could see clearly to the cliff wall above the keep to detect anyone rappelling down Arthur's Drop. Nor was she a risk-taking lad of fifteen.

She relaxed and settled against the cold stones, speaking confidently now. "It's exactly like any other downward drop in the mountains. You use the rock wall and the rope to let yourself down slowlike, dropping by your feet and bouncing out enough to let the rope out a bit at a time.''

''And ye have experience doing this?'' Robert asked.

Again Cassie didn't answer immediately. Instead, she slung her rucksack around and opened it, pulling out a contraption of iron rings and braided rope and a pair of worn leather gloves. The rucksack contained her emergency devices, lucky charms that she always carried with her on every journey. Jamie's gloves were far too big for her hands, but she put them on now.

Robert caught her right arm as she prepared to toss to the rope over the ledge. ''Shouldn't ye thread those through yon loops before ye toss the end away?''

''Aye.'' Cassie pulled back, aware of the mistake she'd almost made.

Again Robert put out his arm, restraining her from any more motion. ''This won't work. There's only one rope. No way to send the device back up.''

''Yes. I'll go down, then I'll tie the loops to the end of the rope and you can pull it back up, then come down yourself. I'll wait for you at the bottom.''

''Aye, and if you've misjudged the drop and the rope isn't long enough? What then?''

Robert threaded the iron loops through the device, making a slip cage of sorts, which could be lowered more efficiently than trying to rely upon hand strength against increasing blisters as a deterrent from killing oneself.

''The rope's long enough to reach the sheep field

edging the river. It's been used for this same drop before.''

''Aye.'' Robert let the corded rope out one coil at a time, checking it for cracks and frays in its length. That was the one thing she hadn't done before attaching the first end to the tor.

He vowed privately not to take any more risks than necessary. He told himself that those nearby spires and the wisps of smoke pouring out the castle chimneys went a very long way into assuring him that there was true warmth at the end of this journey. Warmth, food, hot water and possibly even a hot tub bath like the one he'd partaken of last night. The mere thought of such bounty made the risk taking feel worthwhile.

When the cord was all laid out and tugging from his hands in the pull of the wind, he had Cassie change places with him so he could check the knots and make certain the rope fastened to the tor wouldn't break. Cassie watched him crouch on the narrow landing. Then she held her breath when he actually put his foot out and pushed on the tor, testing its stability. It didn't fracture under the press of his weight. Cassie took that as a very good sign.

''MacArthur's Thumb has been here since the dawn of time,'' she told him confidently.

''Aye, well, God willing it will be here tomorrow and not marking our graves down there,'' Robert said evenly.

''You don't have to do this,'' Cassandra replied. ''You know the way back.''

''And let you go down on your own without know-

ing if you made it safely or no'? I don't think so.''
Robert wasn't accepting that end to this fiasco. "We
do this the hard way—together.''

"We can't!'' Cassie exclaimed over that. "I can't
rappel if I have to concentrate on holding on to you,
and there is only one rope.''

Robert brought his own rucksack around and removed a shorter coil of rope. Rappelling was a trait
as old as high walls and men on mountains. He made
a necessary adaptation to her rappelling belt, then
threaded the new rope into the loops. When he was
done, she was tied securely at the waist to his body,
and he to hers.

"Your job, my lady with the ill-fitting gloves, is to
make certain the rope below us is knot free. Are you
ready?''

"What?'' Cassie gasped the moment she realized
he intended to jump out, dragging her with him in
one fell move. Fell move it would be, too. "No, you
idiot! We don't jump out facefirst! We turn around
and step away, slow and careful-like.''

Robert let the stay rope out, freeing it from the
wall, testing its weight with his stable hand. He memorized that feel, then went on to the next task. Turning
around didn't seem possible in the space available.

His feet could do it, but it took shifting the direction of his shoulders and his head, which seemed impossible when pressed flat against the wall of stone
at his back. Vertigo assaulted him. He laid his brow
against the stones, sweating.

"You know this is mad, don't you?'' He looked to

Cassie and found her just as constrained as he was, hips hugging the wall, feet frozen.

"And necessary if we are to be successful." She stretched her arms as wide as she could, gripping hold of cracks in the smooth stone, and made the half circle turn—as quickly as Robert blinked his eye. He took courage from that, felt above his head until he found something he could grip and swung full about. The maneuver seemed so simple once it was done. He took several deep breaths to calm himself.

"Now what?" Cassie asked, pressing her cheek to the wall. "Do we stay here until we freeze over, or just step back at the count of three?"

"Neither." Robert pulled the slack out of the rope encircling his back and leaned out over the ledge until his head and shoulders felt the true pull of gravity. With his shoulders thus, he tested the rope's feel in his right hand, his leading hand. It was going to be a very tricky descent. He refused to think about possibilities. "I could think of one position that this would be fairly easy in."

"Oh?" Cassie couldn't think of any, at least not in a tandem descent. "What way is that?"

"Like lovers," Robert replied crisply.

Cassie's brow furled. Then she understood what he meant—exactly. She blushed to the roots of her red hair. "Robert Gordon, this is no time to be thinking of such frivolous things!"

"It would work—and it'd be a hell of a way to die." He let out more of the main sheet and pushed away from the ledge, stepping free and coming to a stop only inches down from the edge of the ledge itself. The success of the first maneuver gladdened him right to his frozen toes. "All right, Cassandra, move across me and stand right where I was standing."

Cassie did his bidding, but tensed in the doing. She shook her head. "I canna do this backward. I've got to see where I'm going."

Which brought them right back to where they'd been moments ago. Only she'd shaken her head and that braid of hers was free and loose, being torn more and more apart by the wind with each bitter gust. The rope slipped a little in Robert's grip. He lay almost in a perfect right angle to the cliff. If he were rigging a ship for a first mate, he'd be earning a full ration of grog for his precision.

"All right then, turn around." Robert grinned. He couldn't help himself. She made the switch in record time, but that didn't surprise him. Women did, after all, have smaller feet.

Her face was pale now, every trace of color drained out of it. She gulped and reached out, then literally fell onto him with a death grip, no, a lover's grip, fast and hard and certain.

"Oh, sweet heavenly Father, protect us," Cassie whispered. Her lips grazed his chin.

"He will," Robert said with conviction. "Kiss me."

"Why are you thinkin' of that now?" Cassie yelled.

"Kiss me. It will give me courage."

"Do you lack it otherwise?"

"I dinna think so, but I ken a kiss will inspire me to new heights."

"Verra well then." Cassie caught one hand behind his head, stretched her chin up and planted a facer on his lips.

In that moment that their lips united the elements took flight. Robert let the rope out. Gravity took over and they dropped. An icy wind drove between Robert's legs, up his back and roared in his ears all the while Cassandra MacArthur clung to him, as if they were lovers well familiar with each other's body.

Robert shivered as his cods tightened and slid his tongue between her lips just for the thrill of taking that risk too. She almost withdrew with a jolt from the shock. Instead she clung even more tightly to him. Somehow he had the presence of mind to feel the arc of his bounce decrease and he flexed his knees before the balls of his feet impacted with jarring force into the mountain.

The next hop was slower and more gracefully accomplished. They stopped with a gentle bounce impacting up his legs.

The jolting stop was rather incredible itself.

Robert looked for MacArthur's Thumb and found it caught in the cloudy snow of the mountain far far above them.

Cassie pulled her face from his and looked down. "Whatever you do," she gasped, "Dinna let go again. We'll be impaled, both of us, on Mordred's Spear."

Robert swallowed. "Where is it?"

"Below you, ten feet."

He nodded and pushed out, carrying them both sideways. "Tell me when we're clear."

"Sweet Lord, we're going to die. Pray."

"We're not going to die here. Quickfoot, tell me when I'm clear of it." Robert moved them to the right again. It was incredibly easy.

"Our Father who art in heaven…" Cassie mumbled the words.

"Tell me when we're clear of it!" Robert demanded.

"We canna get clear of it. The rope is tangled all around it."

"Clear it!" Robert commanded.

"Oh, and shall I just climb down there and untangle it with my toes, sir?"

"Do it! Reach under me and bring the rope up then toss it beyond the formation. Do it now, Cassandra!"

"With what?" Cassie asked. "Do I let go of you, I'll fall to my death alone."

"You're not going anywhere. Pretend I'm a tree you've climbed up on. Use your hands to free the rope."

That took more than a leap of imagination to envision, but Cassie did as he suggested, reaching for the rope that dangled loose from his left hand. He'd threaded Jamie's harness perfectly, allowing him control of their descent. She'd never figured it out, and Jamie had refused to show her exactly how to use the tool. She'd have just put it through the hooks once and prayed the friction on her hands didn't kill her before the drop did. Cassie was glad he'd come with her.

She untangled the rope and threw it clear of Mordred's Spear, a deadly granite spike that all the castlefolk bet would fall before the beginning of the new century. Odds were always being given and taken on the exact date in the castle hall.

"It's done," Cassie said with conviction.

"Give the rope a shake and show me how free," Robert requested, gentler voiced now.

She extended her right arm down his left, caught the rope edge and shook it. It felt as if they were in bed together—only no bed Cassie had ever slept in felt this cold and unrelenting as his body did with hers flattened against it.

His hands were numb, but Robert concentrated hard on testing the weight and pull of the rope, the feel of it, judging by that how much rope he had left.

"Exactly how long was this rope the last time you measured it? Be precise."

She had never measured it. Cassie took a deep breath and guessed. "Two hundred yards."

"Six hundred feet." Robert stared at the jutting tor above that kept them from falling to their deaths. It held fast.

"Give or take an inch or so." Cassie wedged her chest back onto his, then wrapped her arms tight around him.

"That's a good lass." Robert grinned again. She felt damn good. Too damned good. "Close your eyes and kiss me again."

"Nay, I dinna want to drop like a stone again."

"It kept your hair out of my eyes and away from the ropes, my hands and the hooks."

Cassie plastered her lips to his again and they flew past Mordred's Spear and sped down the cliff as fast as they had on the first drop. Robert kept his eyes open this time, measuring the distance.

"Kick out!" Cassie shouted, and they did so in unison, bouncing clear of another jutting ledge. Robert slowed the rope and bounced twice more. The air was colder now, heavier with moisture and thick with fast-falling snow pelting them.

"We're almost to the bottom," Cassie told him.

"Good." Robert's hands were about to give out. The rope burned through his gloves as if he wore no gloves whatsoever. "We're almost out of rope."

Robert caught the trailing end, hauling hard on it to stop their descent. It was tricky with the increased weight of two but not impossible. "How far down?" he asked, dizzy now. His ears stung and the drums inside felt imploded. He shook his head and cracked his jaw to rid himself of that sensation.

"Fifteen feet, a caber's length, naught more."

"Oh, for a Highland game, eh?"

"I can jump," she said.

"How many feet of rope left?"

"Verra little, two or three feet at the most."

"Is the ground flat?" he asked.

"Nay, stony, but walkable. And the river's well away, fifteen feet or better."

"Good." Robert nodded. "Drop and roll right when ye land, lass. I'll roll left."

"Wait." Cassie stuck her hand between them and brought up the ropes fastened around their bodies.

She came out with Robert's dirk and cut the rope neatly with a pop.

"What do I do with the knife? I'll never get it back in its sheath."

"Throw it down."

"It's thrown. Now what?"

"Ready."

"No!" Cassie closed her eyes and buried her face in his throat.

"At three. One, two, three! Let go of me!"

Cassie fell the balance of the way, her body slipping away from Robert's only in the last second of the fall. She hit hard, shoulder first, rolling right onto her back where a hundred or more rocks dug into her flesh. Her head smacked the earth with incredible force. She yelped, recoiling from impact, stung all over, certain she was a torn and bloody mess from head to toe.

"Och! Be damned, that hurt," she complained as she sat up.

Robert had landed five feet away, with his back to her. His dirk's handle protruded from his ribs.

"Oh, my God! Are ye all right, Robert?"

He didn't move. He just lay there, paralyzed and groaning. Cassie screamed.

Chapter Eleven

"Mapmaker!" Cassie scrambled on all fours to get to Robert as fast as she could. She couldn't bear losing him when she was just beginning to like him.

"What are ye bleating about, lass?" Robert demanded to know. "I'm the poor bastard's that hurt."

"I'm so sorry!" Cassie burst into tears. Her hands were so cold they were uselessly numb. She couldn't drag Jamie's gloves off anywhere near quick enough, but managed to do so with her teeth. Then she felt under Robert for the entry wound of the blade.

"Ouch!" Robert winced.

"Och! What are you saying 'ouch' for? Aren't you a bloody Gordon warrior?"

"Aye, I am, but that dinna mean I canna complain when a beautiful woman tries to drive a dirk between my ribs. Stop moving the blasted rocks. I'll get up in a minute. Just let me catch my breath."

"You've got too much breath for your own good health, Gordon." Cassie pulled the blade free. There wasn't a speck of blood on it.

"Och, that feels better." Robert exhaled deeply.

"And well it should." Cassie laid the dirk down before his gaze. "You landed on that. Good aim."

"I did?" Robert's eyes widened in surprise. "Dinna tell me I've stabbed myself?"

"I dinna think so." Cassie pulled her hand back after finding no cuts in his jerkin. She crawled around to his opposite side, facing him, looking for injuries, her own aches forgotten. "Do you really think I'm beautiful, Robert Gordon?"

"Aye." He lifted his hand and brushed snow and bracken from her hair. "Verra beautiful."

"You must like freckles."

"You have freckles? I dinna notice."

Cassie rolled her eyes. "Can you no' get up, mon?"

"Oh, aye, I could. But I'd rather I dinna." Robert made a quick reconnoiter of their position in Mac-Arthur's glen as he rolled onto his back. The castle was well away, off in a distant mist where no Mac-Arthur spies could report their doings to the laird. He caught her hand and pulled her down on top of him. She came without any more urging, as close as she had been on the descent, her chest flattened against his. "Kiss me again, Cassandra."

"You're not a mapmaker, you're a scoundrel set upon ruining me."

"Untrue, fair lady. I'm set upon marrying ye."

"Whisht! Now you mock me." Cassie pulled back her head. "No man can meet a woman on one day and decide to marry her the next. 'Tisn't done that way in *these* Highlands."

"Maybe, maybe not. I dinna decide that yesterday and act upon it today. I decided it all the moment I laid eyes upon you skating at MacGregor's pond. I said to myself, 'Now there's a woman worth marrying...one with room to spare for children in her heart and kindness enough to speak to wandering gentlemen.' You are a rare jewel, Cassandra MacArthur, and I'm glad you dinna know your true value. Kiss me."

"Will you shut you up if I do?"

"Och, aye, and then some."

"And you'll get up?"

Robert thought something would definitely get up, but he judiciously didn't say that. She could slug him. It made him dizzy to gaze up and imagine where they had been on that cliff face only a cold moment or two ago. He closed his eyes and felt her lips touch and explore his. His blood flowed more evenly now, warming him, beginning to race with the delayed reactions the cold on the mountain prevented.

He kept the liberties he took to a minimum, careful of the fact that Cassie's innocence seemed so rare and pure. He didn't want to press her too far. But there was no denying the ecstatic joy he felt when the soft fullness of her lips blossomed over his. He wasn't certain when her arms fully embraced him, but they did. That simple completion of a welcoming gesture warmed their kiss into a long, lingering sigh between two new lovers. This was the touch he wanted from Lady Quickfoot. This and more. Yes, much more.

Robert seemed oblivious to the chill of the frozen earth beneath them. But Cassie felt it when his cold fingers touched her throat and laid it bare to the thrilling feel of his mouth beneath her heat-retaining wools. She shivered fiercely as a wave of goose bumps ran across her shoulders.

Robert laughed, realizing what he was he doing. They couldn't stay there making love on the rocks in this weather...in sight of the watchtowers at Castle MacArthur. He didn't know if the laird had glass and metal scopes like his.

Cassie drew back, realizing that same thing. "We've gone mad." She laughed deliciously.

"Aye, we have indeed." Robert grinned at her impudence, delighted that his Lady Quickfoot espoused no prudery. "I'll get up now. I'm firmly grounded back in reality."

Robert lifted his hands from her head and back. A curtain of free hair covered them, glorious red hair that held the delights of Scotland's sunrise in it. How bright and beautiful that tangled blanket was as he drew his fingers through it.

"Och! I'm a righteous mess. My mother would set to coughing and never stop if she could see me now." Cassie sat up, reached for her windblown braid and began to put it back to rights.

"I can well imagine what sort of fit that would turn into does she learn how we arrived on her back stoop," Robert added.

Cassie followed the telling direction of his gaze and saw the dangling evidence of Jamie's rope a mere handful of yards above their heads. "Oh, for a troop of acrobats." Cassie sighed. "I shall have to ponder upon how best to retrieve that before it is noticed."

"You may ponder all you like, but you'll do nothing about it. I forbid you ever to go that route again and I'll have your promise to obey me on the matter, now, if you please."

"That you have," Cassie replied without pause. That said, her teeth set into the edge of her lower lip, her face consumed in the manner of logistical thought. "Though that rope *will* have to be taken down. Then again..." She thought back to Jamie's youth. Very few youngsters in the clan would do anything so daring or attempt to follow in Jamie's footsteps. He'd be the MacArthur after her father, so it wasn't likely to happen in the near future, temptingly dangling rope or not.

Still, it was Jamie's rope and bore his markings. It would be spotted but not so quickly as to give her cause to worry now. Surely her father wouldn't put the dangling rope together with her rapid descent unless he knew exactly how long that descent had taken.

"We must tell my parents that Angus has been lying in the cave since early morning. It's a good four-hour trek from the cave home the long way."

"I'm a precise man, Quickfoot. I'll no' stretch the truth," Robert said to her.

"Verra well, I'll say what's only necessary," Cassie concluded. "Are you ready to stand up?"

"Only if I have to. Give me some inducement I can sink my teeth into."

"A hot supper waiting in yonder hall?"

"Aye." Robert sat bolt upright and bounded smoothly to his feet. He stretched out a hand to Cassandra. She took it and rose to her feet.

"You did that nicely. Verra gallant."

"Of course. I've been well trained at court. Come, fetch your oversize gloves and let's be off."

Their light mood dissipated on the descent from the high meadow. Snow in the hidden glen seriously impeded their progress. Drifts ran sometimes up to their knees and deeper. It had been snowing for days at Achanshiel—a fact that Cassie couldn't help remarking about. Deep snow rarely made it into the Achanshiel.

They were both shivering and cold to the bone by the time they reached the closed castle gate. A guard drew the bolt on the wicket and they ducked inside, stamping sodden boots on the straw-covered ground.

"Milady, 'tis a bitter day to risk traveling." The guard greeted Cassie with a smile. He had a dark scowl for the stranger with her.

No less of a scowl than one her father wore the moment he set eyes upon them entering his hall. "What goes here, Cassie? Where are Dorcas and Angus? Who is this man?"

"Hello, MacArthur, and how are you this fine winter evening? Mother, ah, there you are."

"Cassie, what is going on?" Lady MacArthur cut to the chase. "Where is Angus?"

"At Chattering Otters Cave. Angus has had another attack, a bad one this time. Verra bad. We must send help to retrieve him. That happened just before the storm broke in that part of the pass...."

"Now see here, gel." Laird MacArthur glowered.

"I'll no' be listening to one of yer adventuresome tales. Out with the truth!"

"Lady Cassandra is telling you the truth, sir." Robert spoke in Cassie's defense.

"I most certainly am!" Cassie insisted, twisting her nose up in the air. This wasn't going the way she wanted it. She hadn't planned out her words, and couldn't find a way to keep from explaining who Robert was. "I came as quick as I could, to get medicine and help. Dorcas remained with Angus to tend him. This gentleman escorted me for safety's sake."

"And just who is this bounder?" Her words and Robert's hadn't fazed the laird one bit.

"Robert Gordon, the king's mapmaker." Cassie's chin had joined her nose in a pose full of pride. He deserved it, for he'd been brilliant on Arthur's Drop and probably saved her life and got her here in one unbroken piece.

"Gordon?" Laird MacArthur roared. "By God, no…"

Undaunted by her father's sputtering, Cassie continued until she had finished the introduction. It couldn't be helped. There was no opportunity to dissemble. "Robert, meet my father, John, laird of the MacArthurs, and my lady mother, Claire."

"This bodes ill on my house," Laird MacArthur said, disturbed enough not to offer any welcome.

"I'll sort it out, my lord," Lady MacArthur cut in. "And you may be assured, investigate it we will, thoroughly. For the now, can you not see these young people are frozen to the bone? Let them come in and get warm by the fire. I'll no' have the hospitality of your house questioned by the court. Come in, Robert. Megan, fetch blankets and hot water for their feet. Pray God neither of you have the frostbite. Cassandra, tell us more of Angus.''

Cassie had hoped her mother would intervene. For the time being, her father's rigid prejudices were pushed aside by expedience. Now it was up to her to tell the facts about what had happened, and about Robert Gordon, as best she could.

Cassie first told how Angus came to be injured. Then she related the wondrous rescue of wee Ian and herself at the pool. She talked a blue streak, detailing all of Robert's glowing heroics.

That also made her realize how very deeply she herself was indebted to him and how hard-won was the intimacy between them.

By making it very clear how indebted their family had to be to Gordon for Ian's life if not her own, Cassie had effectively taken all the time that remained before supper. The moment the meal was declared ready to be laid upon the laird's board, Cassie's mother relented and sent them both off with servants to be cleaned up and dressed as befitted Laird Mac-Arthur's table.

A servant provided Robert with a clean, pressed linen sark to wear to supper. While he bathed, his jerkin and kilt had been dried, brushed clean of all stains and pressed. The manservant even offered a spotless lace jabot to tie at his throat. The hot bath went a very long way toward warming his bones. The fine

velvet jacket the servant settled on his shoulders finished the job.

With his hair combed, Robert looked as well as he
could that evening. His lips were badly chapped and
dry as fall leaves. His skin was nigh onto peeled off,
at least a layer or two was gone thanks to the wind
in the mountains.

Cassie also returned to the hall looking like a princess with a sunburned face. She grinned when she
spied Robert at the fireplace, surrounded by her father
and his ever-present tail of henchmen. Robert raised
his glass in a toast to her the moment he spied her
descending the stairs into the great hall.

Robert's courtly bow as she greeted her father
again, this time much more formally with a full
curtsy, was perfection indeed. He cut a splendid figure, in kilt and borrowed jacket with no more polish
to his appearance than a good laundering and scrub-
bing. Cassie's heart did a leap when she remembered
he'd kissed her and said he was going to marry her.
That wasn't possible, not really. It was very exciting
though.

"So you are impressed with Lochaber, are ye, mapmaker?" Laird MacArthur went head on with Robert,
ignoring Cassie's greeting.

"Lochaber is breathtaking," Robert replied, without taking his sparkling eyes from Cassie. Lady Claire
joined them, and a servant brought forth sherry for
the ladies.

A small interval passed of generalized men's chatter extolling the natural beauties of their beloved shire
before Lady MacArthur turned to Cassie and mo-

tioned her away, out of the earshot of the men. "I do
believe you've made a conquest, Cassie. Or are both
of you having a joke at our expense? It seems hard
for me to imagine a MacArthur and a Gordon hitting
it off so famously from the start."

"No one implied that was the case, Mother," Cassie replied hedging. She'd resisted falling under his
spell mightily, only now she realized she had lost the
battle. She was still bursting with pride over his accomplishments. They'd conquered Arthur's Drop in a
tandem descent. It was an unheard-of feat, magnificent, and her blood still thrummed with the pleasure
of the accomplishment.

"Really? So you have been at daggers since he
arrived at Glencoen? How long ago was that? You
seem uncommonly protective of him. Come clean,
daughter."

Cassie avoided revealing the span of time she'd
known Robert, for it seemed unimportant to her now.
"This particular Gordon is rather hard to hate when
he does so many chivalrous things."

"Gordons always do chivalrous things. It's part of
their bloody-minded charm. I've met few who
couldn't talk the spots off the proverbial leopard."
Lady MacArthur paused, then finished her thought
bluntly. "Or for that matter, who couldn't talk the
clothes off a convent-raised virgin with a wink of
their devastating blue eyes."

Cassie colored to the roots of her hair at her
mother's clear-sighted assessment. "Mother, please!
I've met no Gordons before this one, and in spite of
his regal patron's pedigree, papers and endorsement,

I am well aware that the mapmaker is still a Gordon to the core. Though I will admit this particular Gordon appears to have a certain appeal that's rather hard to shake clear off. Millie is in love with him already.''

''Oh?'' the grandmother in Lady MacArthur now inquired. ''And Millie took interest, did she? Now why is that?''

Realizing full well that her mother wasn't interested in what Millie thought, Cassie explained, ''Robert *listened* to her and took questions from her one supper instead of ignoring her like most young men do. That gave me—I mean, Millie—more pause than anything that had happened up to that point.''

''I see.'' The mother lifted one skeptical eyebrow.

''Dinna read more into that than I mean,'' Cassie said stubbornly, damning her fair skin in silence for the telling blush she felt rising across her cheeks.

''Whisht, Cassandra, this is your mother you are talking to, not your father, whom you can trick with one shake of a petticoat. But let's talk of other things,'' Lady MacArthur said with a smile that lit her blue eyes. ''You chose your gown for the evening well. That blue watered silk looks splendid with your accentuated coloring tonight. It's far too pale a shade for me, as I said when I had Beatrice make the fabric into a gown for you.''

''You say that about all pale hues, but it isn't true.''

''Thank you, Cassie. How is my youngest grandchild?''

''You wouldn't believe how fat wee Willie has grown in just a month. Maggie is doing well, too. Have you heard from Jamie yet?''

"Aye, a letter came this past week. It won't make up for a visit, but he claims the king would not give him leave. Word is the queen of England has taken a turn. Jamie gives us to understand our king James is fair to bursting to take off for England and snatch the crown out from under her nose. Restraint isn't James Stewart's cardinal virtue."

"Nor mine." Cassie gazed hungrily at the steaming bowls and platters being laid on the table.

"And your guest as well, I gather."

"Aye, methinks he always has an empty stomach," Cassie quipped, which was her way of telling her mother the slender-looking young man could eat like a horse.

Lady MacArthur astutely broke free from her private conversation with her daughter, went to her husband and inquired if he was ready to dine. At once, Laird MacArthur handed off his glass of whiskey and extended his arm to his wife.

Robert offered his arm to Cassie before anyone else did and escorted her to the table. His eyes fairly gleamed at the offerings, leeks and mushrooms, mutton roasted to a crisp golden crust, haggis, steaming cabbage, peas and squash from the larder, baked apples, bread and four wheels of cheese. Cassie was fairly certain he would pop the buttons on his kilt this time. She'd seen how little he'd partaken of the foods available at midday.

This meal progressed much as the night before at Glencoen, with one or two exceptions. There were no sprightly interruptions from inquisitive five-year-old misses and there was an implication of mistrust voiced early on by her father. Robert, too, seemed less comfortable at the board, since he had to remain on his toes not to offend or take offense himself.

Laird MacArthur was an abrasive man, and his one abiding passion in life seemed to be challenging and testing the mettle of every man he met. Cassie believed he measured his own self-importance by competing with others. Cassie had seen many a young man gullet himself on the first sallies of repartee against her father before the real darts of malice ever appeared in her father's scathing tones.

Before the second remove appeared, beads of sweat had broken out over Robert's upper lip, which he discreetly mopped away with a handkerchief bearing Jamie's monogram. Her father lounged in his high-backed chair and sent forth another volley of words, this one challenging the likelihood that a young pup out of Edinburgh University could prove wee Scotland bigger geographically than mighty England.

"May I take it, my lord, that you are implying that I have attempted to sell a bill of goods to our king?" Robert inquired mildly. "I don't believe I ever stated or implied that Scotland is bigger than England. It is far smaller."

"You may take that any way you like it, laddie. Where's your proof of Scotland's size?"

"My proof is yet to be recorded in miles, sir."

"Aye, and am I not correct in believing the very measure of a mile changes with the arrival of a new monarch on the king's throne? Do we not regard a mile by the measure set out in Henry the Eighth's reign?"

"My lord MacArthur," Cassie interrupted. "Have you forgotten England's ruled by a queen?"

"Don't be impertinent, lass." MacArthur rounded on her, his gray eyebrows nettling. "I'm aware of that."

"Then what's your point in this inquest?" She hoped to deflect her father from his attack on Robert. "A mile is a mile and inch is an inch, are they not?"

"Precisely!" The MacArthur pounded his fist on the oak board before him, rattling the pewter. "Have they not changed all such proportions to match Her Royal Majesty's robust form?"

"Nay, they havena. It remains fixed upon King Harry's mark," Robert informed him as blandly as a presbyter eyeing the collection plate. He cast a more meaningful look to Cassie, one he hoped would tell her he could stand alone against her father.

"Well, then, all the more reason to hurry the changing of the watch. Reform those marks to a better standard. One based upon the fine proportions of Scottish blood. King Harry would have had to climb on a footstool to meet a Highlander eye to eye. Mark my words, the length of the royal mile will change to suit the next king, James of Scotland. It always does."

"Not anymore," Robert replied with absolute conviction. "It is now fixed scientifically, free of the whims and augury of the past."

"Ballocks!" MacArthur snorted.

Then, Cassie kicked him hard under the table. He jolted upright from his waiting-to-pounce slouch and glared at her.

''What was that for?''

''Mother asked you twice to pass the leeks. Are you going to share them or has your hospitality left you?'' Her father blinked and looked to the foot of the table to see his wife's brow raised in a silent question.

''Leeks? Well, why didn't she say so?'' He snatched up the idle bowl and shoved it into Cassie's hands to send back to the foot of the table. Several more resting bowls and platters made the rounds in a hustle of passing victuals.

When the dishes reached the foot of the table, Lady MacArthur nodded to a waiting servant, who set out hot plates of venison and salmon. Cassie's mother did her best to tempt her laird's appetite and get him eating.

Taking her mother's lead, Cassie turned to Robert and told him to eat while he could. Her father would be gnawing on a different bone for the next few moments.

Her father then launched into a tale, regaling the guests at the board with the story of his most recent boar hunt.

''Don't be misled by MacArthur's placid face,'' Cassie discreetly whispered to Robert. ''He's sizing you up for his next victim at the evening's entertainment—arm wrestling.''

Robert groaned beneath his breath. ''I doubt I could grip anyone's hand tonight.''

''Really?'' Curious, Cassie looked more closely at his hands. She saw shattered blisters on his palms.

"Did you ask for ointment?" Cassie asked, appalled at the damage.

"Don't be a dolt, Quickfoot," Robert said for her ears alone. "I'd as soon label myself a coward and a sissy."

Well then... Cassie almost blurted out, *why'd you tell me?* But she knew the answer without asking. "Your streak of ingrained honesty, right?"

"Astutely deduced, milady." Robert grinned in return.

"We can count our bruises later," she responded, then realized what she said.

Robert perked up. Had Cassandra said what he thought she'd said? His attention was riveted on her and blood surged to his privates, reviving them.

He had to change the direction of this conversation—immediately. "Tell me," he whispered, "what's a lovely lady like your mother doing in this pit of Bedlamites?"

"No one's figured out the answer to that in thirty years, but we do all marvel that she stays," Cassie replied, thankful he'd not interrogated her earlier statement.

"Love and loyalty are very compelling traits." Robert managed a straight answer to that.

"Are they?"

"Oh, aye. My own mother is very like that. You'll find out when we go home to Strathspey."

"We?" Cassie jerked, a bit stunned by that assumption.

"Aye," Robert responded, his convictions about

her increasing with each moment they remained together.

Cassie picked up her knife and stabbed it into the slab of salmon on her plate, attacking the fish as if it had done something wrong. "From here on out you can fend for yourself, Robert Gordon."

For a minute Robert made no response, only watched her very adverse reaction. Then he deliberately increased her torment by huskily whispering the word "Coward."

"Realist suits better."

"No such animal exists. Eels, milady?"

"Ugh, send that back to the foot of the table so Mother will have it sent away." Cassie pushed the bowl back under his nose. "I hate those slimy things. They smell vile."

"You haven't lived until you've eaten eels with fried snails in raisin sauce at the king's board," Robert teased.

"Surely you jest, milord."

"Now there's a courtesy I could grow fond of hearing. 'Milord' indeed." Robert put a succulent bite of venison in his mouth and chewed it with appreciable relish.

"With your appetite someday you'll be as big as my father."

"Does that displease you? I eat, yes, but I work it all off during the day."

"Now, aye, but you're young."

"Aye, perhaps. My father's a large man like yours, but size is relative to position and age."

"Unless you're someone like Euan MacGregor.

He's a giant or thereabouts. I used to wonder what Maggie saw in him. I don't anymore. I see his goodness to her above all else."

"You don't think your father does the same to your mother? You don't like your father, do you?"

"I have to live with him."

"Och, ye've got a devil of a tongue on ye, Cassandra MacArthur. Impudent."

"Posh, be quiet and eat. MacArthur will notice you again soon enough." That ended their idle chatter.

Robert actively sought ways to avoid conversation with others by setting others to talking with the same expertise with which he had fired up Euan on crops and pigs.

Cassie began looking for a way to bring the meal to a hasty end.

Her father's physician saved the day by engaging Laird MacArthur in a deep discussion about Angus. She tried to follow it, but their voices were guarded and indistinct.

When Cassie covered her third yawn with the palm of her hand, her mother took pity on her and said they could retire from the table.

That pronouncement brought out the kegs of whiskey again, and the men at the board held up glasses to be refilled.

"Lucky you," Robert whispered, then stood as she departed from the table. "Your servant, always, milady."

"Milord." Cassie blushed, then with a demure glance to her father, she bowed her head and departed, following her mother's swaying skirts up the steps to the gallery.

They hadn't so much as allowed the half doors to close behind them before her mother spoke, "This is all very cozy, Cassandra. I want to know how it is you and a man you vowed to avoid with your dying breath is now your bosom confidant and privy to nearly an entire meal's whispered conversations. What is going on here that I do not know about? The truth, Cassie, and do remember to whom you are speaking."

"My dearest mother, whatever do you mean?" Cassie's yawn had died midstretch and she looked at her mother with wide-open, innocent eyes.

"You know exactly what I mean, my dear. Out with it. I was shut out of the romances of all my daughters until you came along. You have always been an open book to me. Now, I beg you, tell me what is going on before I go out of my mind with worry."

"Is it that obvious?" Cassie asked. There was no forthright answer to give. Could she think of one good enough? She doubted even the plain, unvarnished truth would help her now, because she didn't really know what was happening to herself, either.

"It is as visible as the freckles on your charming face. You flirted with that man outrageously through every course of the meal. Worse, he provokes you to it! Tell me what happened at Maggie's farm!"

Baffled by her mother's interpretation, Cassandra earnestly said, "I honestly don't know, Mother, beyond what I have already told you."

Chapter Twelve

Lady MacArthur stood back, a puzzled look consuming her gentle features. She said, "Those are the facts? Gordon saved Ian's life and then came back and rescued you?"

"Aye. Basically that's the gist of it." Cassie wound her arm around her mother's warm and comforting body, snuggling into that comfort zone that she alone seemed to remember how to get into most quickly and easily.

Lady MacArthur wrapped her arms around her youngest daughter and rested her chin on the top of Cassie's fragrant head. Her hair was still damp from washing. It spilled over her shoulders with gleaming lights, made brilliant by flickering candles in the sconces all along the hallway.

"My clothes dragged me to the bottom and I couldn't get my cloak off. Somehow, I got my skate trapped. Robert dived down to me twice before he freed my foot, and brought me up to the surface. I couldn't breathe, Mother. I mean, it wasn't like drowning anymore—the struggle was gone. I didn't *want* to breathe, I just wanted to close my eyes and drift to sleep. I was so very tired of fighting the cold, the ice and the water.''

The memory made Cassie lift her chin and take a deep, life-affirming breath that filled her lungs with the heavenly air of her mother's sweet scent of rose water and talc.

''I felt his hands press here, hard and with great force.'' Cassie moved her mother's hand to her diaphragm and showed her where Robert had squeezed to expel the water from her lungs. ''I still didn't try to breathe. It didn't seem at all urgent or necessary to do. So he put his mouth over mine and gave me his breath. It was icy cold first, then so very warm and alive that I was shocked by the sensation of it. I don't know how long it took before I could take a breath on my own. Even then breathing seemed so fragile, such a difficult thing to do.

''Even after we were pulled out of the water, I couldna breathe for myself. Robert was breathing for me. I vaguely heard Euan send the children away and tell his men I was dead. Only Robert believed I wasn't. He shivered terribly from the cold and wet, but he kept on giving me his air, on and on and on, until I took each new breath all by myself. Maybe it was like being newly born again, something I had to learn to do to live, do ye ken?''

''Oh, yes, my darling, I do understand.'' Cassie felt her mother's lips press on the top of her head, and her tears dampen her scalp. ''You should have told your father this.''

Cassie shook her head and stared at the flames in the hearth. "No. I canna tell him anything. He never listens. He would just have drawn his sword and started shouting about the effrontery of the man to dare to put his lips to mine. It wouldn't matter to him what the results were. I didn't tell Maggie about it either, but Euan must have said something, because Maggie could not do enough for the mapmakers. There's another man traveling with him—Alexander Hamilton, the marquess's younger son."

"Ah, another personable young man?"

"A quiet man, verra thoughtful. Robert is also. He's been to university." Cassie straightened and her mother's arms fell away.

"What about that troubles you so?" Lady MacArthur asked, concerned.

"Och." Cassie shrugged. "I fear Robert knows a lot—important things. Things I'll never know anything about even if I live to be a hundred."

"But Cassie, you are educated. We had the finest tutors in the land here for you and your sisters. I saw to it we had just as good for my girls as we had for Jamie."

At that Cassie grinned and nudged her mother with her elbow. "You forget, Mother, I was the vanishing child. The one who escaped into the hills every time my tutors turned their backs."

"Yes, but I remember that you passed every test with better marks than your older sisters. Those same tutors praised your intelligence, in spite of your errant ways." Lady MacArthur lifted her head to look into the depths of the gallery to think through her thoughts. "I suppose what I'm really saying is that I am glad to see you showing some sort of interest in gentlemen again."

"Perhaps." Cassie yawned. "I'm very tired."

"Aye, I can see and feel that. You should rest. I'll make your excuses in the hall when I go back, tell your father I've sent you to bed."

"Would you? No, I can't go yet." Cassie shook her head. "I have to keep Robert out of the arm wrestling matches."

"Why so?"

"He's tired, too. MacArthur would take unfair advantage of the blisters on Robert's palms."

Lady MacArthur frowned. "You used ropes to get here in this storm?"

"Mother," Cassie said, hedging quite effectively, "we tucked Angus in Chattering Otters Cave. We had to get back to the path and it was snowing a blizzard by then. If we hadn't used ropes, we'd still be in the pass with the wind howling in our ears right now instead of getting here before supper."

"You have a commendable spirit and more courage than a woman should ever need, Cassie. I'll see that your Robert is spared slapping palms with your father. Go up to bed, darling."

"I canna go to bed now when Dorcas is sleeping in a cave, tending Angus."

"Both Angus and Dorcas are stronger than you realize. I'm sure they'll come to no harm."

"It was essential I get here quickly before the storm broke." Cassie scowled and turned toward one of the windows overlooking the garden.

Her mother looked at the frost built up on her mullion windows. The raw day had turned into a wickedly bitter night. That made her glad her daughter was home and not out there in the elements. She believed this latest crisis unnecessary—another consequence of Cassie's rebellion.

"Dorcas and Angus's situation isn't the real issue needing resolution," Lady MacArthur said. She decided the time had come to speak her mind on Cassie's activities. "How much longer do you intend to evade the marriage contract your father wants resolved between you and him, Cassandra?"

That bluntly spoken question caused Cassie to draw away and regard her mother with wary eyes. "What exactly do you mean by that, Mother?"

"You know what I mean, Cassie. You tell me why you ran off to Glencoen Farm, and you'll have your finger on the source of the problem between you and your father."

"Mother! I haven't been home one day and you're starting in on that again? I've told you a hundred times, I don't want MacArthur to arrange a marriage contract for me. I'll do my own choosing, thank you."

"Cassandra, it's time. Your father is consumed with the worry that something is going to happen to him and there will be no one to take care of you. You canna grieve for Alastair Campbell forever, lass."

"I refuse to talk about this." Cassie abruptly turned away. She wasn't going to be baited, not when this was the perfect opportunity to sneak in a private visit to Robert. Instead of storming off in a fit of anger, she kept her thoughts and temper to herself.

"I'm going to bed. It's been a long day. Good night, Mother."

Lady MacArthur also stood determined. "Cassandra, you cannot continue evading the facts of life. You will be married on the first of May. Your father has made up his mind."

"To whom?" Cassie demanded, shaken.

"Douglas Cameron."

"Mother! He's forty years old and has been married three times!" Cassie lost her composure.

"He's the head of his clan and settled, just the man you need to see that you stick to hearth and home for a change." Lady MacArthur held herself rigid, impervious to attack.

Cassie's lip curled in disgust over the news her parent had delivered. "I canna believe this! Here I have confided in you how I almost died a few days ago. I have spent all of today traveling wicked Glencoe Pass in the worst weather just to get home... Now I have to strike out for the hills again the moment the storm breaks—and you tell me this? It's beneath both of us to talk about marriages or things that have no bearing on whether or not my gillie and my abigail get home alive. Good night, Mother. I must speak to father's physician and organize the rescue before I attempt to get some rest."

Lady MacArthur remained unruffled by her daughter's high-handed manner. "Your father sent rescuers out three hours ago, Cassie. By the time you wake in the morn, Angus, Dorcas and Lord Hamilton's son will be here, safe and sound and resting, God willing, in their beds.''

''What?'' Cassie said flatly. ''MacArthur sent them without me?''

''Of course your father did. Do you think you can actually have the leisure of flirting over an elegant supper while a man is suffering an apoplectic fit?'' Lady MacArthur replied in the most reasonable and practical tone she had, and she was stretching her good nature to the limit to do so and retain her composure.

As shocked as she was by that announcement, Cassie didn't miss the scold inherent in her mother's words. Cassie shook off the hurt, but couldn't get free of it.

''Well, I see that I shall have to thank MacArthur for being so almighty considerate and not bothering to inform me of his august decisions again, won't I?'' Cassie said stiffly.

''Daughter,'' Lady MacArthur said sternly, ''I believe you take too much upon yourself. Your father is well capable of running this shire without your gracious consent or permission. Men had accidents in these hills for centuries before your imaginary 'Lady Quickfoot' took to bending the world to suit her pleasure. I would also thank you to remember that at least ten percent of the time.''

Insulted by her mother's stinging words, Cassie drew up tall and stiff. ''Forgive me for my presumption that I could be of any assistance here whatsoever. I shall retire at once, if you have nothing more to say, Mother.''

"Oh, I have more to say, but for the now, we'd best let it ride. I'm in no mood to start up where we left on the feast of the Epiphany. Good night, Cassandra."

"Good night, Mother." Cassie whirled around, taking the dismissal with all due haste.

Cassie didn't go upstairs to bed immediately. She went to the kitchen, where she could find the castle steward and Cook to make a few requests. After that she was still so angry she deliberately stayed away from her chamber, knowing if she went there, she would only change clothes and immediately head back out into the storm, fleeing everything she hated at Castle MacArthur.

Knowing exactly where her father would house a Gordon, Cassie walked the castles twisting hallways, until she reached the topmost level and the parapet that ran the length of the castle ramparts. Wrapping herself in one of the great cloaks hanging on the pegs near a tower door, she stepped out into the brunt of the storm.

Snow covered the long iron tubes of the cannon there and the stacks of ready iron balls. It even filled the bottoms of the black cauldrons—silent sentinels of doom and destruction that would be filled with hot oil should an invader attack. In her lifetime, the castle had never fallen under attack, but they stayed in a state of preparedness. Her father and his henchmen trained the rest of the clan religiously in the use of the tools and arms of warfare.

It was cold and the wind was fierce, but that did

wonders to bring down Cassie's raging temper. She circled the dark parapet until she saw a lantern bobbing past the window slits in the garret barracks adjacent to the parapet.

She let herself back inside the narrow, cold corridor, closed the heavy door and slid the bolt back into place. Then she removed the cloak, hung it back on the peg. The corridor was silent as a tomb, for no one resided on this level of Castle MacArthur except in time of actual war. She shook the snow off her hems, settled her shawl on her shoulders, smoothed her hair back into place and resolutely marched back to the vacant steward's table to take up her candlestick.

The fat candle in it still burned brightly, casting a flickering gloom over the dark rafters and cold granite walls. Cassie didn't bother to take any precautions against squeaking floorboards. There was no one to disturb on this floor, or the one below it, where all the castle servants were housed. Everyone would still be in the great hall, where fiddlers and pipers had begun to play.

The fifth door down stood ajar. Inside, Robert knelt at the hearth, stoking his own fire. In spite of the chill beneath the slate-and-rafter roof, he'd stripped down to his kilt and his boots to make his own fire.

That stopped Cassie's raised hand from immediately tapping on the partially open oak door. Lord, she wasn't going to lose her nerve, was she? He looked so fine with his bare skin glazed by the orange lights of the fire, she had to swallow her fear of what she was doing here alone all over again.

The musty smell of the peat he had used to ignite

the fire invaded her nose, earthy and aromatic, like an invitation to a cozy croft. The pine kindling and oak wood beginning to burn foretold of steady heat through the night, companionship on a trail and true ease at the end of a hard day's work. She needed all of that very much.

Robert sat back on his heels, dusting off his hands, his back still to her, and Cassie couldn't help thinking how splendid he looked to her hungry eyes. The long, proud length of his spine and the noble set of his head were undaunted by her father's mean-spirited accommodations. Robert had made a frigid garret tolerable and inviting.

Cassie tapped on his door.

Robert spun around, the word "enter" out of his mouth before he'd completed the turn and spied her.

"Don't mind if I do, thank you." Cassie stepped through the opening, a bright smile on her face to match the one spreading on his.

"Good Lord, Cassandra, you pop up in the strangest places. I expected to see you lingering outside your father's hall. What on earth are you doing up here?"

He came to his feet smoothly, still brushing his dirty palms together, and quickly moved to the standing commode where a basin, ewer, towel and pot of soap were ready for his use. Beside the basin stood the basket Cassie had requested for him in her sojourn to visit the steward and Cook.

She moved to the side of the freestanding commode and set down her candlestick there, then unfolded the large linen napkin from the top of the basket as Robert washed his hands.

"Did my father make you have your bath up here?" Cassie asked, the moment she saw him grimace as soap invaded the raw blisters in his palms.

"No." Robert answered the question, glad of the distraction. "As a matter of fact, he was most considerate of the servants' labor and had his steward direct me to the common bath out by the washhouse."

Appalled, Cassie couldn't help saying, "Oh, that was so very kind of him, not to make anyone cart a tub and jugs of hot water up six flights of steps, wasn't it now. Robert, I'm sorry, this is deplorable for you to be housed up here. Here, give me your hands."

"One moment." Robert dipped them in the basin to rinse the stinging soap. Wincing, because the water had more residue than his open blisters could tolerate, he let loose a single complaint. "That must be pure lye soap."

"That?" Cassie looked in the pot of shavings. "It's what's used in the washhouse for boiling bedding and unmentionables."

Robert wagged both of his hands, letting air dry them.

"This will help." Cassie opened the lid on a clay jar of ointment. "Give me your hand."

Warily, Robert presented his right hand, assuming his best bet would be to let her have her way and be done with it quicker. Cassie cradled his hand in hers near the light, and scooped out a generous dollop of the cream. "My mother always put this on our scrapes and bruises. It helps the hurt as well."

She smoothed it into his palm with the softest touch. Robert stood still, quietly allowing her to spread the cool cream over the blisters and onto his fingers and the back of his hand. "You're right. It doesn't hurt, and your gentle touch is mercy itself."

"You might say I've had enough experience with blisters and scrapes to know exactly the sort of touch I can tolerate. I wouldn't treat yours to any less."

"Thank you." Robert presented his left hand willingly for the same ministrations. The cream felt cold, but it did something to dull the sensation of pain very quickly. Cassie didn't stop stroking his hands until all of the cream had dissolved and been worked into his skin and out of sight.

The excess left on her own hands, she smoothed into her own palms and fingers. "Don't go away. There's more." She took out a rolled coil of gauzy cloth and proceeded to wind it about each of Robert's palms.

"I don't think I need bandages." Robert smiled, amused by her serious attention and concentration.

"Do you want your open blisters to be healed by morning or infected and very painful?" she asked, the crown of her head presented closest to his sight.

"Healed, of course, but that's rather presumptive of you, isn't it?" Robert's mouth quirked with a smile. She had twin whorls at the top of her head, cowlicks from which her hair spilled in curly array. And she smelled absolutely wonderful. He leaned closer, sniffing at the clean aroma of her hair and came away with the scent of roses. "Blisters take several days to heal."

Cassie tied the first bandage secure, then set to winding the second. She tied the last knot and used her teeth to tear off the length of gauze that wasn't needed. "There. I'm sure that feels better. You can take the bandages off when you rise.

Cassie picked up her candle and turned, examining the room. There were cobwebs everywhere. Her gaze moved to a stack of rope and frame bedsteads and rolled shuck mattresses, piled to the ceiling in one corner. "My God, there must be rats in here."

One lone rack had been taken down, set near the fire and covered with a mattress and single rough wool blanket. A penitent monk's cell would have been more comfortable.

"I havena heard any rats." Robert dabbed at the grease on his forearms with the thin linen towel provided him, which Cassie would have tossed into the rag barrel. "Rats prefer places where there's food to scavage. Don't think they'd find much to eat up here."

"This is too much, Robert. MacArthur's insulted you putting you here. I'm going to go down and straighten this out immediately with Mother. You deserve better accommodations than this."

Robert stopped in the act of putting his shirt back on, the garment resting open on his shoulders, and moved to catch Cassie's arm as she turned to do as she said.

"Nay, Cassie, you won't do that. I'll be fine right

here. There is a blanket and I have my plaid as well as this great warm fire to take away the chill.''

Cassie slowly looked across the expanse of his chest to his strong face and saw something in the set of his jaw that she already knew about Highlanders—stubbornness.

''I've slept in more than one garret in my travels, and I've seen the rules of hospitality broken a time or two. You'll do nothing to change my accommodations. I accepted this room, and that's the end of it.''

''You're as stubborn as a rock.''

Robert's eyes gentled somewhat and he took her candlestick from her hand and set it on the commode. ''Aye, haven't you told me that before?''

''I'm not certain.'' Cassie held her breath, hardly daring to exhale, caught by the serious expression on his face and the soft echo of his words in the rafters.

''I'm glad you've come.'' Robert's cool hands settled on the sweep of her hair, pressing against her cheeks. ''Mind you, you're not staying long because this is no place for a lady. But since you're here and we are definitely alone…I've been wanting to do this since I first laid eyes on you.''

His mouth descended onto hers and Cassie's resounding heart stopped still inside the cage of her chest.

She had kissed him, on that wild, exhilarating plunge down Arthur's Drop. And again, at his request, she'd planted her lips to his. But this kiss was nothing like the ones before. Those were as cool as the ice freezing on the hills in comparison. His kiss burned hot, full of passion.

Cassie reeled back, caught in the close compression of his arms as they surrounded her. "Open your mouth, Cassie," he drew back to say. "We are not childhood sweethearts timidly exploring one another. I'm a man, and you, my sweet, are the most deliciously tempting woman I have ever met in my life."

With those words, he drew her up against his hard chest and kissed her once more, his tongue plunging into her mouth, igniting a response akin to red-hot coals reacting to the burst of air from a smithy's bellows.

Cassie wound her arms around him, fingers threading through the strands of his hair at the nape of his neck, then raking across his shoulders. His bare skin felt like silk, and beneath that was the wonderfully carved firmness of rock-solid muscle. She lost herself in him, tearing at the shirt he'd pulled on to remove it so that she had more of him to touch and feel. The cloth fell away to the floor, discarded and forgotten.

She gloried in the touch and feel of his chest, roughened by a soft mat of dark downy hair that spread only across his breast like a shield and twisted into a thin line at the waist of his kilt.

She didn't dare let her fingers go farther, certain she'd taken more liberties than any Highland maiden had ever dared.

Robert came to his senses as her fingertips circled his navel. He was hard as a stone, pressing against the full sweep of her gown, aching to finish what he'd begun. He lifted his mouth from her soft, sweet lips and caught her fingers in his hand, holding her exploration at bay.

"Go lower, my lady, and you'll not leave this room with your maidenhead intact," he cautioned.

"Suppose I don't want to leave in the same condition as I came in?" Cassie rested in the crook of his arm, her eyes locked to his, her soul swimming in the grip of his unfathomable eyes. They were as blue as the winter sky in January.

"Why should you want to do that, Cassie?" Robert asked, his passion cooling. Something was wrong. He could feel it in his gut. He searched her face for the answer that wasn't forthcoming. All he found was the glorious fullness of her parted lips, and the invitation to take all that he wanted deep in her eyes.

"I don't know why. It just is. Don't send me away, Robert." She shied away then, her gaze dropping to follow her hand as she lifted it from his and laid the palm flat against his breast.

"Cassandra." Robert caught her chin between his thumb and fingers, nudging it up, seeking eye contact once more. "This is your father's house, not mine. Look at me. Do you realize what you're asking of me?"

"Robert, please, this may be the only chance we have to ever be together. I canna tell you what it is I am feeling inside my heart, for I dinna understand it yet myself. But I want to be with you, forever if it could be possible. Please, kiss me again."

Her hand moved to the back of his neck, to draw his mouth to hers once more. He resisted and caught hold of her elbows, setting her back a pace, needing to slow their passions until he had the chance to think it through.

Her air of desperation swept over him, chilling him more than any February wind ever could. She hadn't said she loved him, only that she wanted him, that she might never have another chance for this. What was she holding back? What was it she wanted from him? She was a Highland maiden, destined to become some lucky man's bride and lady wife. She wasn't the sort of woman a man could love for one night and then walk away from and forget. He certainly couldn't.

"Forever doesn't last one night, Cassie," he said solemnly.

"It could." She gulped, swallowing hard against the tears that threatened to shatter her. "If that's all anyone had, it could."

His fingers tightened at her elbows and he shook her gently. "Say what you mean, lass. What is happening in this castle that I dinna know about?"

"I can't tell you." The rigid rein Cassie had kept on her temper since she'd left her mother's solar split. "Don't ask!"

In a heartbeat, she jerked out of Robert's hold and whirled about, running for the door. He should have let her go, but Robert feared she was about to do something reckless.

He ran after her, out into the narrow corridor, his boots pounding on the wooden floor toward a wide door that could only open onto the rampart. There, clumps of snow melted on the boards underfoot. She yanked open the door as Robert lost his footing in the slush.

He crashed into a wet, dripping cloak hanging on the wall and sank to the floor, his bare shanks connecting with cold snow melting off the cloak. She ran out the door, to do God only knew what.

"Cassie! Come back! That isn't the door down to the family's quarters." Robert lurched back onto his feet and took the precaution of yanking the wet cloak off its peg to cover his bare shoulders.

It was a good thing he did, because a blast of driven snow flew in his face, blinding him as he opened the door. He wiped his eyes clear and stalked out after her.

"Cassie!" He let his voice boom over the ramparts, revealing his temper, not giving a fig if he roused the entire household.

"Go back inside, Gordon. I don't answer to you."

Her voice gave him the key to locating her. But his heart dropped to his boots when he saw her scrambling up on a snow-covered crenel, heedless of the wind tearing at her clothes and her hair. She straightened upright on the edge of the stones, her arms outstretched to the taller upright stone merlon, posing like a diver preparing to execute a graceful swan dive into a sun-warmed pool.

"Christ save us!" Robert prayed under his breath. He couldn't think of what to do, what was wrong with the girl, or what he'd done that had upset her so. The sound of his heart beating hammered in his ears, forcing him into a cold-blooded calm that came only from long experience facing death and battle.

He approached her on a silent tread, his footfalls muffled by the thick snow, and waited till the gust of wind eased. "This is a fine way to leave me, lassie, gut-wrenched with guilt and rejection. And here I thought I was doing the honorable thing, refusing to seduce you."

"Go away, Robert, I want to be alone." Cassie extended her arms straight out in front of her. "I need silence to make my peace with God."

"Why dinna you say that in the first place? What am I then? Your last hurrah? A final fling before you end it all your own way? Come down, Cassie, and I'll make love to you. You can kill yourself while I'm sleeping."

"I'm not afraid to die."

"Neither am I, but the idea of roasting forever in hell lacks a certain appeal, lass." He was close enough that her billowing skirt was within reach of his hands. That wasn't good enough if she jumped and he was left holding only a scrap of torn cloth. "I'm told God can't forgive you for it."

"Maybe you just don't know how to talk to Him."

"Maybe." Robert paused. He took one more cautious step forward. "Maybe you ought to try talking to me about this first. I vow I'm a tad confused at the moment. Aren't you the same woman who was just kissing me? Inviting me to have my wicked way with you?"

She whirled around to face him, perfectly balanced and fearless as the wind battered her gown against her body. "Don't come another step closer!" She had one hand out to ward him off, rocking precariously as she regained her footing.

"What the hell...?" Robert bounded up beside her on the adjacent merlon, a half step higher than her perch.

The edge was right there, beneath his face. The mighty wind struck him at full force, rocking and tipping him. He teetered on that edge, looking down at the long drop—six stories of stone wall—before he straightened and found his balance. When he came to a standstill, he found Cassie's hand pressed against his left knee—as if she could actually prevent his falling with that little touch.

"Why are you doing this?" Cassie screamed. "Get down and go back indoors!" A wealth of hidden rage and frustration came out of her mouth in those anguished words.

Robert gazed lovingly down at her beautiful face. He shook his head, mostly to ease his dizziness. "Would you believe me if I told you, where you go, I go? I meant what I said when I asked you to marry me, Cassandra. But I want to do that in a church. It's what we both deserve. Somehow stolen kisses and a hasty bedding in a tiny garret under the attic eaves pales as my idea of a wedding night."

"I was trying to tell you I'd be content with that."

"Content? Is that all you want from me, Cassie? Contentment? I have to have more."

"Robert, please get down. You've got everything to live for...a future. I don't."

"Why?"

Cassie looked down at the rocks below. "It's too

ugly to tell. Just take my word. Go away and leave me to do what I must.''

'''Ugly' depends on how you look at things. Think how ugly things will get here if I'm left standing here bearing the repercussions of your demise on those rocks.'' Robert deliberately pointed down, hoping to make her look at what waited for her. But her angry, hurt eyes never wavered from his.

''The way I see it, I'm as good as dead if you take the plunge,'' he said carelessly. ''Why? Because there won't be enough pieces left of me to put into a bag to send back to the king once that father of yours and his henchmen get through taking out their vengeance on me. You see, Cassie, I'll be the one blamed for your death.''

Cassie didn't respond, but Robert could see that she was shaking.

''Give me your hand. Let's do it and get it over with. It's bloody damn cold out here and my cods are shriveling to peas.'' He held out his hand to her, noticing that he, too, trembled.

She gave him her hand but he gripped her wrist instead, and his fingers tightened like a vise. She matched his grip, her fingers closing as tightly as they could on his larger bones.

Then without warning, she jumped, backward, yanking on his arm with all her might, toppling him backward into the snowbank on the roof.

She hadn't made allowance for his reflexes or inborn strength, thinking only that she had her quickness and the unexpected to her advantage.

It wasn't to be. Two seconds after she'd made the

move, he was on her, pressing her into the mound of snow, straddling her, wrestling hold of both of her struggling wrists in his combined fists.

''I believe this is the part where we troop back indoors, milady, and sort this out in better conditions.'' His teeth gleamed in the shadows. Their power struggle was reduced to a muted, macabre dance performed while writhing on the snow.

Cassie tried to buck him off of her and unman him with her knee. The less successful her efforts were, the more desperate and urgently she fought his restraint.

''Are ye willing to come along peaceably? Or am I going to have to get rough with you like we boys like to do, eh?''

Cassie's answered by biting his fingers where they crushed her wrists together.

''Have it your way then.'' Robert gripped her wrists in his left hand and made a fist with his right.

Cassie saw the blow coming and panicked, yelling out the first thing that came to mind to prevent it. ''Don't you dare hit me!''

Robert froze. For the love of God, she was a woman. He'd never struck a woman in his life. She was driving him to madness.

''Woman, you leave me no choice, save to use the only weapon I have to subdue you. Sweet God Almighty, do ye realize you've just attempted to commit suicide?''

She went still as a stone then, quieting for the first time since this nightmare had begun. Her lips quivered and she burst into tears.

"Och, Cassie," Robert pulled her to him, cradling her against his chest. She clung to his neck, weeping inconsolably.

Robert lifted her head from the snow, gathering her in to him, rocking and kissing her, to calm and soothe away her terror and anger. When she'd quieted, he regained his feet, picked her up from the snow and carried her out of the storm and back to his chamber. He set them both down on the stone hearth before the fire and began brushing the snow from her hair and face.

Mostly he just held her in his arms as the snow melted away. When her gown began to feel sodden to his touch, Robert gently undressed her from it, spreading it out on another handy bed frame to dry in the fire's heat. Then he returned to his perch at the side of the hearth and lifted Cassie, in her chemise and petticoats, back onto his lap, content just to hold her in his arms.

Neither of them managed to speak a coherent word until after the castle's chapel bell tolled the eleventh hour.

Chapter Thirteen

The last muffled bell brought Cassie's cheek an inch higher on Robert's shoulder. Her fingers shifted in a maddening tickle over his heart. "I'm hungry."

"Mumph." Robert let his all-purpose sound ease up his throat. "Canna help you there. There's no' so much as a crumb to be had in this bloody chamber."

"Aye, there is." Cassie raised her hand to her own neck. Her nails made a soft burring noise as they scratched briefly against her skin, then skittered through her tangled hair, pulling it away from her neck. "Och, this hair of mine. I'm so tired of it the way it is. If you let me get up, I'll fetch the basket."

"Tell me what's in it first?" His hands didn't move from her waist or her shoulder.

"A bottle of claret, I hope. Two crystal glasses, a wheel of cheese, a loaf or two of bread, and whatever meats Cook could gather for me."

"Leeks or eels?"

"None. Apples, maybe pears if there were any left in the larder."

Robert put a kiss on her brow. Her eyes lifted to his. "I'm going to let you go, Cass, only because I trust you. Don't disappoint me."

"I'll just get the basket and come back."

His arms opened. Cassie shifted and stood, her petticoats swirling around her stocking-covered ankles and the neat leather slippers covering her feet. She moved to the commode and picked up the basket, caught the blanket on Robert's bed as well and returned to the hearth. Setting the basket by him, she shook open the blanket, spreading it across the floor in front of the fire, well enough back not to catch sparks or popping cinders. She knelt on that and patted the space beside her.

"Bring the basket, too."

Hang the basket and food, Robert thought. He didn't think he could move, not without jumping on her and tumbling her onto her back. A deep breath calmed his raging blood enough that he managed to lazily set the basket beside her knees. He scooted the short distance, coming to his knees in front of her. She reached into the basket, lifting its napkin cover. Her breasts swelled and furled along the ribbon edging her chemise, rising and shifting with each graceful movement of her slender white arms. Holding her had been easy, hardly any temptation at all. Watching her move, while she was oblivious to her intimate clothing, was the most seductive sight he'd ever seen.

"We should be down in my chamber instead of here," Cassie said, unaware of his torment. "I have pillows and eiderdowns, cushions galore."

"Aye, there's a grand idea. Shall we go down?"

Robert said, only because a walk through the chilly corridor outside would definitely cool his rising passion.

"Och, no." Cassie lifted a bottle from the bottom and set it on the edge of the stone hearth. "'Tis more private here. Quiet, secret, thank God."

"Aye." Robert wondered if she had freckles on her belly, and the thought drove him over the edge. His right hand moved to touch the tiny ribbon tied between her breasts and his resolve was undone. He could not touch her now without making her his own.

Cassie stilled as his touch released the ribbon's tension. His fingers traced the line of the neck, lowering it to expose her nipples. Then they slid under the cloth, pressing it off her shoulders. Loosened completely, her chemise pooled to her waist.

"You're not hungry?" she asked naively, hoping to break the tension between them.

"Aye, for you." Robert let his hungry eyes drink their fill. Her breasts stood out magnificently, firm, round, rosy-tipped and freckled. Not satisfied with a partial unveiling, his hand pressed onward to the lone button at the waist of her petticoats. Garment ties he was used to, tapes and iron hooks galore, but she was the first woman he'd ever touched who had a priceless ivory button on her intimate apparel. He knew why he preferred buttons on his kilts, for speed at dressing and ease of removal. He would ask later why she preferred hers.

Her belly contracted against his knuckles as the button surrendered to his determined hands. She sucked in her breath, tensing, and the petticoat pooled low on her hips.

"Don't be afraid, Cass." Robert kissed her nose, caught her waist and lifted her out of her clothes and onto his lap. She kicked free her stocking feet and settled exactly as he wanted her to, straddling his thighs, exposed and gloriously open to his gaze and his ardent touch.

"I'm not afraid." Cassie laced her fingers together behind his neck.

"Nay, how could ye be?" Robert rested his hands on her gartered knees, smiling, his palms open, the firm flesh of her thighs touching his thumb and fingertips.

He held back as long as he could, allowing her to become accustomed to his eyes savoring her beauty. She wet her lips, anxious, her belly quivering in a lovely rising ripple.

"Tell me what happens next. What should I do?"

"Kiss me, come to me, let me feel all of you pressed against me."

She hesitated, swallowed and whispered, "Your kilt?"

"It won't scare you if I take it off?"

A rosy blush began rising on her breasts, speeding upward to her face. "Och, no. I've seen boys before."

"I'm no boy," Robert replied. "I'm hard as a stone for the wanting of ye, lass."

A shrug lifted her shoulders. "Take it off."

"Your servant, always, love." Robert caught the button at his side and unfastened it, casting the wool aside.

She took only the slightest glance and stiffened. Then she flattened her chest against his, kissing him hard on the mouth.

Robert let her have the lead for a moment, then slowly coaxed it from her by changing ardent desire into demanding passion. He sat back on his heels, letting his hands move slowly up the outside of her legs till they slid round to her bottom and cupped her cheeks with each hand. Then he lifted her, presenting her delicious neck and throat to his mouth to be nibbled upon and teased and kissed until every freckle was memorized.

Only then did he bring her up to her knees so he could take the first taste of her untouched breasts and awaken her sleeping nipples to attention. As he suckled the first one, her head fell back and she moaned, her hips pressing urgently against his belly in need. He locked her in place with one arm clasped tight around her hips. His right hand stroked upward on the soft inner flesh of her thighs till he found her prize.

"My lord, what is happening to me?" Cassie gasped, shaking her head, unable to control the quivering inside her as Robert's fingers explored that place where no one had dared touch her before.

Her hair cascaded across his locked arm, tickling him. Robert laughed softly and sought the other breast, wanting to teach her all the pleasures of love. As he suckled anew, his thumb found the nub of her sex and his forefinger the entrance of her womb.

She was small and tight and very wet, quivering with the building need rising with each new touch. He drew hard on her nipple, giving her the pressure she unconsciously pressed so hard against him to receive. He slid his second finger inside her, stretching her, while his thumb danced round and round on the hardening nub. Her flesh softened more, opening for him. Her fingertips dug into his back, short nails imprinting eight marks on his skin.

Satisfied with the hardened nipple in his mouth, Robert released her breast and drew her back down. Her mouth came to join his again and his tongue mated with hers at the same time that his fingers taught her the rudiments of the strokes to come.

He knew he should give her more time to become accustomed to his demands, but the torment and the urgency of his own need were too much to restrain. With her legs still straddling his, he pressed her onto her back and let her feel the first true hint of his desire.

There was alarm in her eyes when his hips settled in the cradle of hers, his manhood at her gate, her knees more than wide enough to accommodate his need. Robert gave her no chance to ask questions, his mouth having more demands to make on her. He wanted all of her, their bodies fused completely.

Her feet shifted restlessly, and she didn't know what to do with those long limbs that couldn't keep still as he bucked up, adjusting his position. Only then did he begin the slow plunge into her.

He had no need to doubt her maiden status, for the journey had only begun when he came upon the barrier. He thrust down in a hard-won stroke, seated to the hilt, their bodies melded perfectly. She might have groaned in some pain at the tearing, but if she had, she gave it to his mouth in silent witness. Then she found the best place for her legs and feet, bringing them behind his hips, locking her ankles, making their union more secure than his efforts alone could have done.

Robert held his upper body up from hers with his hands and smiled down at her, pleased by the way her hips moved in unison, fused completely to his. "Discovered something, have you?"

"Oh, aye." She smiled a sultry smile.

"I'm not hurting you?"

"Och, no. It feels wonderful now. Tight, mind you."

"Aye, I know."

"What's next?"

"We ride together, love." He smiled and kissed her before she could speak again.

He slid his hands under her shoulders to hold on to her, to explain more eloquently by deed than he ever could with words, exactly what he meant. He expected his own climax to be glorious, but he wasn't prepared for explosiveness of having a woman climax at the same time he did.

It came the moment he planted his seed deep inside her. She tensed and cried out his name, and he exploded into a million pieces.

Sweat fused their skin to the other's. He couldn't move and she couldn't stop involuntarily moving. Trembles flashed up her belly and contractions swept inside her thighs only to start again and again inside her womb. A rhythmic vibrating had begun that Robert had also never experienced in any of his past couplings.

He'd heard about those rare women who gained true pleasure from the mating. But he'd never bedded a woman so endowed or understood what the source of such unrestricted pleasure was. He'd lost his wind and his sense of purpose, and lay on her, collapsed, while her body kept contracting and stroking his shaft inside her, renewing its strength and reviving his need to have her again and again and again.

He realized only as he was coming back to his senses, when they were both spent to the last dram of pleasure, that what had happened between them was magic and, in the end, had exhausted her as completely as it had him.

He caught her chin and turned her face toward his and kissed her soft mouth. "You are my woman now, Cassandra. Mine and no other's. Remember that."

The wood in the fire sizzled and Robert turned onto his back and pulled her up against his side, her head cradled on his bent arm. They touched and talked of childhood, growing up and funny things that happened in their early years. They didn't talk of what to do tomorrow. Robert spoke of the work he had left to finish and Cassie told him about her cottage hidden on Ben Nevis that was hers and hers alone.

When the chapel bell tolled the half hour past midnight, Cassie sat up and told him she must leave.

Robert wanted to detain her, to keep her at his side through the entire night, but he knew he was supposed to practice restraint until she was past the early days of making love regularly. He insisted upon combing the tangles from her hair, then helped her dress and right her clothes without the aid of a mirror or maid.

It only took him a few moments to don his sark and kilt, to throw his plaid over his shoulder and tuck it secure inside his belt.

Then with her shawl close around her shoulders and his arm over that, he walked her down to the third floor and kissed her a sweet good-night at her chamber door.

Neither of them wanted to end the night. "Until tomorrow, then." Cassie pulled her hand from his when she spied her mother's maid coming down the corridor with the pan of heated coals she used to warm Lady MacArthur's bed each night before her mother retired.

"Until tomorrow." Robert bowed over Cassie's hand and kissed it. Impulse made him remove his signet from his own hand and slip it onto the ring finger of hers. "Will you wear this until I have one made for your hand, Cassandra?"

The band of gold was too large for her finger, but Cassie understood the significance.

"Aye." She nodded, accepting it. "But if it would not bother you, I would wear it on a chain at my throat so I do not lose it."

"I will envy its position nearest your heart. Good night, love."

"Good night." Cassie curtsied and slipped inside her room, closing the door as the maid passed. Robert took his leave.

Her chamber had grown cold with no one inside it tending the hearth. She built up the fire then stood before it, examining the gold ring and its engraved face. It bore the stag and crown of the clan Gordon.

She went to her vanity and sat down, searching her jewel box for a suitable chain, asking herself what she would do if her father would not allow her the match. And she remembered the letter she had from the king, the letter that she had not shown to anyone for fear its decree would be enacted against her wishes, without her consent on the match.

She could give her consent now wholeheartedly, knowing that Robert was everything she had wanted in a husband, even if he was a Gordon.

She put the king's letter back in its safe place, and heard her stomach begin to grumble for food. No wonder that. She hadn't eaten enough to keep a bird alive this evening. She left her room and met her mother coming up on her way to bed.

"Where are you going at this time of night, lass?" her mother asked, stopping on the riser below Cassie.

"To the kitchen for food. I'm starving."

"I thought the steward said you ordered a basket in your chamber."

"Not my chamber." Cassie adroitly handled that query. "I had it sent to Robert Gordon in case he should wake hungry after retiring early. I just woke up."

"Aye, I can see that. You must have slept in that gown. It looks rumpled and crushed. Child, how many times must I tell you to remove your clothes before you rest?" Lady MacArthur plucked at Cassie's crushed sleeves, setting the tucks and slashs to rights, then nodded to her. "Dinna be down long. Servants need their rest too."

"I won't," Cassie promised and with a curtsy was on her way down again.

There were many cold poultry legs available to nibble on, and slabs of thick, buttery bread. Cassie ate her fill, washed the meal down with a cup of ale and thanked the steward for serving her. She went upstairs, ready for bed this time.

Her steps were brisk and purposeful on the polished floors of the second level of the castle. She wanted to get to the east wing as quickly as possible and thereby avoid any sort of confrontation with her father.

That was not to be. The canny old fox had one of his henchmen posted as a lookout at his study, who warned Laird MacArthur of her approach. Within seconds, her father appeared at the door, crooked his finger and commanded her presence in his study without saying a single word.

"Milord—" Cassie made one futile attempt to escape the summons "—I was just going to bed. I'm fair exhausted from the day's worries and labors."

"Good," said her father, rolling the vowels about in his mouth for a hearty drawl, "ye'll sleep well then. A word with you first, though."

Cassie sighed and, seeing she was truly trapped, entered the study with little grace.

"Have a seat at one of the chairs by the fire, Cassie. We will be here for a spell." He paused to close the door firmly to protect his privacy, then went to his sideboard and poured himself a glass of whiskey.

Reluctantly, Cassie looked to the three high-backed

chairs set facing the roaring fire. She had hated those chairs as a child, and went to them with dragging feet. Choosing the one in the middle for herself, she stepped around it and discovered Robert Gordon at his ease and content in the leather cushions of the chair to the left.

Startled, Cassie blurted out, "Milord? What do *you* here?"

Robert set aside his own glass of amber whiskey and rose smoothly to his feet. "Milady," he said rather too formally, and bowed, taking her raised hand and kissing it in greeting. "Good evening. How delightful that you've joined us for a nightcap."

Cassie snatched her hand back quickly and glared at him, trying to let him know with head movements that his gallant gesture would be interpreted wrongly by her father. Robert merely smiled at her, his face a mask that gave nothing away.

"Oh, I wouldn't call this simply a nightcap." MacArthur joined them with his whiskey glass full and handed a stemmed glass of claret to Cassie. "Sit down, Cassandra, I have grave news from our king. A letter that arrived while you were off visiting your sister."

More wary now that she had been before, Cassie took the glass with murmured thanks and sat. Both men regained their seats.

"And..." Cassie urged, knowing full well nothing good came from the king's court. "That news is?"

"You are to accompany the king's mapmakers on their tour of Lochaber from now until Beltane, May first." Laird MacArthur took a sip of the amber liquid in his glass, then sat back with the cut crystal nestled in his hand as he regarded his stoic daughter's face.

Cassie already knew that particular news. She delayed responding until she'd savored her first taste of the fine claret. "I've heard something to that effect, my lord."

"I see." MacArthur set his whiskey on the minute stand at his left. His gaze shifted from Cassie to Robert Gordon. "Would you care to tell my youngest daughter the balance of our king's order, young man?"

Cassie stiffened, realizing her father could not bring himself to address Robert by his surname.

Robert ought to have anticipated MacArthur would leave it up to him to explain to Cassie all of King James's devious plan. He didn't want to do this so formally and coldly, in this tension-filled study. He drew a deep breath and let it out between his teeth.

"Well, speak up, mapmaker," Cassie demanded. "What else has our sly king devised?"

Robert cleared his throat and put aside his own glass of whiskey. "Well, milady, simply put, the king anticipated your father's objections to such a plan."

The uncomfortable expression on Robert's face was the only warning Cassie really had of impending doom. "Not to say my own objections matter, but do go on, sir. I wait with bated breath."

"Aye. For my own part," Robert continued, "I want you to know I had hoped very, very sincerely that you would have already been wed by the time I reached Lochaber."

"Oh no," Cassandra said softly, feeling his betrayal like the kick of a hobnailed boot in her gut. He didn't love her. His ring was only a token, and what had come before was a mere parody of love.

"In all honesty, Cassandra, it has been my belief all along that Hamilton and I did not need a guide. The mountains have been rather well documented in the past, though not with the precision and accuracy we expect to bring to the endeavor. All we knew personally of you was gleaned from your legendary reputation—"

"Out with it, mon!" MacArthur interrupted. "The point is, daughter, my reasonable objections to the king's request are to be overridden by immediate marriage to whichever mapmaker I find less offensive to my taste. I am given carte blanche to hand my youngest child over in marriage to families that I dinna trust, nor have any past alliances or history with, to ensure your protection inside their ranks. It goes without question that I have refused such terms. I have other plans for you, and they will be finalized much sooner than the first of May, thanks to this complication from a meddling king."

Cassie swung full around to stare openmouthed at her father. "What?" she gasped.

"You heard me." Laird MacArthur pulled out a folded parchment from inside his quilted vest. "The king's terms are unacceptable. You will marry Douglas Cameron as soon as the man can be summoned to attend the ceremony."

"How dare—"

"Don't!" MacArthur thundered, obliterating Cassie's protest with the pure volume of his shout. "So long as I am alive to prevent it, you, Cassandra, will never marry a back-stabbing Gordon traitor or be tied to a faithless, manipulating Hamilton fop.''

With those words spoken, he tore the king's letter in two and cast the pieces into the blazing fire.

''Is that your final word, sir?'' Robert asked, as calm as the pope's confessor.

''Aye.'' MacArthur stood, towering above both Robert and her in their seats. Sensing disaster coming on her like an avalanche in January, Cassie abruptly stood between the two of them.

Robert drained the last of the whiskey, set the cut crystal cup aside and rose to his full height, with no hint of his earlier serenity in his final stance. Eyeball to eyeball, he and MacArthur stood on equal footing. Only the younger man had the fluidity of youth granting him more grace. Cassie felt her heart sink to her toes.

''You have a quarter hour to depart from my household unmolested, sir,'' MacArthur declared.

Cassie spun back on one foot and broke a vow she'd held sacred for ten years past, naming the man who'd sired her by his truest title. ''*Father,* you canna! There is a blizzard in the hills!''

John MacArthur went rigid with shock over his youngest child's calling him ''Father'' for the first time in a decade.

Robert caught Cassie's shoulder, stilling her. ''Whisht!'' he ordered sharply. To MacArthur he curtly nodded and coldly replied, ''So be it.'' That said, he turned and walked proudly out of the laird's chamber.

"My God in heaven, MacArthur, you dinna know what you've done!" Cassie exploded. "The king wants for only one reason to destroy all of us!"

"I know exactly what I have done." MacArthur caught Cassie's arms and held her fast, staying her from running after the bold Gordon warrior. "I've saved you from a lifetime of misery and heartache with that bounder. Douglas Cameron is the man for you."

More important was the need to keep Cassie from following after her would-be lover. He'd seen all the signs of budding romance he cared to see during supper—the shy looks, the sideways smiles, the whispered words. He would see it end before shame and disaster fell on the house of MacArthur.

He pushed her physically back down into her seat and held her there until she stilled and sat quietly, her fury contained but nonetheless strong.

"You will sit in that chair until I give you leave to get up, Cassandra, else I will do what I should have done an age ago to end your defiance of my will. Understand?"

Hatred burned Cassie's eyes and she tightened her hands into fists on the armrests of the chair. Unable to find words strong enough to alter his decision she nodded once, acknowledging his odious command.

Satisfied for the moment, MacArthur released his fast hold upon her and stepped back. He took his glass in hand, drank from it, then regained his seat. The only sounds in his study came from Cassie's labored breathing as she slowly began to recover and the crackling logs on the coals in the fireplace.

Time crawled on its monotonous path and neither of them spoke. His daughter should have, but MacArthur knew she would die before speaking to him again...if ever. Cassie was that way, too much like him to do herself one bit of good.

Once she took on a grudge she held it forever. It was so regrettable that she had liked this mapmaker, though how much of that admiration was due to his heroism or to the actual man was anyone's guess. Either way, it made no difference to MacArthur.

His duty was to protect his daughter, and he could not protect her in an alliance with either of those clans. Hence, even the king's interest in those clans must be refused.

After an interminable silence Cassie picked up her glass of claret and concentrated upon draining it completely. The fine wine didn't dull her raging temper. She hated his decision and would not accept the resulting consequences—ever.

"May I have your leave to go to bed?" she asked, "or am I to sleep here and use this chair as a privy?"

MacArthur glared at her, his hard gaze measuring what he saw. "You will go to your room and remain there the rest of the night?"

"Where else would I go?" Cassie replied bluntly, her eyes on the red and blue flames consuming the wood in the hearth. "Outdoors into the worst blizzard this year? I don't have a death wish."

"Daughter, look at me and give me your word to remain in your chamber until morning."

"I will no' do that." Cassie stared straight ahead.

"At some point I will calm down enough to want to speak to Mother regarding this."

"Your mother willna sway my decision."

"Nothing ever sways your decisions, sir. That is why nothing has changed between us in ten years. May I have your leave, sir? Else you will have to burn this chair."

"Cassandra...you broke your vow a moment ago." MacArthur softened momentarily, regretting the bad blood between them, wanting his relationship with this child of his to be the way it was before all the troubles began.

"A rash impulse, caused only by the shock of your latest decision, I fear." Cassie interrupted him. "Be assured such a slip of the tongue won't happen again in this lifetime."

He didn't doubt the finality of those words. Still they angered him to the point of violence, which he expended willingly by snatching her glass from the table and hurling it into the brick wall of the fireplace. "Go, damn ye. Get out of my sight before ye tempt me to smash ye into a thousand broken shards!"

Cassie fled his presence with the same dignity that Robert had shown, neither cowering at the threat MacArthur posed, nor giving in to his call for further provocation.

She did actually go upstairs and enter her chamber, undress and make use of the chamber pot. Able to be as devious as everyone else in Achanshiel, she sat down and wrote a letter to her mother explaining what else she knew of the king's plan and how that would affect Jamie and his family in Edinburgh. Last, Cassie made a bolster in her bed and tucked the letter underneath it.

At three o'clock, when the whole castle was asleep, including the guard at the wicket, she set out, following Robert's trail in the new fallen snow.

Chapter Fourteen

Absolute silence followed Robert's proud retreat from MacArthur's study. Had he expected a passionately eloquent defense against his eviction from his so capable Lady Quickfoot? No. In the face of her father's livid fury he'd prayed silently for her to hold her outspoken tongue and let him defend himself. Had he hoped for a plea for mercy based on love and tender feelings on her part? No, it would have shamed him if she had brought that up when her father refused to accept any union.

In all, Robert found Cassie's silence more telling of her total shock. That assured him she could never agree with her father's rupture of the sacrosanct duty of a Highland host. Throwing a guest out into this night's weather was an insult. One that Robert wouldn't forget or forgive.

Granted, Highlanders held grudges for life and generations could carry on the same idiotic feud. But that did not mean that MacArthurs or Gordons could not sit down to the same table and share a companionable meal, suspend their hatreds during bouts of extreme need or work together against a common enemy...such as England. By their very nature, Highlanders had adapted into rugged survivalists who knew how and when to compromise.

About the worst thing Cassie's father could do was to forbid her doing what she thought she ought to do. That bothered Robert the most as he prepared to take on the elements again. Yes, Robert had used the king's power to induce Cassie into cooperating by hinting that her resistance could cause the forfeiture of her brother's life. She had kept silent about that to her father.

Using her brother's presence at court had never been Robert's idea, but he had told Cassie of it freely when the thought of her balking had stopped his progress in getting to know her. A greater good had come out of that. It had caused her to move past the barrier of blanketed clan hatred. That was the purest purpose of King James's prerogative, and brought about an ultimate good.

The king's plan hadn't called for falling in love.

Now where or when exactly that emotional entanglement had soured the sauce Robert wasn't precisely certain, though he wouldn't rest until he made Cassandra MacArthur his wife. But instead of demanding her hand, he had walked out of that study blind with anger at Cassandra's blasted father.

Before Robert had even given his back to the old bastard, he was convinced he should do something as heroically rash and stupid as Gordons of two centuries ago had done, such as abducting the woman he loved right out from under the old rascal's nose.

The impossible logistics of such an act in this castle, in these weather conditions, were so ludicrous Robert almost snorted aloud with laughter at himself. Cassandra wasn't one of the frail, fainting beauties of the past, easily subdued and terrified by the ferocity of an enraged and aroused knight. She'd participate in her own abduction for the span of one heartbeat, no more. Then he'd have a termagant on his hands, not the winsome bride he wanted to love all the days of their lives.

There were no other options at this particular moment save to quit the place before MacArthur and he went at each other with swords drawn and murder in their hearts. Robert didn't give a damn how ferociously the old man provoked him, he was not going to have MacArthur's blood on his hands.

Another thing that troubled Robert greatly on his way downstairs and out of MacArthur's castle was the rapidity with which gossip passed throughout the castle. Either everyone in Achanshiel knew beforehand what their laird's intentions after supper were, or word of his edict was spread within minutes by eavesdroppers after he harshly ordered Robert to quit the place.

Lady MacArthur detained him in the great hall, insisting he come with her to the castle kitchen. There, on the huge split-oak table, all sorts of winter gear were laid out, like offerings to be burned on the ready altar of kitchen fires. She commanded Robert to take food, heavier quilted clothing, boots and oiled tarps she'd collected, else she would not let him exit through the castle gate.

"Milady, I canna carry all of this," Robert protested. It would only slow his progress through the snow to shelter elsewhere.

"My Lord Gordon, give me one moment to compose myself, I beg you." Her trembling hand upon his sleeve stopped his protests. He gave her the time she requested, and she used it by taking a dainty handkerchief from her sleeve and blowing her nose.

With a deep, grieving sigh, Lady MacArthur began explaining herself once more. "I had the most terrible words with Cassandra only moments after we left the supper table this evening. And now this from my husband. I know and understand what drives Cassie—too well. She will be outside these walls before you have traveled one mile in this weather...following you, sir."

Robert thought that an astute assumption. "I'll send her back."

"She won't come. She'll go up to some cave or hut she has in the mountains." Again, the small square of crumpled linen and lace touched the lady's nose and eyes. Then she continued. "She's been doing this since she was eight years old. In years past, Angus and his young nephew, Alastair, could always find her and eventually talk the lass into coming back. We tried everything we could to break her of the habit, which began on the very night my lord husband disowned Cassie's brother and banished him from Achanshiel forever.

"Even after the breach between father and son was

healed, Cassie would not relent. Nothing my lord husband did or I said has changed her.

"Now Cassandra has gotten so set in her ways. My husband believes she has stood up to him so many times she fears no man's wrath. Our years on this earth dwindle and Laird MacArthur hasna seen his youngest and most treasured child settled in a secure marriage. Cassie's future consumes him night and day.

"Trust me when I tell you he sends you away for Cassie's own benefit. We have a guest coming when the weather clears who will marry her and be acceptable to Cassie as a partner for life. She already knows the man well, a Cameron who comforted her greatly after Alastair died. She and Alastair were never more than childhood friends who had become compatible through time.

"When she leaves this time, Cassandra will never come home again." Lady MacArthur finished her lament.

"Aye, she will," Robert responded and placed a reassuring hand on the lady's arm to emphasize that fact. "I will send her back to you does she dare to follow me."

"Empty words, sir." The lady shook her head, negating Robert's well-intentioned assurance. "I dreamed of this moment years ago before Cassie was born. It has come just as I feared it would. Cassandra willna return until the day comes she is accepted as an enemy's wife. I have seen the truth in both of your eyes. Take these paltry goods. My youngest daughter willna go torcherless from my home. I canna allow you to leave empty-handed when a spare plaid and a sack of provisions could well mean survival.''

The items gathered on the table made for a poor man's dowry, and they both knew it. Robert's instincts were to refuse them in spite of the lady's entreaty. The two extra plaids convinced him not to depart with such little grace. There was no telling what Cassandra would decide to do, let alone what she'd wear doing it.

If the mother's instincts erred, the extra gear could be left in the hills if it proved too cumbersome to continue carrying. He wasn't going that far tonight, back to Glencoe's Pass most likely, until he caught up with the rescue party bringing Angus down, or found Chattering Otters Cave, whichever came first. Then he and Alex would set out on their own again.

''Set your mind to ease, Lady MacArthur,'' Robert said in the end, honestly wanting to repair some of the damage his advent into their proud family had caused. ''I will do everything in my power to send her back to you so that she may marry the Cameron— if she will have him.''

''Aye, I believe you will give it your best try.''

At the wicket gate, Robert set his sights on reaching the shelter of the first stand of tall pines beyond the frozen riverbank. The storm had long ago disintegrated into blinding sleet. He set out in as straight a track as possible, intent upon that nearby glen. It took what seemed like a full hour to reach those winter barren oaks and thorns, bent and breaking under thickening coats of glazing ice.

There, he was able to pick up a suitable stick to aid his balance while plowing though the blowing drifts. The lash of the wind never lessened until he reached the shelter of the pines. A little into the woods he was able to make a primitive shelter from the driven snow with the two tarps. He scraped away the snow to uncover solid frozen ground and built a small fire. That done, he waited and watched the castle gate, all the while feeding the small fire.

The work of creating a camp kept him moving and active during the worst of the snow and ice squall. It was well past two when the wind eased and the sleet gave way to simply snow.

While the fire burned away the dampness clinging to the frozen wood, Robert sat staring into the steamy smoke and thinking back to each time he'd seen Cassandra. Her appearance had always registered like a hammer. She hadn't looked or dressed as the same person twice.

As his wait lengthened, Robert took out his spyglass and trained it on Castle MacArthur. It wasn't long before he was rewarded for his efforts. Cassie stepped out the wicket gate, accompanied by a dog. She wore a damned pair of trews covered by a lush and glamorous fur-lined cloak that swirled around her tall boots as she moved away from the castle.

Robert's scope gave him details his naked eyes could otherwise never have detected. For all that she looked more like a boy than she had at any other time, she was a vision of loveliness as she plowed relentlessly through the snowbanks, taking the same path Robert had, straight away from the castle walls.

It wasn't long before Robert heard the baying of the dog as it plunged through the snowdrifts edging the pines, seeking the scent it had quickly lost in the new snow pack. The dog picked up Robert's scent again, thirty yards from his campsite, and stood sentinel, barking a signal to Cassie, who made slower time on Robert's crushed path through the icy drifts.

He lost sight of her for a long, tense moment as she crossed a fallow field sunken below the line of the pines. She came back into sight, climbing the rise, and stayed in his view from that point onward.

She, too, came with a walking staff in hand, skillfully wielding that aid to balance. Robert waited to stand until she'd crossed the barrier of the first pines. His small fire had ceased smoking, reduced now to hot glowing coals that added very little light to his position. He took a step backward, to the icy wall of his shelter, his heart hammering in his chest, and waited.

The rugged collie called Shep ran up beside Cassie as she shook snow off her head, shoulders and the trailing hems of her warm cloak. The dog barked a warning, spying Robert in the wooded shadows. The animal remained protectively at Cassie's side as she picked her way fearlessly to the edge of his make-do shelter.

"I thought I'd find you close enough to be watching the castle gate like a predator," Cassie said.

That greeting left much to be desired, lacking the welcoming warmth Robert had grown accustomed to seeing in her good-humored mouth and eyes. Humor had been replaced by a feminine mask mirroring the same defiant features as those of the laird of the keep. Indeed, apples never fell far from the tree.

Cassandra MacArthur was her father's daughter to the core of her being. Woe unto those caught between their powerful wills. Awareness that he stood in the middle of father and daughter gave Robert no joy; instead he steeled himself to stand against Cassie to the bitter end. He'd made up his mind that the Lady MacArthur's plan was the only logical course. Come hell and damnation for eternity, Robert was sending her back where she belonged tonight.

"What do you here?" His harsh voice laid the restive dog's ears back flat against his head and brought forth a deep, threatening growl.

This was not the welcome Cassie had anticipated.

Robert Gordon made no move to open his rigidly postured arms or gentle his expression in any manner. Cassie snapped her gloved fingers, bringing her animal to heel. The noise ceased and the animal stilled at her side, returning the woods to the deep silence of a storm-strewn winter night.

"We left some unfinished business that needs tending." Cassie rewarded Shep's obedience with a pat on his head, then straightened and faced Robert squarely. "May I come in your shelter? It looks ten times warmer than standing out here in the cold."

"What will you do if I say no?" Robert asked.

"Are you a coward?" Cassie inquired with blunt curiosity. "MacArthur's bark is worse than his bite."

"Both are equally repugnant."

"Aye, well, you canna say you were no' warned of what to expect from that quarter. Take heart, he never gets any better. You've seen him at his autocratic worst.''

"Splendid. Now that you've had your say, turn around and go back whence you came. I do not want you here.''

"Bugger off.'' Cassandra snorted and snapped her fingers in command to the dog. He immediately entered the shelter of the tarps and lay down near the fire. Cassie ducked her head and entered as well. She let the hood drop completely and a gloved hand caught hold of the trailing ends of the cloak, gathering it close. She sat abruptly on the oiled canvas floor, tucking wool about her body. "I've brought whiskey. Are you thirsty?''

She produced a bottle of amber liquid from inside the confines of her cloak. She adroitly removed its plug of cork with her teeth. That done neatly, she put the bottle to her lips and drank deeply.

Appalled, Robert stepped round the fire and snatched the bottle from her hand. "What did you come here t' do—get drunk as a laird, Cassandra MacArthur?''

Her gloved fingers swept across her lips and whiskey-splattered chin, then brushed the droplets glistening on her cloak onto the tarp. "That was boorish of you, sir. I offered to share.''

Furious at her ignorance, Robert shoved the bottle in a drift of snow and yanked Cassandra back onto her feet. "You dinna know the meaning of boorish! How dare you come strutting out here in this weather, chasing after me like a lightskirt from a tavern!''

"I did nothing of the kind!'' Cassie shouted back

at him. "I brought the whiskey to warm my bones, you damned fool. I'd have brought soup if I coulda managed hauling a hot pot of it through this blasted storm!"

"Aye, and you coulda stayed where you belong, did the thought ever occur to you of what you should do, Quickfoot."

"Ballocks!" Cassie spat the expletive in his face. "You havena cause to lecture me upon what I should and shouldna do, mapmaker."

"Dinna start upon that tack, lassie. Your da will be sending out every man he commands, searching for you, the minute he notices your absence. I'll no' go about my business in this shire with that man's hounds and henchmen hot on my heels with murder and bloodlust in their hearts."

"And I'll no' spend the rest of my days burdened by the guilt of causing my brother's hanging at Traitor's Tree because my family cannot obey a simple order from the king! I'm here to do the job the king commands, and I will do it and be rewarded for it with my brother's liberty, or you, sir, will be hounded to hell and back by all the MacArthurs of Achanshiel the rest of your bloody days."

"Shut up, Cassandra!" Robert shook her hard to rattle sense back into her foolish head. "You're going back to the castle, even if I have to drag you every step of the way."

The warning bark from the growling dog cut through the fierceness of both their rising tempers. "Release me, Robert, or I'll let my dog attack you."

"And I will kill it. That will change nothing.

You're going back! I dinna want you here with me. Can you no' get that through your thick head?''

Cassie's fingers snapped once and lessened the dog's ferocious growl.

In the subsequent quiet, Cassie cast scathing words to repel his painful rejection. ''You flatter yourself, mapmaker, thinking I've come after you like a bitch in heat. I've more brains in my head than to settle for that from any man.''

Robert abruptly dropped his hands from her arms. Cassie moved quickly away, taking what distance could be had in the confines of the shelter. She settled to the ground again, with her back to the canvas wall this time.

Shep lay down beside her, put his head on her knee and warily kept his eyes on Robert.

Calmer, Cassie watched as her mapmaker dragged clawed fingers through his hair before he spoke to her again. That same hand passed across his face, rubbing hard at his eyes and mouth before it dropped to his side and burrowed into the warmth of his plaid.

''Listen to me, Cassandra. You canna remain with me through the night. Did you do such an idiotic thing, you would be ruined ever after, and no decent man would have you in marriage.''

''Is that what this outburst is about?'' Cassie asked quietly.

''You know it is.'' Robert's voice was raw and ragged with the truth.

''Why?'' Cassie relentlessly demanded.

He swiveled about, glaring at her. ''You know perfectly well why, lass. I canna keep my hands off you!

I want you myself. But you've got to give me time to work things out my way, time to bring your father around to accepting the match.''

She might or might not have shrugged. Under that thick cloak Robert couldn't tell. ''Oh, I imagine I'll find that a comforting thought some day in the future, but for the now, marriage is the least of my worries.''

''That's the damnedest answer I've ever heard,'' Robert said, sputtering.

''Get used to it,'' Cassie snapped, still wearing that peaceful, permanent smile on her lips that sent Robert mad trying to understand it. ''No one seems to give a damn about what is taking the rescuers my father sent into the hills so long to bring my gillie home. I'm going up to Chattering Otters Cave to see what's wrong. I'm no' going back *there* either way.'' Her head jerked in the direction of Castle MacArthur.

''Aye, you are,'' Robert replied, his voice stern and hard, brooking no argument. ''Cassandra, why didn't you tell me about the husband waiting for you to come home so that he could marry you?''

''Why didn't you tell me that I had a choice to marry either you or Alex Hamilton?''

''Why should I have done that, when you never looked a second time at Alex?''

''Twenty questions is the game, is it?'' Cassie quipped testily. ''Here's a good one. Why did you give me your ring?''

''Do you think I would have done if you'd made it known another man had already contracted for you?''

''He may have done, but I've signed no agreement

with anyone. Do you know Douglas Cameron?'' Cassie's eyes blazed.

"No, and it'd best stay that way if he wants to die an old man."

"Well, that shouldn't be any problem." Cassie snorted. "He's well on his way to marking fifty before I'll see five and twenty. But then, I probably wouldn't live that long if I married him. He's buried three wives and sired a dozen unruly brats, and I'm no' counting the ones that died in infancy or were stillborn. Do you no' want to fight for me, Robert? Am I no' worth that much to you?"

He couldn't answer that question, but his eyes for the first time softened, giving only a hint of the hurt his stoic face and hard manner refused to confide.

"I canna trust what you'll do next, Lady Quickfoot. You're unpredictable and volatile. You've never learned to control your temper or give way to a man's will. One minute you're sinking to the bottom of a pool you had no business skating on, risking the lives of two children. The next you're willing to throw your own life to the devil. Aye, I know what a fine lover you'd be, but the question remains, what kind of a wife and mother follows? And aye, I could still fight to have you, because I want you more than life itself. If only you'd ever told me the truth, Quickfoot."

And there was the biggest lie of all. Cassie swallowed and stood back a pace, pulling off her glove. "I don't believe we have anything else to discuss, Robert Gordon."

She was glad that no tears filled her eyes. Nor did they as she tugged the necklace with his ring on it over her head. When it was removed from the chain, she held it out to him, waiting for him to come and take it.

"Why dinna you tell me the truth, Cassie? Why did you come to me tonight and lie with me when ye knew all along you would leave me for another man? We should never have made love."

She shook her head. "I'll never regret it, Robert. How can you expect me to tell you what I didn't know myself?"

"Aye, but you did, lass. Your own mother confessed to me that she had told you after supper of Cameron's suit. You came to me after that... intending to rob the man of his bridal rights. You did it apurpose."

"Nay, you're wrong, Robert. I stayed because I thought I loved you, and if anyone had bridal rights it is I, not you, not Cameron. It is my choice, mine and no one else's, whom I choose to surrender my maidenhead to and whom I take for a husband. It was my love to give or keep locked away forever. I made my choice and so you have done. Goodbye, Robert. God keep you."

Cassie stepped forward and pressed the ring into his hand. Then she whistled to her dog and turned out of Robert's shelter, walking away from him, away from the castle in the hidden valley. Speechless, he stood watching her go, the ring he'd given her clenched in his fist.

God, if she wasn't going home, where in the world was she going? They were bound together, her life for his life, entwined and eternally bonded till death do they part. This could not be the end. How would he ever find her again? What if something happened to her and she needed help and he wasn't there to lend it to her? What if he couldn't live without her?

Chapter Fifteen

The last time Cassie had looked back over her shoulder, she'd seen Robert kick snow over his fire, killing it. He was breaking down his camp. That made her sigh because it could mean he was coming after her.

She didn't know if that pleased or terrified her. One thing was for certain. Her whole world had been turned topsy-turvy since he'd arrived at Glencoen Farm. For now, she turned her thoughts to Angus, her concern and worry for having left him in others' hands for so long paramount in her mind. Robert could take care of himself—and so could she. She had a good enough life without him.

She was at least a mile down the Oban Road when the crunch of Robert's boots on the path told her he was near. Shep's two barks and backward scurries had given her clues that the mapmaker was closing the distance. She didn't turn or look back or say anything.

Not long after that he came abreast of her, trudging on the opposite side of the wagon ruts that cut deep into the slushy road. He didn't say anything for a long while. Shep barked at him and paused to sniff his boots, then went on about his dog business, trotting ahead, ears up and alert.

"Where are you going, Cassandra?" Robert finally asked.

She pointed ahead at the road that curved around the mountain's flank. "There's a cove up ahead. A niche in the rock that provides a bit of shelter from the wind. It's a good place to wait for Alex Hamilton to come down with the rescuers that went to fetch Angus and Dorcas, if you'd like. Once I'm satisfied that Angus is going to be all right, I'm going to my cottage on the south face of Ben Nevis.

"Actually, my cabin would make a good base camp for your surveying work. It's well situated, and has quite a bit of room, plus good sheds for stabling horses and gear. I was going to offer it to you to use, but I don't suppose you want my help at all now."

"That depends." Robert withheld an outright acceptance.

"If you are worried about the proprieties, I can bring Dorcas with me."

"I have other plans," he said. The prospect of a month or longer confinement in a cabin at day's end with Cassandra's abigail in attendance appealed to him about as much as taking a dead fall off Arthur's Drop or having a healthy tooth pulled.

He still said nothing more, refusing to commit to her offer until he conferred with Alex, but he was not adverse to a momentary fantasy of having it all for once in his life—domestic tranquillity, a beautiful woman warming his bed each night, ample and adequate food each and every day, and good friends to talk away the evening hours.

The temptation kept him silent when he should have stoutly refused her giddy plan outright. "You look tired," she said. "When we reach the cove, you should lie down and try to get some sleep." Small, frosty puffs of air escaped from her nose and mouth as she spoke. If he wanted to sleep, she would make good her escape from Castle MacArthur.

Robert looked for signs of exhaustion in her face, and for the life of him, he couldn't see any at all. That made him realize how very much like him she actually was. She thrived on the outdoor life. What, pray God, was he going to do with her?

Short of throwing the blasted woman over his shoulder, and carting her back to the castle like a hunting kill, Robert wasn't going to get her to return home as she should.

The truth was, he didn't want to be rid of her. He was at cross-purposes, certain that Cassandra's parents' plans for her were what should be, but unwilling to make himself do what was necessary. How could he, when he already loved her so deeply the thought of parting from her forever hurt grievously?

He tramped on in silence, the weighty pack on his back unnoticed save for the slight tilt of his shoulders accommodating to bear it, while his mind continued to struggle with what he ought to do and what he wanted to do. He ought to return her to her parents. He wanted to roll her onto her back in the nearest pine grove and make love to her till they were both finally sated.

They rounded the turn and the cove appeared on their left, a pine-filled level gouge in the rock of the mountain. Just beyond it the road divided into two paths and a cairn of rock at the fork held a worn, faded signpost. North was Caul, south Oban by fifty miles. "Who put that sign there?"

"Why? It's right. Caul is north, Oban, south." Cassie pointed.

"The distance can't be right. Alex and I measured the western shore of Loch Linnhe last fall." He pointed at the long lake in front of them, which stretched as far as their eyes could see. "I'm fair certain the mark is off by five or six miles."

Cassie shrugged. "Five or six miles doesn't make much difference in these parts. Excuse me, but this is a good point for me to take a trip to the woods."

"Aye." Robert glanced at the iced-over pines and oaks, whose limbs nearly touched the snow beneath them. He could glance back and forth and see both ends of the box canyon. It wasn't likely she'd disappear on him now. "Take Shep with you and dinna go far."

"Would it matter to you if I dinna come back?"

Robert paused, his eyes holding hers for the longest time before he nodded and said, "Aye, it would matter a great deal. Don't run away from me, Cassie. If you stand your ground with me, we may be able to work this out for the best for both of us."

"Well, now, there's a question. Just what do you see as the best, Robert? Me married to Douglas the Darling, laird of clan Cameron? You, off wandering and measuring every inch of Scotland for the next thirty years?''

His pencil didn't move on the paper. He lifted his eyes and regarded her as though he were looking over a pair of spectacles on his nose. It was a penetrating look nonetheless. ''Together, if at all possible, but don't push me to act recklessly, Cassandra. I don't take unnecessary chances. Nor was I in any position to make demands to your father back there in his study. Had I done so, I'd be cooling my heels in his dungeon this minute and ye know it. I've got enough on my mind knowing I've compromised you and the consequences that may stem from that. Many a Highland maiden has gotten with child the very night of her wedding to a Gordon man.''

Cassie's head swiveled to a tilt and her eyes narrowed. ''I ken that,'' she said, sputtering. But she hadn't thought about it. Not *really* thought about it. ''A baby...do you think it possible, Robert?''

''For both our sakes this very moment, I pray not. That is why, all things considered, you should never have come after me.''

''Because you wouldn't want the baby?'' Cassie had to run this through to the end, to know his true intentions.

''Nay, of course I would want it, boy or girl. I dinna want to make a baby. There is a difference, Cassie. Do ye ken?''

''Not exactly.'' She frowned.

''Go do what you need to do. Don't stand there giving me puppy-dog looks that make me want to hold and kiss you till I go blind with passion. I'm trying to stick to what needs be done, and you're distracting me.''

"Why don't you just say you don't want me?''

"Because I *do* want you. I can't look at you and not want you. So I'm exercising self-control for both of us, because you don't have any.''

"Why don't you just go ahead and say I'm wrong for leaving the MacArthur's house?''

"He isn't 'the MacArthur' to you, Cassie. He's your father, and you owe him respect and love and obedience to his will. As far as I can see it, he's been trying to do what is right for you. If you were my wife, I wouldn't allow you to walk out of my house every time you felt like doing so to spite me. That's a childish game, one that you should have outgrown before you reached the age of ten.''

"You don't know why I do anything. Until you've walked longer than a couple of days in my shoes, you shouldn't be judging me. I'm not judging you.''

"You were when we first met, and don't say you weren't now. You moved past the blanket hatred of clan disagreements and even war and your Alastair's death. Don't you think your father deserves the same consideration from you?''

"I do try to understand him, but he's impossible.''

"You have to talk to each other, Cassie. Have you even asked him why he wants to marry you to Cameron?''

"No. It'd be like trying to talk to a stone fence and getting just as much response.''

"Well, there is a reason he made that decision. And it'll take an even better reason to change his mind.''

"I'll think about that." Cassie nodded, contemplative for a change. She excused herself and slipped into the woods.

Robert let out a long, frosty breath, amazed that she'd stood her ground and not bolted over his honest criticism. Before the frosty vapor faded, he looked up at the heavy clouds in the sky. The worst of the storm was over, the sky clearing to the north. No hint of the moon showed, but the white snow alleviated the darkness in a way.

He found he could not see any sign of the hidden valley from this juncture in the road. Ben Nevis appeared to have simply folded on its base and obliterated the generous glen Robert knew was behind him. All he saw in the distance was a generous skirt of magnificent pines. No wonder they called it Achanshiel, the hidden glen.

Cassie and her dog emerged from the wood two hundred yards ahead of him. She crouched down conspicuously in a ditch covered by iced undergrowth, furiously waving her arm at him and signaling he should be quiet. Concerned, Robert hurried to her. As he came close enough to her, he saw she had her hand on her dog's mouth, muzzling it.

"What's wrong?" Robert whispered, ducking nearly as low as she did, his sharp eyes searching for trouble in the copse of trees.

"Reivers—cattle thieves," she whispered, jabbing her thumb behind her shoulder, pointing at the stand of woods. "They've got a lot of cattle and hostages tied up. I think I saw Alex...and Dorcas, tied up to trees."

"Dorcas?" Robert mouthed, shocked. Cassie's face was pale as a ghost's. Shep growled and whined, wanting to break free.

"Wait here." Robert shed his pack, setting it on the crackling bracken. "How many are there?"

"Five, six sleeping. One awake standing watch."

"And your father's men?"

"Six, seven with Angus. Gagged and tied to trees."

"Good lass." Robert concluded their hushed conversation. "Stay here, and keep that dog quiet!"

Cassie nodded, knowing the urgency. She practically sat on Shep to keep the spirited pup still as Robert disappeared into the shroud of woods. A job that was, too, keeping Shep from escaping her grip and barking his fool head off. The struggle so absorbed Cassie that she almost didn't hear the blood-curdling battle cry and the first clash of steel as swords met.

There was no point holding the dog back. "Go on then." Cassie released Shep, and he scrambled out of her arms, slipping on the ice. As she stood, he took off, not into the woods to help Robert by biting the throats out of a couple of bandits, but racing down the road back to Achanshiel, barking his fool head off.

"Why ye damned coward!" Cassie spit after him, blaming herself for picking the worst pup in the litter.

Two awful screams and a woman's shriek echoing out of the cove took her mind off Shep's defection. She turned to run to help Robert, drawing her own dirk from its sheath, when a pack of barking dogs rounded the bend at full gallop. Her father's baying bloodhounds headed the pack.

''Jesu Maria!'' Cassie knew with a certainty that behind those dogs with the scent of her boots in their noses would be her father and all of his henchmen, riding hell-for-leather.

She waited until the pack spied her. Shep yapped in recognition, running so close to the lead dogs, the bloodhounds nearly trampled him. Cassie whirled about, her cloak flying behind her as she led them all to the scene of the battle in the clearing.

Soon the sounds of battle were accompanied by the thunder of horses' hooves. Cassie didn't know how many riders there were, but she ran straight ahead, closer to the din of grunting men waging a fearful battle. If she didn't get up in a tree before the dogs and horses reached her, she'd be torn to bits when the pack brought her to ground.

She spied an oak, away from where any of her father's men were tied, and shinnied up in it, slipping as she scrambled desperately on its iced-over limbs to get high enough before the dogs skidded into the clearing.

The sound of their arrival brought an almost instant halt to the combat, as wary reivers turned to find the intrusion. Robert ran a reiver through when he dropped his guard. The man howled and fell on four other fallen bodies, his sword clanging on their steel weapons.

To Cassie's horror, the pack did not gather in a howling, salivating cluster at the base of the tree where she held a precariously slippery grip. A half dozen dogs shot by, intent upon a different quarry than her—Robert Gordon.

"Robert!" Cassie screamed. "Mind the dogs! They're on your scent!"

The advent of the dogs turned the battle against Robert. Outnumbered four to one, he fought for his life, hacking at his attackers as dogs swarmed around them. The dog pack now grew maddened as they trampled over fallen bodies. The sword play ended abruptly. Any man who smelled of spilt blood and made the mistake of moving, became an object of animal attack.

Only Robert had the sense to put down his sword and stand still as Shep skidded to his feet, barking joyously in recognition.

"Hold yer weapons!" MacArthur roared, descending from his mount with his sword drawn. "Round everyone up!"

Another clansman called back the dogs. More Mac-Arthur riders swarmed through every opening in the trees, chasing beleaguered reivers to ground, and cutting loose the hostages. The disturbed trees shed huge clots of snow, burying anyone stupid enough to stand under a canopy.

Cassie's hold failed on her icy branch. The weighted branch tipped, then broke in two and shattered. She fell, landing with thudding impact on her backside, showered by a pelting of snow, ice and broken twigs. The frozen ground stung. It was a minute before she could sit up. When she did, a pair of scarred, grizzled knees and a badger sporran were at her eye level.

"And should I wonder where you'd got off to, lass?" Her father reached down, grasped her arm and hauled her up to her feet. His touch wasn't gentle as he jerked her around, thrusting her into the middle of the melee as he sorted out his men from the attackers.

All of his stout and sturdy climbers he'd sent into the hills to bring Angus safely home wore sheepish faces as they accounted for themselves to the laird.

"All went well, milord," his head man explained, "till we came down the road past the cove here. Four of us were carrying Angus on a litter. The reivers came out of the woods like hornets."

"You let them ambush you?"

"Aye, they did. Came at us from both in front and behind, right opposite the cairn. We never expected it on our own land."

Another spoke up to say, "Young Hamilton fought like a bloody demon, MacArthur. He's a good man to have at your back."

"How many of you are hurt?"

"Dorcas put us to rights afore they tied her up, too. We'll live. Who is that madman that came in here alone and took them all on? He was a bonny sight for sore eyes. Made his sword sing, MacArthur," a kinsman proclaimed.

"I thought he'd be hacked to pieces until ye arrived and saved the day. God bless ye, MacArthur," said another.

Cassie tried to see past the henchmen to find Robert. She couldn't wiggle out of her father's grip to save her soul. It wasn't until MacArthur got around to Angus that Cassie learned her gillie had held his own through the initial confrontation. "I stabbed one of them bastards with my dagger afore they'd tied me up."

"What about your heart?" Cassie asked him, kneeling beside him on the ground.

"Och, wasn't my heart at all, lass. 'Twas a stroke, I fear. But it hasna killed me yet." His proof for that was in the movement of his unaffected right arm.

Dorcas had held up nearly as well as Angus. Other than being exhausted and dirtier than Cassie had ever seen her, she had taken the reivers' attack in stride, as any Highland woman would.

"Och, reivers aren't after blood," she told Cassie before she moved off to bandage up someone else. "They come for cattle to feed their own families mostly."

MacArthur finished Dorcas's thoughts for Cassie's understanding. "Occasionally for booty, horses and the unwary traveler. I'll sort this lot out up at the castle."

Cassie didn't bother to remind him their own kinsman raided—at least the young ones did. He knew that as well as she.

Cassie decided it was perversity on her father's part that made him wait to confront Robert last. She still hadn't laid eyes on Robert since he'd dropped the point of his sword. That worried her terribly.

As the cluster around her father dissipated, she spied both Robert and Alex sitting side by side on a broken tree stump. Dorcas was tending Alex, gently binding his left leg in strips of cloth torn from her own petticoat.

"MacArthur." Cassie dug her own fingers under the viselike clamp of her father's grip on her upper arm. "Let go! Dorcas needs help tending the mapmakers' wounds."

MacArthur's head swiveled halfway round to her, and he growled through his teeth with a vehemence that scared her. "You are not leaving my side for any reason, do you hear?"

"You're crushing my arm."

"Aye, and I'll crush more than that, lass. I'm fed up to my eyeteeth with yer running every time my back is turned. Cross me if ye dare. I'll take a strap to ye, here afore God and all his people. Interrupt me in my work again, and I'll beat ye just for the pleasure of skelping the devils out of ye. Shut up and be still!"

Which was exactly what Cassie did from that point on, since MacArthur's roar in her ear had brought every seated man, even the prisoners, to their feet.

Robert remained grimly silent. MacArthur swaggered his way. Cassie followed like a rowboat in tow behind a sailing ship.

"Gordon, it appears I'm indebted to you again. I don't like it now any more than I liked it earlier. From what my men tell me, if it wasn't for your friend there, Hamilton, and you, seven of my kinsmen and a woman would be lying here with their throats slit come sunrise. Thank you, both of you. Lochaber is yours to measure and all of my kin will aid your endeavor as best we can."

That news caused Cassie to jerk forward because she impulsively wanted to hug Robert. She got yanked back to her place at MacArthur's side before she'd taken a full step forward. She didn't say anything though.

MacArthur cleared his throat roughly. "My house is open to ye both from this day forward, and I'll provide ye the best guides I have, but not my youngest daughter!"

Robert and Alex looked at each other, then back to MacArthur and grinned. Robert whipped his hair out of his eyes with a toss of his head and extended his hand. "Thank you, sir. Not even the king could ask for more."

"Aye, well, the meddling fool did. But I'll take that up with him when next I see him. The two of you see about checking your horses and your kit. We'll be going back to the castle anon."

Cassie was at once relieved and irked. Her father had no right to keep hauling her about like a rag doll or to treat her with so little respect. Did she have to slay four bandits like Robert had to earn MacArthur's admiration?

She knew Robert couldn't ever free her from her father's controlling hold, so she didn't really blame him for not trying. Oh, she did blame him in a way, but she knew she was asking for the moon.

There were only two of them and her father had ridden out with no less than twenty of his strongest henchmen. Cassie certainly didn't want to see Robert hacked to pieces. So she desisted from further attempts to gain her release, even on the short, silent tandem ride back to the hidden valley.

Her compliance ended when her father did not let

go of her arm on entering his great hall. MacArthur's intent to keep her separated from Robert became absolutely clear at about the fourth flight of stairs to the castle's ramparts.

Even then, Cassie only feared MacArthur was marching her back to the scene of her and Robert's lovemaking. Had there been a witness? Had she left telltale evidence behind that she'd given away her virginity? Blood, a piece of clothing of hers?

Soon, however, MacArthur's purpose became absolutely clear, when his harried steward fumbled with a ring of keys, trying to open the lock on the south tower door. Too late she realized she'd made the biggest mistake of her life in not fighting for her freedom the moment MacArthur had laid his hand on her. Cassie began to fight for all she was worth.

Her mother and the rest of the castle that crowded in their wake appeared ignorant of MacArthur's true purpose. Cassie knew his purpose. The sorry cretin was going to lock her in his bloody tower.

He slammed the iron grate at the very top of the tower stairs shut in her face, slid the bolt in the stone wall and put the lock on with his own hands, then tossed the iron key out the arrow slit, right in front of her eyes. Cassie clutched the heavy iron bars, shaking the gate, not that it budged an inch with her puny strength.

"I'll never forgive you for this!" Cassie yelled in his face.

He stood opposite her on the very top step, breathing hard as he raked his fingers through his hair and wiped his sweat off with his hand. "Talk to me about forgiveness some day in the future, when yer own flesh and blood, that ye've loved from the day they were born, betrays ye. Until then, we've nothing to talk about."

He turned around and glared at the crowd pressing closer to see what he would do. His booming voice scattered them in a panic of retreat. "Get out of my way, every one of ye!"

Only Cassie's mother stood her ground. She refused to budge as he came down to the same riser as she. MacArthur didn't say a word to explain himself. He did offer Lady MacArthur his arm.

"You will come down with me to the hall, wife."

It wasn't a request, it was a command. Instead of socking him in the jaw and sending him tumbling down 102 stone steps, as Cassie would have done, her mother put her hand where MacArthur expected it to be put and accompanied him down the steps without a backward glance at Cassie.

If they said anything to each other, Cassie couldn't hear it for the clatter of hundreds of shoes filling the cold tower with deafening sound.

Cassie slid to the stone floor, staring at the dark, gloomy cell, which was no more than ten feet across from wall to wall. When the sun rose she was able to see that it was furnished with a minute wardrobe-commode, a cot, a table and a stool.

A cupola roof topped it, which had exposed rafters and beams six feet above her reach, even when she stood on the stool stacked on the table. Four orb-and-cross windows were cut into the stones in each of the cardinal directions, north, south, east and west, just as in the three other towers in the castle.

Cassie could see out those windows to the hills beyond Loch Linne and up to Ben Nevis's crest. Crossed iron bars cemented inside the orb and the narrow cross below it prevented her from reaching out any farther than her elbow. There was no escape.

Shortly after sunup a steady procession of lone, red-faced servants began making pilgrimages to the top of the tower, stopping at the iron gate to heave and catch their breath. Once they had recovered from the climb, each lone servant would begin to push through the long narrow rectangle at the bottom of the heavy gate whatever it was her mother had ordered delivered to her.

First it was blankets, linens, a narrow feather mattress, enough changes of clothes for Cassie to wear a different gown for a sennight. Water was brought to her and the large bucket sat on the topmost step outside the gate. She had to dip out what she needed to fill her own pitcher, basin and ewer inside the gate. That made her come out of her deep silence to ask the water boy, "Am I going to have to spoon out the waste water and garbage the same way, one scoop at a time?"

"Och, no, milady." The boy tugged at his cap. "There's a drain right there in the center of the room. Ye can lift the small grate aside with a spoon or such and simply pour it away. It goes out to the river just like in the castle proper."

"How clever," Cassie said dryly. "All the comforts of home."

"Save for a fire, Lady Cassandra, but I heard they were working on something, a brazier maybe."

Grand, Cassie thought. *I'm in here for life.*

Chapter Sixteen

Toward dusk, Robert made the long climb to the top of the south tower. The guards at the door on the rampart did not ask him to surrender either his sword or his dirk, which he found odd, so he asked about it.

"There's no need, sir," the stouter of the two said. "I hardly think you're going to harm milady, and MacArthur threw the key to the top gate out the window. You can't possibly aid an escape. You may leave them with us if you like. A sword gets in the way on them steps."

Which gave Robert much to think about as he climbed up, up, up and up more stone steps. There were so many he made three full revolutions before he reached the top. And he'd banged the tip of his sword's sheath on the stones and his shins more times than he cared to count.

He set his lantern on an iron hook in the wall after holding it up for the light to shine through the bars into the dark chamber at the top. Cassie lay with her back to him on a cot, her fine fur cloak tucked up to her chin. A soft audible cadence to her breathing told him she was asleep. He moved a nearly empty water bucket down to a lower riser and settled to the step and took out his pocketbook and pencil.

The light was ample for him to make a drawing of the layout of her prison and a more detailed one of the lock and bolt keeping the gate shut. He wondered if MacArthur had really thrown the key away, or if he'd just palmed it in his hand. The only orb-and-cross window right here at the landing faced the inner ward. To be sure, Robert took out his compass and checked. His drawing finished, he stood and checked the hinges on the opposite side of the gate. Then he spread his arms across the iron bars, gripped them and gave them a sound shake, looking for signs of plaster or mortar drizzling out the hinge sockets.

They were solid, with no appreciable rust or limestone disintegration. They appeared to be deeply set and bolted on the opposite side of the stone jamb.

"Robert?" Cassie sat up on her cot, facing him. "Is that you?"

"Aye, sleepyhead. 'Tis about time you woke up. I've listened to you snore a good hour."

"Gads." Cassie bounded to her feet and ran to him, pressing her whole body against the iron bars, her arms clutching his shoulders and her face pressed as far as she could push it out the square nearest her head. It was far enough for a kiss, which Robert gladly initiated. Then he held her back at his arms' length, looking her over from head to toe for bruises or cuts that would have given him reason to go after

MacArthur with no holds barred. "Do you have the key?"

"No. Should I have?" Robert let go of her arms and let her come back to the bars. "You'd better fetch your cloak, Cass. You can't stand here in a nightrail freezing to death."

"Kiss me again, then I'll get it, I promise."

He couldn't resist doing just that—or holding her even with the damned bars between them until a shiver from a draft rising up the tower shaft made gooseflesh break out across her shoulders.

"The cloak, Cass." Robert pushed her back, and she went to get the cloak. She brought a fur rug along with it, spreading the rug on the floor before she sat down wrapped in the warm cloak.

Robert settled opposite her, his face serious to Cassie's eyes. "Did he hurt ye, Cassie?"

"Aye, he's killed me putting me up here. I canna believe it, even when I open my eyes and see this anew. I'll die locked up. I canna stand it. When I haven't been shivering, cursing or praying, I've slept." She put her chin on her knees and wrapped her arms around the limbs. "And you?"

"I slept a lot, too. Fighting and chasing after quick-footed women kind of wears a man down."

Cassie laughed briefly, then she grew as solemn as he and her smile faded. "Robert, we're going to have to talk about this Quickfoot business, but for the now I've got more important things on my mind. I've got to find some way to get out of here. MacArthur threw away the key...."

"Who did, Cass?"

"Look, Robert, I'm mad at him right now. I'm no' going to call that man 'Father.' I'd choke on the word. Can you bring a file or a saw of some kind? These bars are thick, but there has to be a way to cut them or to break the lock."

"I know you're angry. Everybody in the castle knows you're angry, but somebody has been sending an awful lot of stuff up here so you won't suffer unduly or lack for things to do to occupy your mind and your time. I see books on your table, and you're sitting on a bearskin rug. Looks like you had ample food to eat judging from the tray of empty dishes to the side of your feet."

"My mother sent all of this up here."

"Maybe, but somebody else is allowing her to do that." Robert wrapped his hand around the inch-square iron bars. "This looks pretty stout and sturdy. It isn't that old, either, and it's been kept well oiled. I'm certain I can bring you a file, but you'd still be filing away at the same bar six months from now."

"Six months?" Cassie wrapped her fingers next to his. "Oh, Robert, can't you get me out of here, somehow?"

"I will try, but without that key..." He looked pretty defeated before he'd even tried. Cassie's disappointment couldn't be contained. Her arms rose to hide her face as she bent her head and cried. "Do you think maybe he has another somewhere?" Robert asked.

"The steward has all the keys...." Cassie lifted her head, and wiped the tears coursing down her cheeks on the sleeve of her nightrail. As she did that, Robert could tell that this wasn't the first time she'd cried this day. "I'm so lonely up here, Robert."

"But you're used to being alone in the hills, aren't you, Cass? Leaving here when the people bother you and going off wherever you like."

"That's different. Then, I have my freedom. I can come down when I want, talk to anyone I want to or no one if I don't want. I'll die here, Robert. I know I will."

He caught her hand and held it. "You mustn't give up, Cassie. Look, I've come to see you and I'll be back again, I promise you that."

"Aye, I believe you will, though I can't believe you're really here and MacArthur allowed you to come up."

"Anyone can come up. There's no list of forbidden visitors tacked to the guards' door on the rampart. Alex told me his leg would be fit to give the stairs a try in the morning. He's found a present for you. We've all been pretty tired today so you'll have to excuse us for letting you languish all alone up here. Come here. If you turn about one quarter turn, I believe I can put my arm around you. I have something important to tell you."

Cassie scooted as close to the gate as she could, turning so that their shoulders almost touched. He was right, he could reach through the grate and embrace her shoulders. If they each tipped their heads just so, their brows could touch as well. Cassie threaded her right hand through the bars and clasped his other hand. "Tell me what is important?"

"I spoke to your father about marrying you."

Cassie sighed. "What did he say? No?"

"Not exactly."

"What do you mean, 'not exactly'?" A worried frown creased Cassie's brow.

"He said he is most concerned about your future." Robert gave her the bald truth.

"That's what he always says." Cassie exhaled a sigh.

"Aye, then he asked about my future, how long this mapmaking was going to be the only thing I thought about. First, I told him that wasn't true. Yes, I'm a wandering vagabond now, but not without direction. I have set out to accomplish a certain goal. I do have a home, a very nice home, as splendid as this castle, albeit on a bit smaller scale. Strathspey only has four floors and a cellar in it and no towers to lock up errant daughters in because I didn't have any daughters to lock up."

"You didn't tell him that."

"Oh, I did. He laughed over it. I didn't get the impression that he's angry at you, Cassie. I came away thinking he was worried sick about you."

"That's ridiculous. MacArthur's never been sick a day in his life." Cassie snorted.

"Maybe so, but he keeps a physician on retainer for someone and I don't think it's all for Angus. That rascal was limping about the hall this afternoon as if yesterday never happened."

"That's Angus, at death's door one day, ready to hunt badgers the next. It's baffling." Cassie shook her head, then put it right back where it had been, touching Robert's brow. "He never did give you a straight answer yes or no, did he?"

"Who? Angus?"

"MacArthur! Robert, stop pretending you don't know who I mean just to get me to say what I don't want to say. It isn't fair. I'm the prisoner here."

"It takes more than stone and iron to make a prison," Robert said earnestly. "Your freedom's here, Cassie—" he touched her breast "—in your heart and the way you've chosen to love. I admire that, Lady Quickfoot. Dinna despair."

"That's beautiful. How did you become so wise?"

"I dinna know that I am, but it's important now. Remember it, Cassie. I'll be moving on tomorrow after I visit you. Alex and I have to get some work done while the weather is good."

"Well, for now—" Cassie stood up, stretching her back and rubbing her bottom, which couldn't take a lot of sitting on the cold stone flagstones "—I'll be here."

Robert chuckled at her cheerful response. "I'll be back," he promised as he reached in and pulled her up to the bars. "Why the grimace when you rub your bottom? You said your father didn't harm you."

"You probably didn't notice, since you were occupied keeping four or five reivers from cutting you to pieces, but I thought the dogs were chasing me and climbed an oak tree to keep from getting mauled. The limb was slippery and covered with ice. It—"

"Broke," Robert finished for her.

"Exactly." Cassie reached for his shoulders and

pulled him to her. "I've gotten stiff is all. It'll be better tomorrow."

Robert changed his arms to the lower slot, so that he could hold her bottom while he kissed her. Cassie didn't want that kiss to stop so he lingered, taking a long, heady kiss from her that would carry him through till dawn.

Robert and Alex Hamilton came to visit Cassie at the crack of dawn the very next morning. Each carried a bulging cloth sack, which immediately made Cassie think of masons' tools, sledges, chisels and hammers. Poor Alex looked pretty forlorn standing there, his mouth open, staring at the size and formidable strength of the iron door.

Cassie put down her hairbrush and tied her robe at her waist before getting up and coming to greet them properly at the gate. For Alex, that meant her hand pressed through the bars to hold his ever so briefly, just long enough for a brief, courtly bow and the barest touch of his lips to the back of her hand. Robert received a heartfelt hug and a happy kiss.

There wasn't room for them both to sit on the same step so they stood and visited, but after a while, Cassie brought her stool over and held court seated on a soft cushion, listening to their plans for the days ahead.

The sky, they informed her, was going to be perfect all day, just as it had been the day before. They hoped to measure Ben Nevis's elevation from its sea-level base on Loch Linnhe to the summit. Cassie inquired who their guide was and nodded approvingly when she was told which of her father's men had been selected for the honor. "It won't be the same without me leading you, but Jacob will probably acquit himself well. You'll probably make good progress, having more bearers going with you to carry your tools. That will keep your strength in reserve.

"You will mind the snow, won't you, Robert? The sun sometimes causes avalanches and they can be deadly. There's no way to tell when a pack will break free and slide down on top of you."

"We will most certainly be careful, Cassie, and yes, you will be missed. Alex, you had a favor to request of Cassie." Robert turned the floor over to his friend.

Alex held up his sack. "These…this is something I found in Chattering Otters Cave, sort of adopted, I suppose. Would you care for it while I'm gone? Who knows when we'll really get back?"

He extended the sack through the bars, and whatever was inside it, moved. "Not a snake, I hope." Cassie wasn't certain she wanted to take the sack.

"No, definitely not a snake." Alex brought his other hand inside the bars as well, and opened the rope at the top of the sack, holding it open so Cassie could look inside the dark interior.

"My, it is definitely not the hammer and chisel I prayed all night for." She reached inside and drew out the small ball of fluffy fur. At first, she didn't know exactly what the sleepy animal was, then she figured out its markings. "An otter! Where did you find it, Alex? How did its mother let you take it?"

"She had an altercation with another resident of

the cave—a wild cat. I saved the kits from becoming dinner, but was too late to be of any service to the mother or the rest of the family.''

Cassie cradled the small creature in her hands. She could cover it completely with her two hands cupped. ''What do I do for milk or food for it? What does it eat? I haven't the foggiest idea what to do for that.''

''They like any kind of milk—goat, cow, sheep. I specifically asked that Cook send you plenty for them. I'll show you how to feed them after you meet the others. When they're bigger they'll eat bits of fish and crabs, things like that.''

''Others?'' Cassie crooked a brow, looking at Robert's sack dubiously. That bag was definitely more active, hinting that there was a sibling war going on inside. Robert passed the sack in to her and Cassie sat down to see how many animal orphans Alex expected her to look after. Three, it seemed, all total. Cassie turned the sack over, and the knot of animals slid onto her lap. They were sucking each other's toes and squeaking loudly.

''Hear that? They're chattering. Aren't they cute?''

''Cute, aye, but I don't know about this. I've never tried to raise an animal infant, let alone three of them.''

''I'm sure you'll get along just fine.'' Robert reached into her lap and picked out one of the toe-sucking fur balls. He asked Alex for one of the wet rags of milk he'd brought with him. Alex produced that from inside his sporran, along with several others. ''I even learned how to feed the greedy little mites last night in self-defense. They'll chat all night and keep you awake to boot. We took turns after we got the method down pat.''

He folded the rag and made a point out of it, then squeezed a drop of white fluid against the struggling baby's nose and mouth. It caught on to what was going on quickly. Alex waited for Cassie to hand him a kit, giving her a sopping rag in exchange and he soon had his kit suckling as if there were no tomorrow where this food came from. Cassie took a little longer to get the hang of it.

"Amazing," she said.

"That's all there is to it," Alex assured her. "They sleep in the sack and do that most of the day. They do get a bit more active at night, but so long as you've got milk to feed them, they're no trouble at all. I reckon they could be lapping milk from a bowl in a week or thereabouts.''

"Speaking of animals, have either of you seen Shep?''

"I thought I'd take him with us," Robert suggested. "That is, if you don't mind.''

"You may as well. I won't be able to train him or give him any attention.''

"Cassie." Robert's gaze was intense when she met it. "In all likelihood, we may be gone longer than a couple of days. You won't fall apart or turn into a madwoman here, will you?''

"Probably." Cassie nodded, half joking, half serious. She didn't know yet how much of this she could take. "Do what you need to do. Don't think about me.''

"I canna do that." Robert grinned, the most wistful

look ever in his eyes. His kit let go of the rag and yawned, curling up into a ball in the cup of his hand.

"This certainly gives me something to do." Cassie gathered his kit with hers and Alex's and tucked them all back into the sack on her lap. Alex took a short walk down a few risers to give her and Robert privacy.

He held her and caressed her, driving her mad with revived desire. As difficult as it was, Cassie told him to go before the sun rose any higher.

Robert hesitated a moment longer then stepped away from the iron bars. He opened his doublet and withdrew a narrow package. Cassie's eyes grew wide with surprise as he unwound the clothbound package and exposed its contents—a chisel, a short-handled hammer and a diagram.

"Here's something to keep you busy until I return on the tenth of April. Wait for me, Cassie. I will come for you. Sooner if I can. Read my directions first."

Chapter Seventeen

Hamilton's otters were fat, frisky creatures, who scooted at will up and down the tower steps, before any change in Cassandra's status ever became so much as a rumor at Castle MacArthur. The three rascals, as Cassie thought of them, woke her every day by starting a fight over who was going to sleep first in their nest of splintery wood chips.

The woodpile had once been her three-legged stool. She had sacrificed the stool rather than allowing them free rein with the balance of the few and simple furnishings of her cell. Their food, which now consisted almost entirely of fish, was kept in a bowl several steps down the stairs. The smell of fresh fish first thing in the morning had been making Cassie sick for quite some time.

The new placement of their ready food supply turned out to be all right with the otters. They preferred finding their own food now. It was quite a sight for Cassie to see them leave each night by hitching a ride in the water boy's empty bucket.

They were water creatures, and Cassie had insisted they know where their natural home was from the start. The boy was agreeable, even if it did mean an extra trip up the long flights of steps to bring them back from their wee frolic in the cold stream behind the castle to MacArthur's loch.

When it had become time she deemed they should be learning to hunt their own food, the boy brought her minnows in a bucket. Hamilton's otters fished most unsuccessfully. That is, until the bucket tipped over with all three of them on the same side. The mess was as appalling as it was hilarious, with minnows flopping here and yon and young otters chasing them all over her floor. The otters pounced upon the fish and toyed with them in much the same manner kittens learned from their mother to catch mice. Two nights of that sort of entertainment were enough for Cassie. Thereafter, they went down to the loch for a swim and a hunt.

The first time they did not come back with the boy, she worried the whole night through. She found the water boy was worried too; he stayed by the loch late into the night, calling them and waiting for them, to no avail.

They returned at daybreak, racing one another up the steps. They also raised havoc for an hour afterward over their happiness to find her and their familiar nest before they settled to sleep away the entire day.

Awakened as usual by their commotion, Cassie rolled upright on her cot, pausing a moment to test the stability of her stomach. This damp spring morning all seemed to be well.

Cassie scooped up the first noisy cellmate she could reach, holding it by the scruff of its sleek, dark brown silky coat. "Tsk, tsk, tsk, when are you boys going to learn to come and go without all this fuss? Ye make more racket than would a whole nest full of bantling owls."

The fat young otter twisted around her hand and forearm and clung to it, scolding her for all it was worth. Its two brothers scrambled up Cassie's nightrail to her shoulders and began playing and nibbling on her hair.

When they tired of the game, they were off to run the racecourse made by her few clothes hanging on a rack of wood pegs set high on the wall. Try as she might, Cassie could not help laughing at the wee creatures, even when all they did was wind up tumbling all of her clothes to the floor.

As she shook out the last gown and hung it up again, she heard footsteps on the tower steps—the water boy coming with her morning ration of water. Before he had her bucket on the stoop filled, Hamilton's otters each clung to a perch on the iron gate, curiously watching the splashing water, anticipating an extra swim that the water boy prevented by setting a wooden lid on the top of the bucket.

"There is news, milady," the boy said, scattering a handful of nutmeats from his pocket on the top step for the otters.

"Aye, what news?" Cassie asked, pausing as she brushed otter tangles from her hair.

"There's talk about the second reading of yer marriage banns at the kirk. All of us in the castle thought ye set to wed the Gordon that saved yer life, but the minister says it's Douglas Cameron ye'll wed come Beltane. Is that true, milady?"

"Och, well, I believe MacArthur thinks I will." Cassie staunchly refused to go into that with a boy.

"I dinna believe it, but…Cameron is here. He came roaring in hungry last eve. I hear tell he and MacArthur had strong words last night."

"Aye, what words?" Cassie asked, setting down the brush and listening carefully, all the while taking up her flint and stone to light her candle wick. As few visitors as she had, she pleaded for information.

"The baker's boy told me he heard the steward tell Cook it was no one's business that the lairds argued over ye being here in the tower. Cameron said it wasn't right t' lock ye up here. Like ye were some wee bird in a cage. The baker said Cameron told yer da he should ha' skelped ye and ha' done with it."

Cassie shook her head wryly. The minute Douglas did something to redeem himself, he managed to ruin it.

"They say Cameron and MacArthur will be coming up t' see ye afore they ride t' hunt boars."

"How appropriate for them." Cassie laughed and caught an otter just as it headed south with her slipper to gnaw another hole through it.

After a few more inane tidbits of castle gossip, the boy departed, and Cassie completed her morning ablutions. She considered her sparse wardrobe and chose her green worsted gown. It fit her best, and tying the laces of the weskit that went with it was easiest. That snug-fitting outer garment lessened the ache in her perpetually sore breasts more than any chemise, stomacher or gown she had hanging on the pegs could have done.

Then she sat with the morning sun falling through the eastern cross and orb onto her table, the end of her cot her only available seat. She sharpened a quill, dipped it in the inkstand and began the laborious work of penning another Lady Quickfoot story for her niece and nephews.

Maggie was due to visit, as the MacGregors would all be coming to spend Easter at the castle. Euan MacGregor was another who stood against her father's harsh decision to keep Cassie contained in his tower prison. According to her sister, Euan and MacArthur had nearly come to blows on their visit a month ago, on the occasion of Cassie's birthday. Yesterday was Palm Sunday. She prayed Robert returned no later than Holy Monday, a week hence, April 10, for her wedding to Cameron could happen any day after the third posting of the banns.

Of Robert Gordon, Cassie had heard only that the weather had cleared the day the mapmakers rode out of Achanshiel. Both Angus and young Jacob Innes accompanied them to act as their guides. A good half dozen other MacArthur kinsmen had voluntarily enlisted to assist in completing the king's commission.

She suspected that there was more news, but none of the servants she saw on a regular basis knew any to tell her. She saw her parents infrequently. The trek to her airy abode was difficult for her mother.

Cassie had her days mapped out perfectly and stayed very busy. In the beginning she had stood on her lone table top and worked with frantic determination on removing those two cut blocks of stone from the east-facing cross-and-orb windows. Robert had been absolutely right. Once the mortar was gently chipped away, the stones slid out of their housing, like a hand easing from a well-made glove.

The iron cross bars that had prevented pressing her arm farther out the window than her elbow had remained fitted in the stones. But it had only taken a bit of determined pushing and pulling on each stone she was removing to fracture their topmost seat and slide them from their housing as well.

She could—if she had wanted to at any time in the past three weeks—have escaped from this odious prison. She had decided to wait for Robert. Beltane was almost three full weeks away yet. Cameron's presence at the castle did not worry her unduly, since no marriage could be performed in their chapel until the banns had been read three times.

So she sat at her table entertaining herself, writing down yet another of the Lady Quickfoot stories for her siblings to read to their children. She also awaited the arrival of these visitors she was to have today.

MacArthur she always recognized the moment he entered the stairwell. His brisk, heavy step would falter midway. By the time he reached the top, his face was always red, and sweat would be running freely on his cheeks and neck.

A commotion on the steps far below told her more than one man was attempting the laborious climb. Sometimes, Cassie could hear a voice below and recognize it, as the stone cavern transmitted the sound of a single person's speech very clearly. Most often what she heard was no more than a shout of hurrah as one of the guards at the door below greeted a visitor, or won a round of dice against his mates.

This time it was more than one booming voice, and the voices were engaged in an argument. But through the swearing and fussing accompanying the climbers on their way up the circuitous steps, the words were not clear.

Cassie finished sweeping her flagstone floor at the gate, collecting a pile of lint, dust and otter mud to be scooped up and taken below later. Then she hung her rush broom on a peg where the rascals couldn't reach it to chew it to bits. She settled on her cot, ready to play the part of the damsel in distress.

Just when she was deciding it had to be her father and Douglas Cameron, along with their attendant henchmen, the noise stopped quite suddenly. She cocked her head, certain that a serious thump had preceded the silence, as though someone had fallen and slid down many of the steps.

The myriad voices rose in alarm and some panic, and shouts went down to the guards below.

As suddenly as it had started, the noise abated and her tower reverted to its normal quiet-as-a-churchyard-before-dawn demeanor. It remained that way throughout the entire day.

It was one of her guards who brought her meals and water later that day, telling her the usual boy was busy serving the guests in the hall. Shortly after dusk, she had one visitor, her sister Maggie, who arrived as red-faced as any visitor Cassie had thus had.

"Sweet Saint Ninian, Cassie!" Maggie exclaimed, holding her lantern high so she could see into Cassie's cell. "This is a climb that would put an end to me, were I to have to do it twice in a day."

"Maggie, I didn't expect it to be you!"

"Och, well, we got started late once the rain ceased this morning and have only just arrived all in one piece. And ye, Cassie? Are ye keeping yer spirits up?"

Cassie reached out to embrace her sister. It was an awkward way to greet anyone, but it was the best she could do. Cassie winced as her tender breasts contacted the cold iron bars, then stepped back a pace, studying Maggie's flushed face. "The children are with you?"

"Aye, the wee monsters. I fair wanted to strangle all of them with their fighting and fussing, and whining 'weren't we there yet' all of the long weary afternoon. The rain this morning threatened to hold us off another day, but I was determined not to be waylaid from getting here when I planned. Lord, this is a dark cell at night. Have ye no candles or lanterns?"

"One or two stubs of candles, but I dinna expect company and dinna think to ask for replacements. There's a hook just above your head you can hang the lantern on."

"Good, my arm was beginning to ache." Maggie hooked the lantern on the handy fitting. "You look thinner, Cass. Are you pining for Robert?"

"'Twouldn't do me any good if I was, would it?" Cassie hadn't admitted any relationship with Robert to Maggie, but it was commonly believed that she had run off to elope with Robert Gordon. Only her father's dogs catching up with the two of them had prevented the marriage, or so Maggie had informed Cassie on her birthday, February 29. "MacArthur goes ahead with his own plans regardless, doesn't he?"

"Tsk." Maggie clicked her tongue. "Euan asked me to give you this packet of letters from the children. They enjoyed the stories you sent them so much. I think Millie drew Lady Quickfoot, but the truth is, I haven't had time to look at it. Both Ian and William came down with the croup, and I haven't had a single night's sleep through in a week. I'd trade places with you in a heartbeat, were it possible.''

''You dinna mean that. This gets old in a hurry.''

''Aye, but…to be able to do nothing but rest and sleep for a while…'' Maggie's voice trailed to a stop. ''Ah, well. I'd best go back before Willie wakes, screaming his head off for want of nothing good to eat.''

''Mother will see to him,'' Cassie argued, hoping to prolong Maggie's visit.

''Ahh, she sort of has her hands full at the moment,'' Maggie replied, starting to reach for the lantern, then changing her mind. ''I can leave you the lantern, Cass. There are two torches burning above the steps as they circle below. It's only here at the top that there isn't any light.''

''No, you'd better take it with you, better safe than sorry, Maggie. It sounded to me like someone had an accident on the steps coming up here this morning. Gad, that was ages ago. Was it MacArthur?''

''Nay, 'twas not. 'Twas graceful Douglas the Darling, and he's injured his bad leg. I swear, Cassie, I dinna know when to believe you and when not anymore. The mon does smell like pigs, and worse, he's a terrible patient, a great big overgrown baby, moaning and complaining about the MacArthur's being out to murder him. Father looks to be at his wits' end, and Mother doesn't appear to be speaking to anyone. The whole household has gone topsy-turvy. So I really canna stay longer for the now. Do read Millie's letters. Euan was most insistent that I urge you to do that tonight.''

Maggie took down the lantern to take it with her on the descent to the castle proper.

"Wait a moment," Cassie asked. "I'll fetch my candle and light it from your flame. 'Tis easier than finding my flint and steel in the dark, what with these otters about.''

"Ye still have Hamilton's wee creatures? They dinna die?''

"Nay, they're fat as seals, sleeping in the corner still each day. 'Twon't be long before they wake up and start looking for the water boy, who gives them a ride to the loch each night.''

"Millie will be delighted to hear that and love to take a turn at the task, I vow." Maggie kissed Cassie's brow and hugged her, then opened her lantern for Cassie to put a punt to the flame and light her small candle.

"Tell Millie thank-you for the drawings. Good night, Maggie. I'll see you all in the morning.''

"Sleep well, Cassie." Maggie lifted her lamp and picked up the hem of her skirts and went down, her light bobbing on the circular stone walls as she descended the steps.

Cassie took her candlestick to the table and set it down, then sat down with Millie's packet, turning the parchment toward the light, chuckling over the small figures drawn on the folded square of parchment. From somewhere, the girl had found sealing wax and carved her initials in the blob of wax sealing her thick, folded packet. Cassie broke the seal and opened the drawing, and a sealed letter slid onto her lap.

A letter that was written in ink and did not come from a child's attempt at correspondence. Turning it over, Cassie read the seal and recognized the face of Robert's signet ring impressed onto the wax.

She put aside Millie's drawing of Lady Quickfoot ice skating, and tore open Robert's seal.

My dearest Cassandra,

The days grow long and I fear I am never to see you again. Euan MacGregor came to my camp on Loch Lochy this morning, bringing word that the first of the banns, announcing your marriage to Douglas Cameron, was read at services in your father's chapel yesterday morning. Does this mean you have consented to the match? I wish I were there to talk to you, to hear your answer myself. I cannot leave my work now, not even to hear so important a decision from you with my own ears. Only the Spey River as it courses through Lochaber remains to be charted, and our fieldwork will be done. It was my hope to return no later than the tenth. Euan's visit has altered my plans, filling me with a sense of urgency to get back to you before the sun rises on Easter morning.

Euan believes MacArthur will press the wedding forward immediately following the third reading of the banns, Sunday, April 9. Easter, not Beltane, May 1, as MacArthur had told me. I had written to the king, begging his intercession and aid, but my greatest fear now is that it will not come soon enough for us. I regret my innate caution, which kept my sword arm down when it should have been raised in defense of you, and my trust in God Almighty answering my prayers in his own good time. But I could not force myself to raise arms against the father of the woman I most desperately want for my wife. I could not bear the hard feelings you would have for me, did I shed one drop of Mac-Arthur's venerable blood. I beg you to forgive me for not having found another way to prevent his taking his wrath out upon you.

Cassie, I think about you day and night and cannot believe we have come to this. That you would consent to marry a man you do not even respect. I do not know what to believe anymore.

Have your made any progress at the orb and key? Is it possible you can escape your prison unbeknownst to those within the keep? If so, on the night you receive this letter, tie the rope I gave you securely to the gate, let the rope out the window at the hour of midnight. Euan and a trustworthy man of his choosing will be waiting to come up and assist you down to the parapet. They will see that your escape is complete. I will meet you at a prearranged site, where a priest will be waiting to marry us. It is up to you, Cassandra. The decision is yours. I love you with all my heart, soul and mind. If you feel as I do, then you will be there at the kirk to marry me.

> I remain your humble servant always,
> Robert Gordon

Stunned, Cassie read the letter through three more times, memorizing it before she touched the corner of it to the flame of her candle and burned it to ashes. She began to make ready to escape. Cassie would have done so long before the midnight hour Robert had suggested, if her father had not chosen to do the unthinkable. He came up to the tower at the stroking of the tenth bell. Without preamble he told her she was free to leave whenever she liked.

MacArthur produced a key to put in the lock and twisted it full round. Cassie approached the gate, wondering what new trick he was playing. She couldn't stop herself from falling into his trap, if that what this was.

"Why the change of heart, MacArthur?" Cassie asked. "Have not seven weeks passed and you have withstood all entreaties and refused to relent? Why this sudden change of heart? Does Douglas the Darling no' want me?"

"Aye, he does. The mon has rocks for brains and would find a way to buy the moon if that were my price for him to have ye. Yer sisters and all of their husbands have descended upon the house, and have begun to squabble amongst themselves, deciding who your mother will go to live with. She vows to leave me if I dinna give you your freedom, so that ye may decide for yourself who ye want to marry."

He moved aside the water bucket and swung the gate wide open, then sat down wearily on the very top step, his back to Cassie, his shoulders slumped in defeat.

It was quite the biggest shock of all.

Cassie couldn't move for the longest time, and just stood looking at that wide-open gate and the defeated man with his shoulders hunched. She truly didn't know what to do. Finally, she caught up her slippers and put them on her bare feet and stepped out past the barrier as far as the second step. Then she sat down at his side, quietlike, waiting for something, though she hadn't the foggiest idea what that something was.

After a bit her father's big head turned her way and he glared at her with eyes that seemed to glisten in the lantern's light. "What do ye wait upon? Yer brothers-in-law, Lord Appin and that worthless Sinclair, wait at the bottom of these steps. They'll escort ye down to the hall."

"Roslyn's here?" Cassie gulped, naming her eldest sister, who had eloped to marry Elliot, the Earl of

Sinclair. Cathy, the next oldest, had handfasted for a year and day with her husband, George Mansfield of the clan Murray.

"Aye, the whole damned family, save our own James, is here with their squalling bantlings and demanding husbands, the whole sorry lot. Every one of them stands against me, siding with yer wicked-tempered mother. 'Tis the blackest day of this mon's life. I'd rather stay here where there's peace and quiet if ye dinna mind."

"Aye, it is quiet." Cassie nodded. "A good place to think and sort things out. Would you tell me why you locked me in here, before I go, Father? Was it to force me to marry Douglas, or to keep me away from Robert Gordon?"

MacArthur looked at her for the first time since she'd sat down at his side. "Humph! Gordon!" MacArthur snorted in disgust. "Bah! What good is he to ye, lass? I dinna want ye wasting yer time on the fop, that's true. Ye saw for yerself how much he did to stop me from incarcerating ye. He never lifted so much as a finger, did he? Ye'd be happier in the end with Douglas Cameron."

"But *I* don't think I would," Cassie told him.

"So everyone in my hall tells me," MacArthur grumbled, jamming his fist into his jaw, propping his dejected head on his arm. "I dinna want that Gordon bastard blinding ye with his handsome, courtly ways, but I see now I acted too late and the magic done the moment the two of ye bid eyes on one another."

Cassie blinked, her jaw sagging, not knowing whether to believe what she had heard or not. Then she swallowed and said boldly, "In all truth, Father, it was I who had to seduce him, and a job that was to accomplish in and of itself."

His head shook back and forth against his fist. "I'm no' surprised to hear that, lass. Yer lady mother did the same to me thirty some years ago, and I, fool that I was, fell for her like a stone. She's held me bewitched ever since and I can no' live if she leaves me here alone in this pile of rock. Tell me, are ye carrying his child, Cass?"

"Aye, a fine son, I believe, another grandson for you. Is Robert here?"

"Nay." MacArthur sighed deeply and put his arm around her shoulders, holding her gently to him. "I had hoped to prevent that, but I see I failed, lass. I fear the mon would kill ye, indulging yer wild whims in the hills."

"He's really very cautious, Papa, more so than I am," Cassie said in defense of the man she loved. "You could learn to like him in time."

"I could if I knew I'd never see ye take another chance, like the one ye took coming down Arthur's Drop on a rope that dinna even reach to the valley floor."

Cassie started, looking at him, really looking at his careworn and wrinkled eyes. "You know about that?"

"I saw the two of ye high on the cliff with my own two eyes. I had been out tracking the reivers that stole the cattle, when the storm broke and drove me back to the castle. My heart was in my throat when ye walked in the door of my hall, for I knew there was only one way to arrive in so little time. And neither one of ye had more than a scratch or two on ye.

"Aye, I locked ye here to keep him from killing ye with his exploring the hills and measuring the lochs. Until today, I would not admit the truth. It isn't Robert Gordon who is the reckless one. 'Tis you, Cassandra. He desna want a wife climbing the mountains any more than I ever wanted a daughter of mine taking such risks. I did it to protect ye from yourself, Cassie, because I love ye with all my heart."

MacArthur stood up then. "Come, lass, will I have to drag ye down to the hall to face the music?"

Cassie threw her arms around him, peace made between them at last. She kissed his cheek and said, "Aye, come on then, drag me down to the hall. Let's finish this the way we started it."

"Y'er a strange lass, Cassandra, baffling ye are." MacArthur hugged her close, kissing her brow in return. "Do ye forgive yer auld father for only wanting to do what's right for ye?"

"Aye, I can if ye'll allow me some say in the matters of my heart."

"'Tis that important to ye?"

"Aye."

"Well, then, let's go down and ye can tell poor Douglas ye dinna want him as yer husband."

Yes. Cassie was to have her freedom and to see all of her sisters and their husbands. It made her even happier to tell poor Douglas to look to another house for his fourth wife. The blot on her happiness was

Robert's absence—and the urgency of his desperate letter.

The moment she could, Cassie approached Euan MacGregor.

"What have ye decided to do, Cassandra?" Euan asked quietly.

"Elope and marry the man I love. Can you still help me?" Cassie replied.

Euan nodded, marveling that the hour had not gone past midnight yet. His man would still be waiting outside the castle walls.

"Aye, but we've made my man wait long enough." He caught her hand and pulled her along with him, sneaking her out a side door into the larder. They left the castle and fled across the ward to the postern gate that Euan earlier had made certain could be open, just in case.

A mounted man waited there on a restive horse.

"Ho, Connor, ye know where to take the lass?"

"Aye," the stranger replied curtly.

Euan lifted Cassie up by her waist and set her on the man's saddle before him. "Godspeed, Cassie. All will be well."

"God bless you, Euan. Dinna tell anyone where I've gone before the morning, and tell the water boy to mind Hamilton's otters till I return for them."

"So I will do," he promised. Then he slapped the horse and sent it bolting into the night.

Chapter Eighteen

Despite the ease with which Cassie departed from Castle MacArthur, the building tension inside her brought back her nausea in full force. She fought valiantly to control it for several hours of constant motion on the swiftly moving horse.

She could only thank the Lord the silent rider stopped to water his horse and rest it a moment. Cassie bathed her face several times in the cold clear water of a swiftly moving stream coursing through the pass of Glencoe.

"What's the matter with ye, lass?" Eaun's man asked. His voice sounded harsh and rough, as though he'd struggled recently with his own bout of the croup. "Have ye lost yer courage?"

"Not exactly. I'm feeling a bit nauseated, and riding on that horse isn't helping."

"Christ and Him crucified save us," the man prayed. "Y'er as wan as last week's moon. Are ye that sick? We dinna have much time to do this."

"Not sick...breeding." Cassie swallowed hard.

"Och!" The man choked, then cleared his throat and hoisted Cassie back onto his saddle. "All the more reason for haste, lass, and to stand ye afore the priest as soon as possible."

She caught a glimpse of his face as he moved to mount behind her. He wasted no time spurring the stalwart horse into motion. He wore a cap pulled low over his brow. A black cape obscured his clothing. Other than seeing his thick, dark beard, Cassie had no idea which of Euan's sturdy workers this man was. If he got her to Robert without incident, she'd be eternally in his debt. Hence, she said nothing as he put spurs to the horse and set off on the last leg of the journey to Glencoen Farm.

Two hours more passed before a late-rising moon illuminated their way. No welcoming lights burned at Maggie's farm as they would have had the family been at home. They sped past it, on the downhill run toward the settlement of MacDonalds at the bottom of the valley. The horseman turned up the flower-strewn path to the little church at Kilchurn.

Though a small light glowed in the vestry of the stone chapel, to Cassie's dismay there were no horses tied at the church door. Her escort drew in his reins and halted his horse before the hitching post and ring.

"But where is Robert?" Cassie asked, looking off to the distant hills for a rider, seeing no one where any rider could have been seen coming to the kirk.

She dismounted unassisted and stood there, her legs

feeling strange and unsteady underneath her. Then, disheartened not to see the man she loved so dearly waiting for her, she made herself turn to face Euan's man. She must thank him for his assistance if for nothing else.

Without Robert this whole fiasco of eloping was just that, a fiasco. What would she do if he wasn't here? If he didn't come soon? Was this man going to desert her shortly, to return to his chores at the farm? A hundred questions all grounded in the uncertainties of love assailed her.

The man threw his cape behind his shoulder, revealing a swath of green, blue and black plaid folded across his breast. He pulled off his cap and ran his fingers through his dark hair, raking it back the way Robert was wont to do.

Then she looked at his bearded face, really looked, and thought for the first time since their silent ride had begun that she knew who he was. And he hadn't said so much as a word to give away the game!

Cassie threw her arms around him, before he'd even finished pressing his hair out of his eyes, tackling him and tumbling him onto his back on the soft, fertile earth. "You devil! Why didn't you say it was you? Do you have any idea how sick I've worried myself, wondering where my Robert was? And here you came all along with Maggie and Euan, as bold as a thief stealing inside Castle MacArthur, intending all along to spirit me away from my own father right beneath his proud nose!"

"Wait! Hold on there, lass. Before ye kiss me and drag me in to say vows before yon gawking priest, ye better ask me which Gordon I am. I think the one ye'll be wanting to marry is the free devil, standing in the door of the kirk right now."

Cassie drew back, becoming very still, intently staring at the man's bearded face, and in particular his eyes. They were Robert's and they weren't. The realization of what she had so impulsively done hit her as hard as a fist in the belly. "No, don't tell me I've done this in front of a priest," she whispered. "Or Robert?"

"As you like it, milady." The man beneath her flashed an outrageous white-toothed grin just like Robert's. "It isn't so and ye havena flattened me on my back in a rosebush in front of the king of Scotland either. Or does the king matter as well?"

"King?" Cassie gulped.

"None other than His Royal Majesty, James the Sixth." The damned fool laughed.

"Dear God in heaven, let me die right now." Cassie dropped her face to the man's shoulder, wishing the earth would split open and swallow her whole.

"Up to your old tricks again, eh, Connor?" a lady's sweet voice asked.

"Ah, not exactly, my dearest." Connor cleared his raspy throat. "Though I admit the lass does seem to have caught me in a compromising position."

"Who is that?" Cassie whispered, more embarrassed than she'd ever been in her life.

"I'm his wife, darling, and I do hope you aren't planning on marrying him. I would kill him if he even dreamed of committing bigamy while I'm in this condition of carrying his third child. Robert, quit standing here like a useless wart on a frog. Go help your charming bride off my husband."

As Robert lifted Cassie off his brother's body, Cassie winced, expecting an explosion. "Let me guess," he said, planting a kiss on Cassie's lips. "Connor's sore throat kept him from introducing himself, right?"

"He never said a word until we got here," Cassie lamely explained. "Then when we got here and I saw his eyes as he took off his cap, I thought for a second he was you with a beard."

"That great ugly beard of his is the reason I shave every opportunity I have," Robert quipped, kissing her warmly. "I'd hate to look that ugly."

"Can we get on with this?" King James demanded testily from the doorway of the church. "I've been awake the whole bloody night. You, I take it, young woman, are the renowned Lady Quickfoot?"

"Your Majesty," Cassie gave him her best curtsy, despite the shakiness of her knees. "I am Cassandra MacArthur. Lady Quickfoot doesn't exist. She is naught more than a legend of my clan."

"Is that so? Hmm, Robert, what do you make of that? And do my ears serve me right, was that not humility neatly voiced by none other than your

Highland maiden? A rare woman this maid must be, rare indeed.''

''Oh, Lady Quickfoot exists, Your Majesty,'' Robert reassured him. ''Cassandra is as close to being the real Lady Quickfoot as any Highland maiden is ever going to be. May I?'' He proudly offered Cassie his arm to escort her down the aisle to the priest waiting at the altar.

''Well, all I can say is that her exploits make for fine, adventuresome reading,'' the king called out to a lone man standing in the shadowy corner of the church. ''Wouldn't you agree, MacArthur?''

Cassie's head swiveled to the right, to spy her brother, James, stepping forward from the shadows to stand at the King's side, and murmur an agreement. He looked up at Cassie and cast her a reassuring wink that all was well.

Robert kept a firm hand on Cassie's fingertips, continuing to take her to the altar and the priest.

''First things first,'' he said. ''You promise to love, honor and obey me all of my days, and I will swear on my honor to love, protect and cherish you all the days of my life. When that's done, you may kiss your brother and continue your efforts to conquer our king. They're going to adore knowing the real Quickfoot as much as I do.''

''But there really isn't any Lady Quickfoot,'' Cassie insisted, wanting to make a clean breast of things once and for all. ''And I already love and honor you, and even obeyed you—as much as it annoyed me to do so. I patiently remained inside my blasted prison until the opportunity to resolve things with my father appeared.''

"Did ye now?" Robert replied blandly, his mouth twitching at the corners. "That's excellent news. Have you healed the breach?"

"Aye, it's all settled now, and it wasn't necessary for me to climb out the window, or risk our babe with a descent down the tower wall from a rope."

"Truly?" Robert turned to look at the priest, nodding at him to begin.

The moment the priest began to speak the words of the ceremony, Cassie's message sank in, and Robert's head jerked back to rivet her with startled eyes.

"Babe?" he asked, stunned.

"Aye." Cassie grinned. His arm tightened at her waist and he lifted her palm in his hand and kissed it gallantly. The priest frowned and cleared his throat, then with the bridal pair quiet for once, he began anew.

"Brothers and sisters in Christ, we are gathered here this night to celebrate the union of this man in holy matrimony with this woman..."

And thus it was, Cassandra of the clan MacArthur, married Robert of the clan Gordon, on the fifth of April, 1598.

When the ceremony with the king as their witness ended, they rode leisurely back to Castle MacArthur to join her family for the wedding celebration of their lifetime. The two of them lived happily after in Straloch, Aberdeenshire, where Robert finished his map and saw it published for all of Scotland's use.

* * * * *

Dear Reader,

Long after Robert Gordon died in 1661, his map of Scotland lived on as the finest cartographic record of his homeland published until modern times. Scotland's border at the time began at the Cheviot Hills, Berwick-upon-Tweed in the east, and the infamous Gretna Green in the west. In comparison to the space-age charts we now rely upon for accurate maps of all landforms, Gordon's comprehensive charts and maps are amazingly accurate, which I, as a historical writer, find absolutely fascinating.

Although little detail was available regarding this relentless cartographer's private life, I was able to uncover a few concrete facts. Robert was considered the "doyen of geographers" by none less than his peer publishers, Jean Bleau, whose atlas of c.1660 quickly replaced those compiled in the late 1500s by Gerardus Mercator.

If you should travel to Aberdeen, be prepared to come across a college named Robert Gordon University. One of the first things you might learn there is that the university's founder, Robert Gordon, born in 1668, was named for his famous grandfather, the same Robert Gordon who gave Scotland its rightful place on the map of the world.

A finer legacy than that no man could ask.

Elizabeth Mayne

www.romcom.com/mayne

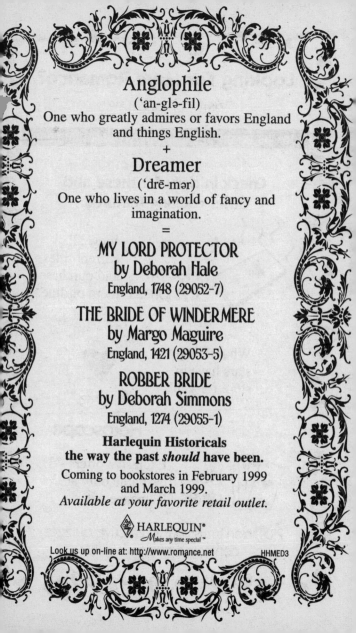

Anglophile
('an-glə-fil)
One who greatly admires or favors England
and things English.

+

Dreamer
('drē-mər)
One who lives in a world of fancy and
imagination.

=

MY LORD PROTECTOR
by Deborah Hale
England, 1748 (29052-7)

THE BRIDE OF WINDERMERE
by Margo Maguire
England, 1421 (29053-5)

ROBBER BRIDE
by Deborah Simmons
England, 1274 (29055-1)

**Harlequin Historicals
the way the past *should* have been.**

Coming to bookstores in February 1999
and March 1999.
Available at your favorite retail outlet.

Tough, rugged and irresistible...

THE AUSTRALIANS

Stories of romance Australian-style, guaranteed to
fulfill that sense of adventure!

This March 1999 look for

Boots in the Bedroom!

by **Alison Kelly**

Parish Dunford lived in his cowboy boots—no one was going
to change his independent, masculine ways. Gina, Parish's
newest employee, had no intention of trying to do so—she preferred a soft bed to a sleeping bag on the prairie. Yet somehow she couldn't stop thinking of how those boots would look
in her bedroom—with Parish still in them....

*The Wonder from Down Under: where spirited women win
the hearts of Australia's most independent men!*

Available March 1999
at your favorite retail outlet.

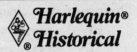

COMING NEXT MONTH FROM

HARLEQUIN HISTORICALS

DON'T MISS THESE FOUR GREAT TITLES
AVAILABLE NOW!